"We Norsemen," said Voldar, "are a proud, courageous people, bound by family and honor, protected by the gods, enriched by the plunder of our forefathers."

"Plunder," said Dane, a question forming. "You mean 'kill,' Father?"

"Yes, Son," said Voldar, sharing a look with the other men. "To survive, at times, a Norseman must kill. To feed his family. To fight to defend them. But 'tis my fondest wish that you never have to follow the path of the sword."

Dane had oft heard of his father's exploits, of the blood spilled with spear and broadsword, of the screams, sobs, whimpers, and whines even the bravest of his enemies made as they met their ends. He had memorized the locations of his father's many battle scars, and in his dreams had seen vivid scenes of the violence he might one day do. For countless generations, he knew, his forebears had survived by invading and raiding foreign lands, breaking men's spirits by forcing them to wear their undergarments backward while barking like dogs and other such humiliations. It was conquer or be conquered, as Voldar liked to say, and Norsemen weren't keen on being on the losing end of anything, much less a good fight.

Also by James Jennewein and Tom S. Parker

RuneWarriors: Sword of Doom

Shield of Odin

James Jennewein and
Tom S. Parker

HARPER
An Imprint of HarperCollins*Publishers*

For Allison, Jake, and all those who believed

—J.J.

For Laura Noelle

—T.P.

RuneWarriors
 For information address HarperCollins Children's Books, a division of HarperCollins Publishers, 10 East 53rd Street, New York, NY 10022.
www.harpercollinschildrens.com

Library of Congress Cataloging-in-Publication Data

Jennewein, Jim.

RuneWarriors / by James Jennewein and Tom S. Parker. — 1st ed.

p. cm. — (RuneWarriors)

Summary: In an ancient and mystical time, teenaged Dane joins forces with his rival, Jarl the Fair, to retrieve the Shield of Odin and Astrid, the girl they love, from the tyrant Thidrek, fulfilling a destiny long foretold.

ISBN 978-0-06-144938-3

1. Vikings—Juvenile fiction. [1. Vikings—Fiction. 2. Adventure and adventurers—Fiction. 3. Voyages and travels—Fiction. 4. Fate and fatalism—Fiction. 5. Fortune telling—Fiction. 6. Humorous stories.] I. Parker, Tom S. II. Title.

PZ7.J4297Dan 2008 2008000775

[Fic]—dc22 CIP

AC

Typography by Carla Weise

10 11 12 13 14 LP/CW 10 9 8 7 6 5 4 3 2 1

❖

First paperback edition, 2010

NAME	PRONUNCIATION
Astrid	"ASS-trith"
Blek	"BLECK" rhymes with "deck"
Drott	"DRAHT" rhymes with "hot"
Fulnir	"FULL-ner"
Geldrun	"GEL-drun"
Grelf	"GRELF" rhymes with "shelf"
Hrolf	"Huh-ROLF"
Lut	"LOOT" rhymes with "boot"
Orm	"OARM" rhymes with "dorm"
Prasarr	"PRASS-ahr" rhymes with "fast car"
Skogul	"SKOE-gull"
Thidrek	"THIGH-dreck" rhymes with "high tech"
Ulf	"OOLF"
Voldar	"VOLE-dahr" rhymes with "coal tar"

PROLOGUE

Wherein the Reader is Forewarned

'Twas long ago, in ancient times, when the mystical powers of heaven were one with the earth . . . when fantastic beasts strode o'er the land, swam the seas, and soared through the skies, inspiring fear, wonder, and nervous indigestion . . . a time when the voices of the gods could actually be heard by mortal men if one were to listen carefully enough to one's heart or to the whispers on the great north wind. . . .

1

A Lesson is Learned While Peeing in the Snow

The boy was alone in the woods and the snow was falling fast, big, fat flakes twirling down out of the darkening sky, drifting higher. The sun had sunk from view, and the towering trees had thrown deep shadows over the snow. Stopping to rest, he gazed upward into the spruces and pines, their great limbs moving in the wind like giant arms that might reach down and grab him. He caught some falling snowflakes on his tongue, and the fun of it made him feel less afraid.

He had turned nine years old that day, and as was the custom, his father and other village eldermen had taken him on his first hunt. They'd been tracking a herd of elk when the boy, bored by the waiting and the watching, felt the call of nature and wandered off behind a tree to relieve himself. While watering the tree, he had spied a trail of fresh tracks in the snow, what looked to be paw prints of the rare white fox. Knowing this creature's pelt to be highly prized, the boy had pulled up his trousers and followed the trail, bow and arrow in hand, eager to make his first kill. But the tracks had led to an icy stream, where he had soon lost his way. He had watched the fat snowflakes as they fell upon the water, amazed that they stayed so long there before melting. He had listened to the *pocka-pocka* of a woodpecker and peered up into the blue-shadowed tree limbs to find where it was perched. It wasn't until the bird flew away that the boy looked round and realized he had wandered off too far, and his people were gone. He had hurried back to where he thought they were, but the winds and rising snow had covered their tracks and they were nowhere to be found. He had cried out for his father, but the empty whistling of the wind was all he heard in answer.

The boy had wandered alone through the forest for what seemed a long time, and now he felt small, helpless, and alone. He was cold, scared, and—not wanting to believe it—utterly lost. He drew his coat tighter and began to walk on, the snowdrifts now nearly to his knees. He heard a sound. A huffing, snuffling sort of noise that seemed to be coming from a copse of trees just a few paces away. He listened. There it was again. Was it the fox? A wolf perhaps? No, the rustling branches were too high off the ground. It had to be something . . . bigger.

His heart thumping, he tried to run but fell facedown in a snowdrift. When he sat up, brushing ice flakes from his face, the thing came out of the trees—a giant brown bear, with steam gusting from its jaws and bits of glistening ice visible on its dark, shaggy fur. For a terrible moment the bear just stood there on all fours, eyeing the boy. Clearly ravenous, having just awakened from a winter-long hibernation, it reared up on its hind legs and let out a roar, a sound that chilled the boy's blood.

The boy took off, scrambling and falling in the snow, moving with everything he had, when all at once another great furred creature came out of the trees in front of him—and the boy ran straight into its arms.

He let out a scream, and behind him the roar of the bear grew louder. At any moment his head and limbs would be torn from his body, and he braced himself for the certain death he knew was upon him. But then the furred creature that held him pushed him aside. He saw the creature's sparkling blue eyes, red beard, and long iron-tipped spear, and the boy realized he had run into the arms of his father.

Dressed in a long, thick coat of gray wolf fur, his father bravely stood his ground as the great beast charged. And when his father reared back with his spear and gave a war cry, the bear, too, stopped running and reared up on its haunches and let out a sickening roar of its own, as if to say, *You're* mine, *old man.* The boy cried out, fearing his father would be devoured. But then, with one sure, swift thrust, the bearded man hurled the spear through the air—and there was silence. The spear had gone straight through the bear's heart, and with one whining groan, the great beast fell over dead and its roar was heard no more.

Other men of the hunting party, all very hairy and scary looking, with their spears and knives and other implements of destruction, now came out of the trees to attend to the bear and to congratulate Voldar the Vile, the man who had killed it.

In truth, the boy knew Voldar wasn't *really* vile; *testy* would better describe him. At times, his mother called him Voldar the Vile and Irascible and Peevish and Cranky, but never to his face. He was a broad-shouldered, bushy-bearded man with a flinty gaze that could strike fear into the bravest of men. And when he spoke, his voice had the ring of steel in it. The fact that he also had the breath of a rotting walrus carcass may have further explained his powers of intimidation.

The boy blinked in awe at his father, crying tears of joy, astonished that they both still lived. The great man turned and glared at his son. For a moment it seemed Voldar might erupt in anger, as he often did, exploding in colorful oaths such as, "What in Thor's befouling backside!" or the ever-popular "I'll be dipped in weasel spit!" But instead, he turned to the men and said with a good-natured growl, "Somebody grog me! My throat's afire!"

A man rushed over with a goatskin bag filled with barley ale. Voldar held it aloft and hungrily squirted the home brew straight down his throat. He thrust a fist into the air and let out a loud, ripping belch.

"Vikings, one; bears, nothing!" he said, and the men

burst into laughter, drawing out more goatskins of home brew and drinking them down in great gulping drafts. Soon they were in high spirits, gathered around Voldar, their chieftain, laughing at his ribald jokes. His son, too, gazed up in wonder at the great man, marveling at his courage and capacity for drink.

It seemed to the boy that all knowledge of how to survive in this world flowed from his father. "Self-reliance," the old man often told him, "is the greatest gift a father can give to his son." So he'd taught the boy how to build fires and hunt with a bow and arrow, how to track game by following prints in the snow, and how being downwind from your prey would let you smell them without their scenting you.

In winter, Voldar had shown him how to fish by hacking holes in iced-over lakes. And in spring, when snows were melting and the rivers were full and wide, his father had taught him how to spear and gut the silver-pink fish and smoke them over fires of oak and alder, the smoky-sweet tang of the fish on his tongue of particular pleasure to the boy. By daylight and by firelight, the son had sat beside his father, taking in his stories and his bladework, whether it was the skinning of badger and fox pelts or the carving of reindeer antlers into hair combs and eating utensils.

"Life tries to kill you," his father had always warned him, referring to the many perilous forces of nature and the wild beasts of the forest that could end a life with a swipe of a paw. This is why village rule number one was "Never hunt alone," and why men usually went hunting in groups. And why, if a man ever *did* go out alone and never came back, he was forever referred to as "that idiot."

The boy now quivered as his father approached, bracing himself for the punishment to come and hoping *he* wouldn't be called an idiot.

But all Voldar said was, "Don't run off." And he gave his son an axe and together they cut down a tree, helping the men to build a wooden pallet upon which they could carry the bear back to the village, where food was scarce this season. The boy worked hard, chopping and splitting and helping to bind the planks with cords of leathered sealskin to form a sturdy platform. The men then heaved the bear with some difficulty onto the pallet and carried it off through the forest toward home, singing as they went.

For a while, the boy walked beside his father, listening to the songs of the men, the smell of the dead bear adrift on the chill night air. When the boy tired of walking, his father lifted him onto his shoulders, and the boy rode that way, holding on to his father's furred hat, dangling his legs down onto the great man's chest, feeling safe and on top of the world. And later, when they finally reached the edge of the forest and the boy saw the warm welcome of the village torchlights twinkling in the distance, the baying hounds announcing his return, he knew that he was home.

2

Tales of Gods and Monsters

The boy was hailed a fine hunter. "Dane! Dane! Dane! Dane!" the villagers chanted as he waved from atop his father's shoulders.

In honor of his first hunt, Dane's father presented him with a string of bear claws to wear as a charm round his neck. Her eyes ashine with pride, his mother, Geldrun, gave him a beaver coat she had sewn, with a wide belt and a rabbit-fur collar. Then the hooded figure of Lut the Bent—the village *sannsigerske*, or soothsayer—came forward. An ancient stick of a man with nut-brown eyes and worn, leathery skin, Lut was one hundred three winters old and still active with the ladies. His face crinkling into a smile, Lut laid a bony hand upon the boy's forehead and in his croaking voice declared him now worthy of being called "warrior." Dane beamed. *Me? A warrior?* His heart soared.

Dane felt a special kinship with the old one. For years, Lut had taken him aside and treated Dane as his own private pupil, teaching him about the gods who ruled their lives, and the healing properties of various flowers and plants, and the storied history of their people. Dane treasured these talks and sometimes felt that Lut had selected him for a purpose, that he was watching him, *preparing* him for something. "Learn to read your own dreams," Lut had often said, explaining that the gods spoke to men in dreams. Once Dane had even been allowed to watch Lut cast the runes, divining the future as writ by the gods, something no other child in the village had seen. Yes, Lut was both teacher and friend, and it felt good to receive his blessing.

That night, amid a large circle of stones, a heroic fire was built, and Dane, son of Voldar the Vile, grandson of Vlar the Courageous, was allowed to sit beside the council of elders as they gave thanks to the gods. They stripped the bear of its hide and divided its meat among the families.

The snow had stopped falling, and the fire's warmth felt good after so long in the cold. Dane watched as skewers of sizzling bear meat were passed round, the women and children feasting first and then the men. He'd dreamed of this moment for years, and now it was here. His first hunt. At last, he was a warrior!

Other boys were soon ushered over and allowed to sit by the fire, among them the snotty Jarl the Fair, Orm the Hairy One, and Dane's good friends Drott the Dim and

Fulnir the Stinking. No one cared where Drott sat; he was a good-natured sort, always good for a laugh, and he bathed regularly. Fulnir, however, was made to sit downwind, the elders all too aware that even a whiff of the boy's feculent fumes would foul the festivities.

Seated beside Voldar under the starlit sky, Dane listened to the elders tell stories—brave tales of their fathers' fathers and their fathers' fathers' fathers and their fathers' fathers' *fathers'* fathers and—well, they told a lot of stories. Tales of yore being the way wisdom was passed on to succeeding generations—and a fine way to brag to the womenfolk as well. Fathers told tales of magic trolls who dwelled in marshy bogs and fed on children, of fire-breathing elves who rode serpents, of wolves that walked upright, and other creatures large and small that did the bidding of the gods. Lut spoke of other mysteries, like the Ægirdóttir—the Nine Daughters of Ægir—god-spirits who were said to dwell beneath the sea, preying on sailors and schools of wayward herring, and the legendary Well of Knowledge, a secret spring whose waters would greatly expand a man's mental capacities, though knowledge of its location had long been lost.

Finally it was their chieftain's turn to speak.

"We Norsemen," said Voldar, "are a proud, courageous people, bound by family and honor, protected by the gods, enriched by the plunder of our forefathers."

"Plunder," said Dane, a question forming. "You mean 'kill,' Father?"

"Yes, Son," said Voldar, sharing a look with the other men. "To survive, at times, a Norseman must kill. To feed his family. To fight to defend them. But 'tis my fondest wish that you never have to follow the path of the sword."

Dane had oft heard of his father's exploits, of the blood spilled with spear and broadsword, of the screams, sobs, whimpers, and whines even the bravest of his enemies made as they met their ends. He had memorized the locations of his father's many battle scars, and in his dreams had seen vivid scenes of the violence he might one day do. For countless generations, he knew, his forebears had survived by invading and raiding foreign lands, breaking men's spirits by forcing them to wear their undergarments backward while barking like dogs and other such humiliations. It was conquer or be conquered, as Voldar liked to say, and Norsemen weren't keen on being on the losing end of anything, much less a good fight. But one day, after years of warring, Voldar had been persuaded at last to lay down his broadsword. It was Geldrun, his common-sense wife, who had convinced him.

"Face it, Volie," she'd said, "your fighting days are done. Your eyesight's gone, your knees shot. There's no future in raiding and pillaging. It's time to put down roots, live off the land, be sensible."

Like most men who fall under the civilizing influence of their women, Voldar grumbled and put up a fuss and even kicked the furniture a bit, but eventually he saw that his wife was right. One summer after snowmelt, he and twenty other fathers built a circle of thatched-roof homes in a lush, flower-dotted meadow that lay between the base of a mountain and the waters of a coastal inlet. And it was this very heathland—near a freshwater stream and a forest rich with game—that Dane had come to know as home.

"Father?" Dane asked now. "Do Vikings ever lose?"

The fire crackled as Voldar paused to reflect on this.

"Well . . . there have been one or two defeats," he answered, "but nothing too ignominious, and nothing I'd tell your mother about. The unofficial record, I believe, is Vikings five hundred and three, enemies nil. But some stories may vary."

The older men chuckled. Dane had another question.

"Father, when a Viking dies in battle," said Dane, "where does he go?"

A gleam came to Voldar's eye. He rose and gestured to the sky with a flaming stick from the fire. "He goes to a place more glorious than man can imagine. He goes to Valhalla, a shining palace above the clouds. The Valkyries—great beauties who ride cross the sky on winged horses—come down and take the spirit of the fallen warrior up to the heavenly Hall of Heroes, where he sits beside the gods in glory forever." Voldar paused. "But it's not *dying* that brings a man honor—it's how he *lives* that counts. What most defines a man isn't the sword he carries; it's the beliefs he carries in his heart."

For a long moment, the men stopped their work on the

bear and gazed up at the stars, their eyes full of wonder.

Drott spoke up. "Can we eat treats up there? Honeyed nuts and sweetmeats?"

"Of course," Voldar said, indulging the boy. "All the sweets you can stomach!"

Then Fulnir had a question. "My father says Odin is always watching us, so we had better do our chores and mind our elders, or Odin'll smite us and smite us good."

"That's right, boy," said Voldar, giving Fulnir's father a smile. Odin, it was said, had lost his own eye in order that he might see with a more godly sight, and thus he became the god of prophecy, poetry, and war. And it was to Odin, Father of the Battle-Slain, that the Valkyries would bring the fallen heroes of war.

Voldar raised the sacred Shield of Odin, and the boys were instantly mesmerized by the flickering firelight reflected in it. It was a circular disk forged of a secret alloy, and it held in its center a precious stone. The stone, known as *Óðinn Auga*, or Odin's Eye, was reputed to give the Shield special powers, making whoever held it invincible in battle. In times of peace, Voldar and his tribe believed that Odin's Eye watched over the village, protecting them from invaders, and that if the Shield were ever lost, his people would be without protection from famine, disease, and widespread tooth decay. (Toe fungus was another much-feared pestilence, but easily cured with a poultice of yarrow root.) "The Eye sees all," Dane had oft been told, and having nearly lost his father that very night, Dane was comforted to know someone so powerful was watching over him.

Voldar laid down the Shield. "But Thor," he said, his eyes boring into the boys, "Thor is the mightiest of gods, for he has *Mjolnir*—Thor's Hammer—the fearsome weapon he hurls across the sky, unleashing lightning and thunder to smite our enemies." At the mention of Thor's name, Dane noticed Lut and other elders touch the charms they wore round their necks. Of all the gods in Valhalla, Thor was the mightiest. He could topple mountains with a single blow of his Hammer—a weapon so large, it would take a score or more of Norsemen to carry if it were ever to fall to earth. Though said to be the son of Odin, Thor possessed none of his father's cunning; but when it came to brute battle strength, Thor beat all. So men prayed to father Odin for wisdom and to Thor the son for power. And as father-and-son combinations go, a man was believed to be unbeatable if he had both on his side.

Transfixed, the boys gazed at Voldar as if he were Thor himself. They'd heard the tales of Thor and Odin many times over but never tired of hearing them told again. And Voldar never tired of telling them, dancing about, eyes alight, gesturing grandly with his hands. Then he narrowed his eyes and spoke in a hushed whisper. "But that's not all, boys! Did you know that far, far to the north, there are known to live giant men made entirely of *ice*?"

Dane's eyes went wide with wonder. "No!"

"Ah, yes, frost giants, they are! *Hrímþursar!* Marvelous

magical creatures, they say, some over twenty feet tall, who dwell atop the highest snow-capped peaks of Mount Neverest—a place so terribly cold and remote, no Norseman has ever reached it, nor likely ever will."

Voldar towered over the boys, waving his torch, his war necklace of wild boar tusks jangling on his chest.

"It's the cavorting of these very creatures," he continued, "that causes the deadly avalanches that bury entire villages. The mountain they live on is so high, some say, frost giants can reach right up into the clouds—into the halls of Valhalla itself!—and wrestle with the gods! Legend has it that someday a frost giant will steal Thor's Hammer—and the man who steals the Hammer back for Thor will bring his people a hundred winters of peace and prosperity, give or take a few years."

An elder spoke up, saying he thought the story was a prophecy, not a legend. Voldar replied that if memory served, he was fairly certain it was a legend. There was more disagreement back and forth. Finally they looked to Lut the Bent for a decision.

As Lut had oft explained to Dane, there was a distinct difference between a legend and a prophecy. A legend was a story created by *men* about the *gods*. A prophecy, or *spá*, was just the opposite: a story created by the *gods* about *men*. And it was the seer's belief that Norsemen should take prophecies far more seriously than man-made legends, given that the prophecies came directly from the gods and legends from mere mortals. But as tales got handed down from one generation to the next in the mind-numbing cold, the Norsemen flat out forgot which stories were which and came to believe in all of them just to be safe.

"Truth is all that matters," Lut said gravely, "and if we seek it, we shall prosper." The men nodded, Lut's wisdom ending the discussion and reminding them all of the higher things. The boys fell silent too, staring up at the stars, visions of dwarves and elves and giants made of ice alive in their minds, the only sound the crackling of the fire.

Later that night at home, as his father put him to bed, Dane's mind was still astir with questions. "Does Thor's Hammer really exist?"

"Of course, Son."

"And the giants made of ice?"

"So they say."

"Tell me another story, Father," said the boy.

"No, no, it's time for bed now, son. Go to sleep." And he kissed his son good night and rose to leave.

"Father, are you angry with me? For getting lost?"

"No, not angry," his father said. "I feared for your safety, boy. Because you're so dear to me." Dane saw the shine in his father's eyes, and it made him feel a special kind of warmth inside.

The old man turned to leave again, but the boy had one more question.

"Father?"

"Yes, Son."

"When I grow up, will I be as brave as you?"

Voldar smiled and looked deep into his son's eyes. "When you grow to be a man, you will be *twice* as brave as me, son. You'll be a Rune Warrior." Dane knew this to be the name Norsemen gave to those whose deeds were so great and selfless, their exploits were carved on giant granite slabs called rune stones in celebration of their heroism. And hearing Voldar speak these words gave him a sense of deep tranquility, for he knew his father never lied and was the wisest man in the village, perhaps even wiser than Lut.

Lut the Bent couldn't sleep. The stories round the fire and the celebration of Dane's first hunt had stirred feelings and brought forth images long buried. But now, as he lay alone in the darkness of his hut, it all came flooding back: haunting scenes from the boy's earliest days passing through his mind—memories most awful.

The Winter Longer Than Odin's Beard, it had been called. Six miserable months of blizzards and ice storms the villagers had endured, without a glint of sunlight, the skies so gray, they seemed to be made of impenetrable ice, the people weak with hunger. Then one bleak morning, a baby had been born to Voldar and Geldrun, the boy who would come to be known as Dane. Lut remembered visiting the hut that first morning and being struck by the thick tuft of red hair atop the boy's head and his tiny smile. Lut remembered, too, the joyful shine he'd seen in Voldar's and Geldrun's eyes. As was Norse custom, Lut had then taken the newborn outdoors and raised the fur-swaddled infant to the sky to present him to the gods. And as he began to pray, asking them to look with favor on the child, the wind abruptly died, the air grew still—and then there was light! The clouds had parted and a shaft of golden sunlight shone down from the heavens. Lut had felt the warmth of sunshine on his cheeks as the villagers danced in merriment, cheering the child's every squirm and squall. "Is this a sign?" they asked Lut. A *tegn*, or omen? "Is the boy a gift from the gods?"

"Every child is a gift," Lut had told them, not wanting any burdensome pressure placed upon the boy. There was no significance whatsoever to the baby's arrival, he'd said. Spring had finally come and their long ordeal was over. But later that very night in his hut, he'd had a dream, a terrible nightmare so disturbing that thinking of it now, so many years later, made his insides churn in dread. Women with their hair and limbs on fire . . . decapitated human heads impaled on spikes . . . an ever-widening shadow hole devouring the huts of Lut's village one by one . . . and at the center of all the destruction, a red-haired warrior, a demon resembling Dane.

As the village seer, he had a duty to alert the elders of ill omens his dreams might foretell. But the possession of foreknowledge was a dangerous thing, and often it was best to keep silent until certain a thing was true. And so he had told no one, especially not the boy's parents, believing that the dream had been nothing but the foolish ravings of his aging mind, or perhaps caused by a bad batch of mutton stew. And besides, the boy was but a baby! What harm could come from a wee infant?

But now, awake in his hut after the celebration round the fire, listening to the wind sighing in the trees and the high, lonely whine of a wolf howling in the distance, Lut had an uneasy feeling that all was not right. Something about the firelight dancing in Dane's eyes. But no, he told himself, how could he think such things about someone so beloved? And to banish any further doubts, he thought of the boy's hearty laugh, his delightfully inquisitive nature, and his uncanny talent for mimicry. And in the warm glow of a teacher's pride in his favorite pupil, Lut's mind wandered back to his own now-distant boyhood, to faded memories of his mother and father and other Norsefolk he had known and loved. And soon, adrift on a new sea of memories and growing drowsy, he sank back into the comforting arms of sleep.

3

The Boy Discovers Girls

One morning, soon after his first hunt, Dane was play fighting with his wooden sword in the livestock pen behind his family's hut. He leaped about, dispatching a dozen Goths, shouting, "Hie, *skum-bøtte*!" and "Death's too fine for swine like thee!" when the sound of laughter startled him. He looked up to see his father standing over him.

"Defending the village, are we?" his father asked. Dane nodded, afraid he was soon to be scolded for not having milked the goats and mucked out their pens. But his father grinned and said, "Well, why not do it proper, then, eh?" and unbuckling his leather-belted scabbard, he handed it, sword and all, to his son, nodding for the boy to take it. Dane could scarce believe it: his father's own sword! Dare he even touch it? The worn silver of the hilt gleamed in the sun, seeming to hold the secrets of a thousand battles.

Dane gripped the hilt, the steel icy cold in his hand as he drew it free of the scabbard—the blade so heavy, the sword point fell to the ground. Dane used his other hand to lift it, and his father then showed him how to hold it aloft in both hands, and how to thrust and parry without losing his balance. And then, taking up the wooden sword as his own, Voldar encouraged Dane to fight him one-on-one, man to man. Much to Voldar's delight, Dane barely hesitated. Hard he came, bringing down the blade so quickly, Voldar scarce had time to raise a defense, and backward he stumbled, falling through the fence, wood splintering on top of him, a bit of blood appearing on his arm.

For a moment Dane thought Voldar was dead. *I've killed my own father*, he thought, panicked, and burst into tears. But then he heard his father chuckling as he rose and brushed himself off, showing Dane that there was nothing but a scratch on his arm, nothing serious at all. And then Geldrun came out and began scolding Voldar for fighting with the boy, and as his parents argued, Dane scurried off to join his friends and brag about what his father had let him do.

As skilled as he was at play fighting, Dane was even better at making friends, Drott and Fulnir being two of the closest. The times he spent with them were the very best times of all. One winter, before the lake had fully frozen, the boys not yet nine, Dane, Drott, and Fulnir went fishing without permission. Drott, not the sharpest of blades, ventured out too far and, being of generous girth, fell through the thin ice into the freezing water. Unable to climb out, he thrashed about, crying for help until Dane, afraid his friend might drown, crawled out onto the ice and pulled him back to safety. After the boys had been scolded and told never to do it again, the villagers laughed at Drott's stupidity—for this wasn't the first time he'd shown ridiculously poor judgment—and he was ever after known as Drott the Dim, a name he himself found amusing.

Dane's other boyhood chum, Fulnir—who loved to play in mud and filth, rarely bathed, and loudly and frequently emitted farts so dense with stench, they made bystanders want to retch—naturally became known as Fulnir the Stinking. But this nickname in no way gave a full measure of the boy. For Fulnir, son of Prasarr the Quarreler, was a solid sort, loyal as the days were long, and as strong of heart as he was of scent. And, in truth, Dane was comforted by the odor, for he knew these other virtues came with it, and it was these strengths that most defined his friend.

Then there was Astrid, the fairest in the village, but every bit as tough as the boys. While other girls sat home with their mothers, learning to cook and sew and wait on their fathers hand and foot, Astrid was out playing with the boys, having fistfights and *snøballkrigs*, with tightly packed balls of ice. Once, after getting hit in the face with one of Dane's iceballs, Astrid had run home in tears and Dane had felt a pinprick of pain in his heart, the first stirrings of love. Days later, while sitting in a tree together, Dane had stolen a kiss and she'd punched him in the face, which only made him love her all the more. Soon after, Astrid discovered an affinity for playing with axes, and the boys pretty much left her alone. And though the sight of a girl hurling hatchets at high speeds may have seemed odd to some in the village, her father, Blek the Boatman, having no sons, encouraged her, and over the years she grew to be quite handy with them, using trees for target practice and only occasionally threatening to throw them at one of the boys.

In the spring of Dane's eleventh year, Dane, Drott, and Fulnir left the village just after dawn to hunt with their bows and arrows. The mist rose off the early-morning frost as they moved through the forest, talking of game they might kill, and of girls. Though the high grasses were thick with summer quail, Dane could think only of Astrid.

Whenever she was near, he couldn't take his eyes off her. What was happening to him? He could think of her and her only. And there were things about her he'd never noticed before. Like the way she chewed her bottom lip when thinking. How the sunlight put a kind of glowing halo round her golden hair. And her scent! Ah, sweet as wildflowers after a summer rain. And her eyes. Her smile. "The greatest beauty in the fjordlands," her father oft proudly said of Astrid. And it was true.

But never did she put her nose in the air or pretend to be above anyone else. If there were fish to be cleaned, she would gut them; if there was wood to be chopped, she'd be the first out of the hut with her axe. And daggers, cleavers, carving knives—she had mastered them all. She'd become so adept with her blades, in fact, that she'd learned to shave men of the village with nary a nick and to make crude ice carvings of Odin and Thor as yuletide gifts. Dane knew he wasn't the only boy in the village who admired her, but the thought of anyone else holding her hand or walking beside her always gave him a cold ache in the pit of his stomach. Just the day before, he'd seen Jarl the Fair giving her a lesson in archery, and the familiar way that he'd put his arm round her to guide her hands made Dane sick with anger. The schemer! Jarl always wanted what others had, if only for the pleasure of taking it away from them.

A loud *skreek!* interrupted Dane's thoughts. He saw that Drott was taking aim at a black bird perched high in a tree. "Don't," said Dane. "It's a raven." Lut had oft said that ravens were the kin of Odin, and that killing one would bring ill fortune. Drott lowered his arrow, and the boys turned away to continue hunting, and that's when Dane spied them. Wolves. Five big grays had come out of the trees behind them and quickly circled the boys, yipping and howling. Dane caught flashes of their yellow eyes and long dark tongues through the high grass.

Dane let fly an arrow. One wolf fell, the arrow sunk in its side, a spurt of blood staining its fur. But the four other wolves crept closer, and the boys, shooting the rest of their arrows and missing, scrambled to find what weapons they could. Fulnir drew a knife and waved it, hoping to keep the wolves at bay. Dane jabbed his bow at the beasts as they lunged, growling back at them in a vain attempt to scare them off. The wolves stood their ground, dancing back and forth in the grass, easily ducking the stones the boys began to throw. And then the biggest of the four sank its jaws into the end of Dane's bow and pulled it from his grasp.

"What do we do?" Fulnir cried. "Run for it?"

Dane's heart raced. The wolves drew closer, snarling and baring teeth. He knew it was useless to run. Their only chance was to stay and fight, to make the wolves believe that they were bigger and more dangerous than they really were and to scare them away. But how? The boys were running out of stones to throw.

All at once the boys heard an angry *crawk!* and, like an arrow shot by the gods, a raven swooped from above and began to attack the wolfpack. It was the very raven Dane had saved. Down it came with surprising ferocity, cawing and clawing and swooping and swiping, heroically pecking at their heads so viciously, the four wolves had to turn from the boys to fight off the bird. The wolves tried to swat the raven with their paws, but this only intensified the bird's attack. And with the boys yelling and hurling stones, and the raven attacking with unrelenting ferocity, the wolves finally retreated back across the stream into the trees. After a few desultory yips, they hung their heads, turned, and slunk off, disappearing into the deeper shadows of the forest, defeated.

The boys continued their yelling, slapping hands in victory, until they spied the bird hobbling around on the ground, unable to fly. Dane saw that the raven had been injured in the fight, its left wing broken. Lifting the bird with care, he set it upon his shoulder, and the four of them began their trek back to the village. The raven seemed at home perched beside the boy's head, and it squawked as they walked along, Dane laughing and mimicking its cry.

After a time, boy and bird had grown so at ease with each other that whenever the raven gave Dane's ear a nudge with its beak, Dane would take a berry from his sack and feed it. The three boys walked through the summer-scented forest, happy to be alive, and Dane happiest of all to have made a new friend in so unlikely a way. And though he couldn't have known it then, it was a friendship that would last the rest of his days.

4

Our Hero Goes to War with his Father

The moons rose and fell, and by the time he entered his teens, Dane had ripened into a strapping young man, stalwart and strong, with glittering blue eyes, a big, easy smile, and a shock of unruly red hair just like his father's. A skilled swordsman, adroit with bow and arrow, he could also play a lively tune on the wooden pipe. And if not exactly picture-book handsome like Jarl, he was what Astrid's father had once described as "a lad not lacking in charm."

A young man of impulsive good humor, Dane always looked to make others laugh. He would mock the explosive sound of Fulnir's epic farts or walk into a tree, imitating Blek's poor eyesight, and he could mimic the voices of most everyone in the village, especially his father's.

But one bitterly cold day at winter's end, just after he had turned thirteen, he got his comeuppance. Eager to amuse his friends, Dane hid in the outhouse, imitating with surprising accuracy the colorful oaths his father made when his bowels were stopped. "By stinkers!" he groaned. "My innards are in knots! No more horsemeat, woman! You're killin' me!" And to his delight, he heard his friends explode with laughter. But then came another voice—

"Well, I'll be dipped in weasel spit!" The outhouse door flew open. It was Voldar, come to use the privy. He'd heard the shenanigans, and now Dane was caught in the act. "I'll teach you to respect your elders!" He'd tried to grab his son, to knock some sense into him, but Dane had slipped free of his grasp and run off laughing, pulling on his long bear-fur coat as he disappeared into the woods with his friends.

"You forgot your chores!" Voldar called after him, seeing that the tree limbs he'd stacked against their house had yet to be chopped into firewood.

"I'll do it later!" came Dane's faint reply and then more snickering. Voldar fumed. Once again his son had chosen play over work, and it steamed him no end. He was all of thirteen! When would he grow up? Voldar stood there, watching the snowflakes fall in the soft afternoon light, wondering if perhaps he himself was to blame for his son's soft character, and this thought vexed him even more.

So when Dane came home an hour later without his fur coat, shivering cold and stamping his feet in front of the fire to get warm, Voldar ordered him to go chop the wood. Dane said he would, just as soon as he got warm again.

"What happened to your coat?" Voldar asked.

Dane looked sheepish and said he'd lost it.

"You *lost* it?"

Dane explained that he'd taken it off to climb a tree, but then the coat had fallen into the river and been swept away. His mother, Geldrun, said it was all right, he could use her coat. Voldar said, no, he'd go out and chop the wood wearing what he had on.

"Hey," Dane said, "it's freezing out there."

"Yes, and the cold can kill," said Voldar. "A man can easily freeze to death for want of proper clothing. You were given a coat of the finest furs, a coat your dear mother slaved for weeks to make—skinning, cutting, sewing. But you? You throw it away as if it were nothing. You appreciate nothing. And so to learn this lesson you will go out only with what you have on and do what you should have finished hours ago. Chop the wood. And you'll stay out there until it is done."

Then Dane, being headstrong, made another mistake. He said he wouldn't do it. It was too cold, he said, to go out without a coat. And it was then that Voldar rose from his chair, forcibly removed the rest of the lad's clothes, and pushed him out into the snow, shutting and barring the door behind him and shouting that because of his insolence, he would do his chores without any garments at all.

Dane stood bare naked in the freezing twilight, the falling snow and icy air so cold on his skin, it was only a few moments before he took up the axe and began to chop wood, desperate to do something to keep himself warm, as the voices of his parents continued arguing inside.

"Have you completely lost your mind?" he heard his mother ask.

"A father stern is a lesson learned," came Voldar's reply. "He *defied* me."

"But 'tisn't healthy—"

"Serves him right, disrespecting us. Discipline! *That's* what he needs."

"But," said Geldrun, "how's he to learn if he freezes to death—"

"Woman!" barked Voldar, losing patience. "It's decided!"

So naked Dane stayed out there, hacking away at the wood, his hair frosting white and lips turning blue, further humiliated as the village children appeared, jeering and pointing at his privates, receiving even worse ridicule from those his own age, particularly Jarl the Fair.

But no one laughed harder than Astrid, comely daughter of Blek the Boatman. Yes, Astrid had flowered into a fetching young lady with long blond hair the color of sunshine and a smile that lit her face whenever she laughed, a laugh so bright, it seemed to Dane the most beautiful music on earth. Whenever he heard her voice in the village or saw her at work with her axes, chopping firewood or hacking meat from a carcass, his vision grew misty and his heart filled with a feeling much like a flower in bloom, and he found it hard to speak. So when an iceball of her own hit him hard in the buttocks and he heard her giggle, it was truly a dagger to his heart.

My father doesn't understand a thing! Dane silently fumed as he stared into the fire, covered in blankets, eating the venison stew his mother had made, ignoring Voldar, who sat across the table. The cozy warmth inside reminded Dane just how bitterly cold he'd been outdoors. *How dare he humiliate me like that? In front of my friends? And Astrid? Leaving me out there a whole hour? The man's a monster!*

His father's lips were moving, but Dane refused to listen. Something about it being time to stop his foolish ways and grow up. Be a man. Time to choose what to do with his life. Be a swordsmith. Shipwright. Farmer. A trader of furs. A tender of livestock. A maker of maps or cheese. All were respectable trades, he heard his father say—

". . . and I just pray you choose the right path."

"Oh? And what path is that, Father?" Dane asked sarcastically. "Follow in *your* footsteps and become village leader?" Dane scoffed. "Uh, I don't think so."

"Well, make some decisions!" his father exploded. "A so-called man of thirteen and still no nickname? The festival is just weeks away! You haven't practiced. If that's not irresponsible, I don't know what is!"

The Festival of Greatness, competitive games held every year in the village, was a ritual rite of passage for those moving into adulthood. It was common practice that if by his fourteenth year a man had not yet received his nickname, he'd choose one of his own and keep it the rest of his days. But Dane, much to his father's shame, had yet to pick one. Dane the Dangerous. Dane the Amuser. Over the years he'd been called many names, but none had ever stuck, perhaps because, as Dane liked to believe, his positive traits were too plentiful to pin down.

"Actually," said Dane, "I *have* picked a nickname."

"Is that so," said Voldar. "And what name have you chosen, son?"

"From now on I shall be known as . . . Dane the Insane."

His father just looked at him and nodded, saying nothing, appearing to give serious consideration to what the boy had said. "You've given this a lot of thought, eh?" came Voldar's calm reply.

"Yeah. I guess. I just like the sound of it. 'Dane the Insane.' When people who know me hear it, it reminds 'em what wild fun it is to know me, and they'll laugh. And when strangers hear it, my enemies in battle, it'll make 'em think I'm insanely violent, and they'll run in fear and wet their pants in panic. 'Dane the Insane.' Pretty good, eh?"

Dane grinned, expecting it to be met with hearty approval. But the grin quickly disappeared when Voldar rose and roared at the top of his lungs, "That's doubtless the most *asinine* thing that's ever come out of your mouth! 'Dane the Insane'? Are you really *that* backward, boy? You may as well call yourself 'Dane the Idiot Son of an

Embarrassed Village Elder!'"

Dane froze, momentarily speechless.

"D'ya hear this, Geldrun? What your boy is saying?" cried Voldar, beside himself with rage. "*This* is the best you can do? What about 'Dane the Despicable'? Or 'Dane the Destroyer'? Or 'Dane the Fierce'?"

"Oh! So the only name I can pick is one of *your* choosing?" Dane yelled, now finding his tongue, his anger spilling forth. "Killing is the only thing that makes a man?"

"Of course not! But at least it's got character! Iron! 'Dane the Insane'? That's a joke. A fart in a windstorm! A—"

"But I like being funny and carefree! It's who I am!"

"You're my *son*, that's who you are!" Voldar exploded. "Don't you *ever* forget that!" His father erupted in a fit of swearing, overturning the kitchen table, his eyes afire. Dane feared they'd soon come to blows, but Voldar caught a reproachful look from Geldrun and, bottling his rage, made a supreme effort to sit back down and speak in the calmest, most well-reasoned of tones.

He explained that he'd been the same when he was young. He too had defied authority. All he'd wanted was freedom. To blazes with responsibility! But he'd been wrong, Voldar admitted. He'd come to realize that freedom itself was nothing without a family, that taking responsibility, for himself and for others: This was the true road to manhood. And he wanted this for his son more than anything.

Dane nodded, feeling stupid but not about to show it. His father laid a hand on his shoulder, blue eyes ablaze with love.

"Son," Voldar said, "it's not just having a name your enemies will respect. It's having a character your people will look up to and follow." Dane listened now, his anger subsiding. Voldar explained that the strength of a man's character, the wisdom that lay in his mind and heart, were far more valuable than the brute power found in muscle and bone. "Violence. Killing. Destroying things," said Voldar. "That's easy. Anyone can do it. But building something—a home, a friendship, a family—and making it last? That's hard. It takes a real man to do that."

Voldar rose and left the room soon after, and Dane sat for the longest time, staring into the fire, pondering what his father had told him.

"'Dane the Insane'? You actually *told* him that? Are you crazy?"

Dane was walking in the forest with his pals Drott and Fulnir, hunting quail. Klint the raven flitted about through the treetops above. (Dane had named his bird Klint after one of his own great-grandfathers on his mother's side, who had lost his wits at age thirty and fallen off a cliff while trying to fly.)

"Not a name I'd have chosen," said Drott.

"Oh, and 'Drott the *Dim*' is so heroic?" asked Dane defensively.

"No," said Fulnir, "but it's accurate."

"So is 'Fulnir the Stinking,'" said Drott with a smirk.

"Hey, I know what people say," said Fulnir. "I should feel shame for my name. That there's no dignity to it. But the way I look at it is this: On the rare occasions I *don't* smell, people are pleasantly surprised. They're thinking, 'Hmm, he doesn't smell half bad.'"

"So you're saying," said Dane, "a name shouldn't promise too much."

"Yeah. Like if your name were, say, 'Dane the Magnificent,' you'd be expected to always *be* magnificent. But c'mon, even on your best day, folks would bound to be disappointed."

"I never thought of it that way," said Dane. "So what name *should* I choose?"

They walked awhile in silence, their sealskin boots crunching over the now sun-softened snow that carpeted the forest floor. Drott suddenly stopped. "I know! You shall be known as 'Dane the Nose Picker!'"

Dane and Fulnir just looked at him. "Don't you see?" said Drott. "When you meet people and you're *not* picking your nose, they'd be favorably impressed!"

Fulnir burst into laughter. Even Klint gave a derisive squawk. Dane shook his head and walked on, his pals hurrying to follow, Drott continuing to spout more names, each more ridiculous than the last, like "Dane Fish Breath," "Dane the Strangely Warted," and "Dane the Kisser of Sheep."

Then, as Drott paused to take a breath, Fulnir said, "Why get upset? It's only a name, Dane. Just a few meaningless words thrown together to define you the rest of your days and the way generations of Norsemen will remember you long after you're dead. What's the big deal?"

Dane caught sight of the big grin on Fulnir's face and realized his friend was just messing around. "Right," said Dane. "It's only a name. I'm sure to hit on a good one by the day of the games."

Then, cresting a hill, Dane stopped in his tracks. Before him lay the snow-frosted valley, his village appearing far below like a collection of small gleaming stones beside an uncoiling ribbon of river that ran into the bay, the flower-buds dotting the trees and green shoots breaking through the melting snow crust a welcome reminder that spring was nearing. Dane and his friends gazed out in silence, absorbing the breathtaking beauty of the place they called home.

"Sweet, eh?" Dane heard Fulnir say. Dane agreed it was.

Then they slowly became aware of another imposing presence. Following the shoreline to the southernmost rim of the bay, their eyes were drawn to a great castle perched ominously on a distant cliff top overlooking the sea, its dark ramparts faintly visible above the veils of gray mist hugging the rocky shoreline.

There in his great princely castle, Dane knew, lived the man who lorded over these lands, a man to fear, his presence like some never-sleeping sentinel, ever watchful, seeing far and wide, as if this ruler's vigilance were as constant as the sun, moon, and stars themselves.

"Talk about names," said Dane softly, his voice having lost all sense of fun. "Prince Thidrek has trumped us all."

"Yeah," said Fulnir flatly. The three then fell silent, possessed by thoughts of the man in the castle, the man whose name was Thidrek the Terrifying.

And then they started homeward, threading their way through the high whispering pines, the lightness returning to their boyish hearts as they began to race each other down the rocky hillside, their laughter echoing. None had any notion of the perilous turn their lives were soon to take.

5

Enter the Villain

The hooded figure moved up the stone steps, his pace quickening, for he carried a secret so great, he could barely contain his excitement. Up the curving castle staircase he went, his torch casting a dancing light onto the steps ahead. A flurry of thoughts tore through his mind as he climbed, wondering what this might mean for the future of their fiefdom and his own future as well. As the prince's second in command, this certainly would reflect well on him, he mused; it was the kind of moment every man-in-waiting waited for, all too aware that most might wait a whole lifetime and never get a chance like this.

And Grelf the Gratuitous—for this indeed was his name—was not a man to squander opportunity. Orphaned as an infant, Grelf had grown up under the shrewd tutelage of a spice merchant who plied his trade in a large port town far to the south. The many years of indentured servitude had given Grelf a worldly education; he'd learned to cipher figures, to read and write in Latin, the Roman language, and to practice the greatest art of all: the art of listening.

Reaching the door to his master's chamber, he paused and gave a knock. A familiar voice issued forth, uttering a sharp command. Grelf put his weight against the door and it creaked open.

Peeking inside, he saw only the silhouette of his lordship seated in his grand chair before the fire, the flames licking up to form a flickering orange halo behind his head. Grelf crept closer and waited, knowing not to approach until given permission. He'd made that mistake once—invading Prince Thidrek's privacy—and he'd nearly paid with his life. Ever after he was careful to tread lightly and never speak until spoken to, and especially never to mention the knitting.

Yes, his lordship was fond of knitting, as he'd explained to Grelf, because he needed a meditative outlet to calm his violent nature. Which was perfectly fine as far as Grelf was concerned; he cared not a fig what a prince did in his leisure time behind closed doors. But then he'd witnessed the shockingly despicable and violent acts his master had committed with the knitting needles themselves, and this had given him grave doubts that the knitting had any calming influence whatsoever.

"Yes, Grelf? What is it?" The voice was dark with

irritation. Grelf saw the half-completed sweater that lay in Prince Thidrek's lap, but knew better than to offer a compliment.

"Sire . . ." Grelf began, suddenly unsure of his words.

"Well—*out* with it."

"A scouting party, sire . . . information has been uncovered. . . ." His voice trailed off. Catching a sharp look of impatience, Grelf drew closer and whispered the rest of his news directly into his lord's ear. Thidrek's eyes shot open, electrified. Could it be? Was it possible?

"I'll need more men. A lot more. And I'll want a meeting with the Berserkers. As soon as possible."

Grelf gave a nod and waited, seeing bits of firelight aglitter in his master's eyes.

"This is big, Grelf. The chance of a lifetime. The stuff kingdoms are built upon . . ."

"Yes, sire, leave it to me," said Grelf, bowing eagerly. "I'll arrange everything." Now happy to have an excuse to leave the room, Grelf backed out and pushed shut the door. He paused, taking a breath to steady himself, and then went flitting down the passageway, flush with a kind of boyish thrill about that which lay ahead. After all, it wasn't every day that the greatest power of the gods fell within reach of man.

Grelf had never seen a meaner, viler-looking group of warriors in his life. The Berserkers—eight of them, each over six feet tall, one more vicious looking than the next—

stood gathered a few yards away on the crest of a hill, the pink light of dawn glinting off the battle-axes, spears, and daggers they held at their sides. The streaks of red and yellow war paint smeared across their cheeks and noses gave them an otherworldly appearance, as if they were already dead and therefore could not be killed. Scarred, toothless, with many missing fingers—and one missing a whole arm—these men emanated a kind of casual brutality that made you glad they were on *your* side. (At least Grelf *hoped* they were to be on his side—you could never be sure of another man's loyalty until it was too late.) They also gave off an odor so ripe, it made Grelf want to hold his nose and turn away in disgust. But he knew better than to insult their lack of personal hygiene, for fear he might lose an appendage or two of his own, and he felt fairly certain he'd like to keep his arms and legs attached to his body for as long as he could.

Prince Thidrek, tall and slender as a knife, stood calmly among the beastly lot, showing not a whit of fear. He rubbed his thumb against his clean-shaven chin, speaking in a low murmur to the tallest of them, who was clearly their leader, a glowering guy whose right eye was missing and who sported a scar in the shape of a skull on his left forearm.

Grelf busied himself with watering the horses for a bit, thinking back over the events that had led him here. He'd sent a horseman the night before with a message for the Berserkers to meet His Lordship this morning here on Spiker's Hill, a neutral spot not too far from the forest where the Berserker clan made their home. Thidrek's messenger had promised there'd be no other soldiers in attendance, and he could see that this precaution had put them at ease. He caught sight of more Beserkers in the woods, no doubt waiting to see if the negotiations went to their advantage.

Not that Berserkers feared anyone or any*thing*. They were a peculiar clan of men who kept to themselves mostly, peaceable away from battle. But when called to fight, there were no men more fearsome. It was the concoction of bog myrtle and frenzy-inducing mushrooms they ate before battle that caused them to foam at the mouth and go berserk. (As Grelf knew, the word *berserkir* meant "one of bearlike strength who drinks the blood of wolves." But it being hard to get one's hand on the blood of wolves whenever one wanted to, they sometimes had to make do with bog myrtle and mushrooms to get their juices flowing.) For hours at a time they lost all reason, howling like wild animals, biting their shields, and indiscriminately butchering everything and everyone in their path with blind ferocity—even women, children, pets, and livestock of friend and foe alike (the loss of a man's livestock at times being worse than that of a wife). No doubt about it, when the Berserkers went berserk, blood did flow and you'd best be gone or lose your own head into the bargain.

Grelf heard a sudden clang of iron and voices raised in anger. He turned to see that two Berserkers were brandishing their weapons, and that Thidrek and One-Eye were in something of an argument, their words sharp and heated. One-Eye had taken a menacing step toward Thidrek and was kicking the ground with his boot, kicking up the snow. The prince calmly stood his ground but kept a firm hand on the hilt of the dagger at his belt, ready to draw and strike if need be.

"Must we be so beastly in our doings?" asked Thidrek, a touch of disdain in his voice. "Showing such lowly lack of faith?"

"Faith?" One-Eye said, and he spat out an oath to tell Thidrek what he could do with his faith.

"What's become of trusting a man's word?" asked Thidrek with a hint of judgment in his tone, and he finished off with a light chuckle.

"We trust in silver," came One-Eye's reply. "Silver speaks louder than words."

Thidrek moved not a muscle. He held One-Eye's gaze for a long, tense moment, and then he said, "So be it." And from beneath his cloak he drew out several small coin purses. He tossed the largest one to One-Eye and the others on the ground for the rest of the men to pick up. The Berserkers looked on keenly as One-Eye opened the purse, drew out a silver coin, and inspected it in the sunlight. Then, satisfied of its authenticity, One-Eye grinned and banged a balled fist to his chest, this being the common gesture of trust and good fellowship that men gave when business had been concluded satisfactorily.

Breathing easy once again, Grelf watched as the prince

and One-Eye grasped arms and shook, relieved they had at last come to an understanding. The other Berserkers followed suit, he saw, banging their chests, pocketing their purses, and walking off toward their waiting horses, muttering oaths so colorful that Grelf made a mental note to write a few of them down back at the castle so that he might commit them to memory and reuse them on special occasions to impress friends and irritate foes. Such was his love of the well-chosen phrase.

Their war mates from the woods now joined them, and they all rode off to the sound of thundering hooves. Grelf and the black-cloaked prince watched them go.

"I trust your negotiations went well, my liege?"

"Well enough," Thidrek said. "I now have a score of the fiercest mercenary soldiers at my bidding. I'd say the day's begun to my advantage."

Grelf agreed that it had, and they mounted their horses and rode off in the other direction, toward the castle and a destiny that Grelf could scarce wait to discover. With the wind blowing hard against him as he rode, it occurred to Grelf that most leaders, through sheer force of character, could instill the kind of loyalty in their men that would make them want to fight and die for their liege lord. He wondered how long the loyalty would last when it was paid for in silver rather than earned by honor.

Many men were soon to die, many innocent men, Grelf knew; but when and how many, it was too soon to tell.

Like most men who covet power, Thidrek had not amassed the lands of his fiefdom by his own effort; he had inherited them. His father, Mirvik the Mild, had ruled the land in a spirit of kindness and generosity, and so was beloved by the people. Beloved by all, in fact, except his own son. Thidrek had felt his father too weak, too sensitive, too lenient. He especially loathed the fact that his father had ended the practice of beheading, Thidrek believing that merciless brutality went a lot further than lenient compassion in building a thrifty working class. Above all, Thidrek had hated his father's name. The word *mild* represented everything he hated about Mirvik's forgiving ways, and he forever wanted to erase it from the minds of his subjects.

And so, upon his father's death, when Thidrek took command of the fiefdom, he'd taken the name "Thidrek the Terrifying" in order, as he said, "to set the right tone." From then on he'd ruled with an iron fist, torturing those even a day late with taxes and reinstituting his beloved beheadings. He even hosted Saturday execution matinees with free admission for those under ten. For while it was good to be respected, he reasoned, it was better to be feared, to have your subjects quavering at the very sound of your name. Yes, to have them shaking in their boots, that's what he craved.

He knew that fear had the power to turn fiefdoms into kingdoms. His spineless father had lacked the ruthless impulse to crush his enemies and acquire neighboring lands; hence, Mirvik the Mild had never been a king. But that did not stop his son from audaciously taking the title *prince.* As he told Grelf, "A prince is a king-in-waiting, and after a well-planned reign of terror, my waiting will be over."

But Grelf, ever crafty, was of a more politic nature. He'd heard rumblings of revolt and convinced Thidrek to ease up on the executions, if only to keep people guessing what he would do next. Keenly aware of the power of language, Grelf knew words to be the greatest weapons of all. To reshape His Lordship's image, he'd suggested with consummate tact that Thidrek's insistence on being called "the Terrifying" might be lathering it a bit thick. Stubbornly resisting, Thidrek at last agreed to drop the name from all public speeches and royal documents. Yet in his heart he still believed this to be his full and proper name, and whenever he heard *Thidrek* spoken aloud, he would—due to force of habit and his colossal conceit—sound the words *the Terrifying* to himself and hear them echo inside the vast and empty chamber of his soul.

6

A Darkness Beclouds Dane's Fate

Lut the Bent had all but forgotten the harrowing birth dream he had had about Dane so long ago. The redhead's flashing smile and sunny disposition—his innate good-heartedness—had made Lut feel nothing but a deep, abiding affection for the boy. But shortly after Dane had had the fight with his father, a vague sense of foreboding again descended upon the seer, and then, just before the Festival of Greatness, the doom dream came again. . . .

Lut stood in his village, horrified as a glistening river of blood rolled toward him. He saw a half dozen human heads stuck on spikes, the eyes and mouths shrieking in pain as their own headless bodies danced before them. Women opened their mouths to scream and black smoke poured forth. And then a humongous wolf-monster, black as pitch, rose from the sea and descended on the town, its jaws devouring everyone in sight. As the children fled, the wolfen thing gobbled one, two, as if they were mere morsels. With one whipping blow of its tail, it obliterated the flaming huts, sending fiery debris shooting into the night sky to form stars. And then Lut saw Dane, the red-haired one, riding atop the wolf-monster! The boy rode as if on horseback, in full control of the beast, his gleaming sword held high. Dane and the wolf-creature then bent their heads in unison to look down at Lut. Lut backed away, frantically trying to escape, but the boy gave a chilling cry, and next he knew, the wolf-thing was upon him. Snatched in its jaws and swallowed, Lut felt himself plunging into the very belly of the beast, tumbling amid the blood-wet bodies of others who had been eaten, engulfed in screams and—

Lut awoke, his heart hammering, his body bathed in sweat, barely able to breathe. He sat up, trying to clear his mind, but the nightmarish images wouldn't leave. He bolted down some warm ale to settle his nerves and clear his mind. Each of the agonized faces in the dream, he realized, was a person of his village. Worse, it was the same dream! The same one that had visited him on the night of the boy's birth so long ago! *And* the same dream he'd been having just the night before and the night before that!

Three nights in a row now, the same horrid nightmare had visited him, each time more vivid than the last. Lut shuddered. He could no longer ignore it; there was no doubt anymore. The dream had deep significance. But what exactly *did* it mean? Alone, the wolf could have signified any number of things. The coming of an invading army. A deadly avalanche. A nasty bout of crotch rot. But the redhead riding the beast! That *had* to be Dane! Did it mean, as Lut feared, that the boy was ill-fated? That he was destined to bring death and destruction to them all? Lut didn't want to believe it—it was too disturbing; but he knew there was only one way to know for sure.

Turning to a small altar, he lit a tallow candle and a sprig of rosemary and took out a worn sealskin sack. Opening it, he drew out the sacred runes, small discs of elk bone and antler, each the shape of a large coin and worn smooth on both sides. Each runebone had letters of the runic alphabet carved into it, each of which corresponded to key aspects and elements of the Viking world.

For Norsefolk, reading the runes was the most reliable way to interpret dreams and thereby divine the future as writ by the gods. Handed down by his forbears, divination was the most sacred act a seer could perform for his people, said to allow men to listen to the very whispers of the gods.

As always, Lut the Bent went about his runecasting with great reverence. Cupping the runes in his hands, Lut bent over his furs and closed his eyes, slowing his breathing, clearing his mind, becoming an open vessel. He began to chant the names of his forefathers, calling upon the gods and beseeching the runes to speak. And then, when an inner voice told him it was time, Lut tossed the runes into the air. One by one they fell and came to rest on the earthen floor, the symbols that had fallen faceup forming a message. Lut opened his eyes, and there he saw, illuminated in the flickering candlelight, the future written in the bones. His awful dream was true! The boy indeed would bring catastrophe to the village and everyone in it, though the when, where, and how of it were not revealed.

Lut's mouth went dry. He felt a dizziness in his head and tightness in his chest. He knew it was his duty to pass this foreknowledge on to the village elders—*and* to Voldar—but for a moment he considered not telling anyone. After all, wasn't it possible he was wrong? That he'd misread the signs, and it was all a colossal mistake? He was old, he knew, and prone to periodic bouts of befoggery and forgetfulness. Lut sighed in deep resignation. No, he wasn't wrong. Painful as it would be, he had to go to his chieftain and tell the truth about the boy. But how would the great man react? His own son a danger, fated to destroy his own people?

Lut knew Voldar would have no choice but to banish the boy from the village, send him out to fend for himself in the wild, like other ill-starred children Lut had seen abandoned in his youth, a gruesome sentence that few survived. And with the Festival of Greatness being held the next morning, the timing could not have been worse. But so be it. Lut was old and nearing death, he knew, and so his final act on earth would be to honor his people. To do what must be done and say what must be said. To cast out one life in order to spare the lives of many. For generations they had lived and died by this code, and so it would be again.

Pulling on a sheepskin for warmth, he rose and shuffled to the open door of his hut. Outside, a light sprinkle of rain fell, veiling the moon in a silvery glow. Yes, he would tell his chieftain, he would have to. But first he would have some rye cake and cider. And sleep. Yes, more sleep. He was aged and weary and in desperate need of sleep.

7

Dane Receives a New Name

At last the day came for the Festival of Greatness, gray blustery dawn skies turning sunny and warm. Dane rose early, meeting his friends in town, as he always did, to watch the festivities unfold.

The games being a great source of entertainment, Norsefolk came from miles around to watch, and to snack. That morning, Dane watched as a dozen longships from outlying villages came ashore, bringing scores of onlookers both young and old. Gathering then in the village, the women shared gossip and recipes for pickled herring, while the men drank copious amounts of home-brewed ale, told raucous stories, and headbutted each other senseless. A few laid wagers on who could vomit the farthest. And all this by nine in the morning.

Being spirited young men, Dane, Drott, and Fulnir eyed the women in their foxtail furs and feathered finery, bowing politely to the older, already-married ones and acting even friendlier to the younger yet-to-be wed ones. It was customary to marry in one's middle-teen years, life being so short and there being no reason to wait on starting a family. (Average life expectancy was so brief, a man of thirty was considered all washed up.)

Male elders sat by themselves on the north side of the field, it being expected that the sexes sit apart during high ceremonies such as sporting games and divorce proceedings to keep fighting and hair pulling to a minimum. And as the females filled the rows of benches on the far side, Fulnir went from girl to girl, chatting them up and asking the prettiest ones if they'd dance with him at the feast that evening, Dane all the while marveling at his boldness.

Drott, ever bashful in the presence of the fairer sex, took a slightly different approach. When he saw a girl he liked, he threw stones at her to get her attention. If she scowled and ran, he knew she wasn't for him; but if she picked up the stone and threw it *back* at him? Well, then he'd really found a girl worth knowing. On this particular morning, as the ladies paraded past, one of Drott's stones found the rump of a rather hefty girl. She whirled and, spotting Drott as the culprit, spat an oath and threw a stone right back. A look of joy spread across Drott's face. Then, to his surprise, she gave an animal growl and charged like a wild boar, yowling and running straight at Drott, intent on doing him bodily harm. Drott gleefully ran off, the girl in hot pursuit, leaving Dane smiling and shaking his head as the two disappeared into the crowd.

And Dane? Though he pretended otherwise to his pals, he thought only of Astrid. He scanned the crowd for a glimpse of her, hoping to have a moment together before the games began. He had something to say to her. Something important. And he yearned to be alone with her, away from the prying eyes of his parents. Like Lut, he too had had a dream the night before, a troubling dream in which he and Astrid were afloat on a cloud, blissful and free. But when he went to kiss her, he accidentally knocked her off the cloud and she fell screaming earthward. Dane was unable to save her from a death he feared he'd caused.

Dane had awoken early and left before his parents arose. He hadn't spoken to his father about his name since the day they'd fought. He hadn't wanted to think about it, or to face him; something in him still refused to give in or to grow up. His mind in turmoil, Dane couldn't quite make sense of it all. And then he spied Lut the Bent. His old friend had been avoiding him, it seemed to Dane, but now there he was, rounding a corner, shuffling along at what, for Lut, was a rather high speed. And Dane felt the urgent need to get the old man's counsel.

"Lut!" Dane called, raising his voice above the raucous din. But Lut didn't stop. Dane fought his way through the throngs. "Lut, it's me!" he said as he caught up and took Lut's arm. "I need to talk! I had a dream—"

Lut dropped his eyes, darting them this way and that, not wanting to meet Dane's gaze. "Not now, son, I—" Lut fell silent, unable to give voice to his thoughts. "I—I have to go!" And with that he sped off.

Dane felt stung. Rebuffed by his closest confidant when he most needed to talk? Why? What had he done? What had spooked Lut so? Dane had seen something in the old one's eye, and it disturbed him. What made Lut run off?

Dane's mood would have darkened further, but the sudden blare of a horn struck all thought of Lut from his mind. He sensed a tension in the air, a murmur of fear amid the commonfolk. The horn announced the arrival of Thidrek the Terrifying, lord and ruler of their northern fjordlands.

From out of the trees he came, the twin red flags bearing his black wolf's-head emblem. The flag bearers themselves rode horses draped in the royal colors. Next came a marching phalanx of some twenty guardsmen, in leather and coats of mail, their heads helmeted in iron, their long spears held at their sides and pointed skyward in warrior fashion, sunlight glinting off the tips. Then, astride a shiny black stallion, his long black satin cloak rippling, Prince Thidrek himself rode into the village, quieting the raucous crowd.

To Dane he looked ever so lordly and imperious atop his horse, and even more imposing walking among the commoners. He stood six foot four, with long, black hair, finely combed and worn in a ponytail. His piercing gaze was said to be so penetrating that it made men's bowels squiggle in disquietude. People bowed and averted their eyes as he passed, fearing that to meet his gaze would incur Thidrek's displeasure, a thing to be avoided at all costs.

Dane stood at the rear of the hushed crowd, watching. Growing up within sight of the castle, Dane and his friends had heard tales of Thidrek's cruelties: Far to the south he had terrorized entire villages, making men dance while wearing their wives' clothing before he had them executed. And he took special pleasure in watching things die: Men, women, horses—even children and their pets, if the mood struck him. It was said that, just for entertainment's sake, he would force doddering old folk to fight to the death with nothing but knives, and even wager on which one would win.

They'd also heard tell of his own terrifying skill with weaponry. A master archer, Thidrek was rumored to be so skilled, he could shoot an arrow straight through a man's heart at a hundred paces. Even more daunting was his swordsmanship. As a youth, Thidrek was so deft, he'd lopped off the heads of two men with one lightning-quick swipe of his broadsword. Knowing of his athletic prowess, Voldar had once invited Thidrek to compete in the games, but the prince had graciously declined, citing a schedule conflict.

Dane had heard talk among the villages that something was afoot, whisperings to the effect that Thidrek had plans to expand his empire. He was hungry for more land, more taxes, more power. Recent comings and goings at the castle had set tongues a-wagging but, as yet, no one really knew what Thidrek was after. All the village elders, even Dane's own father, were careful to say nothing against Thidrek. And though Dane knew full well why fear had silenced them, he couldn't help recalling that it hadn't always been this way. There'd been a time in Dane's boyhood, soon after Thidrek had launched his reign of terror on the northlands, when Voldar had spoken ill of Thidrek without fear. Dane remembered the night he had awoken in his bed-straw to hear the voices of Voldar and other elders of the village, gathered round a fire outside his home, drinking and discussing Thidrek's doings.

"Bloody dung eater," he'd heard his father mutter. "I'd sooner piss down his throat than bow to his wishes." Dane had been shocked to hear these words come from his father, but had been excited by them all the same. Voldar had continued fuming and fulminating against Thidrek's oppressive reign, bemoaning the loss of Mirvik the Mild and the lost days of his own reckless youth, when no man who dared disrespect him would live to see the dawn of another day.

Unaware his boy was listening, Voldar had gone on to vividly describe the many ways he'd like to bring discomfort to Thidrek, something about having him trampled by horses and thrown into a pit aswarm with poisonous vipers and then having his fingers chopped off, one knuckle at a time, then his toes, and maybe each of his ears, and then when Thidrek lay bleeding and pleading to be put out of his misery, Voldar would lash him to a tree and smear him with honey and leave him for the bears to finish off one limb at a time. And when it was all over, he'd remove Thidrek's head and have it mounted on a spike outside his hut with his eyes propped open, and every time he went in or out, he would smile and say hello and then spit in Thidrek's face and ask how he was feeling.

There'd been more uproarious laughter, until Dane's mother had discovered him listening in. She'd scolded the elders and bidden them go home to their wives. She'd upbraided Voldar for having used such foul language in front of the boy, and Voldar had then explained to Dane that it had all been in fun and that it was something men did when they wished to impress one another and that he hadn't meant a word of it. But Dane knew the truth, and had been proud of his father for speaking out so fearlessly.

Now, as Dane stood with his father and mother alongside the council of elders, welcoming the self-proclaimed prince, Dane was saddened to see what his father had become: a servile supplicant. He saw the dark pleasure Thidrek took in seeing these grown men—men Dane had looked up to his whole life—bow to him and touch their forelocks in fealty. Dane, his insides aboil with fear and shame, in turn bowed in obeisance before his liege lord, the prankster in him fighting the urge to make light of it all.

The prince was presented with gifts: casks of mead, doeskin slippers, and a long ermine coat with the name THIDREK stitched across the back. But as Thidrek's gaze fell upon his name, his smile withered. His eyes went cold and, drilling Voldar with a look, he said gravely, "Where's 'The Terrifying'?"

The crowd went silent, all fearing Voldar's blood would soon be spilled. Dane feared it too as he saw his father's face go pale. It angered him to see this once-great man, his own father, forced to cower like a child.

"Well, my lord . . ." choked Voldar, fumbling for an answer that would keep him alive, but not having one. "It's—it's—"

And Dane was as shocked as everyone else when he found himself stepping forth and blurting, "It's only a lounging jacket, sire."

Oops. Too late. The words were out.

"A *lounging* jacket?" intoned the prince, eyes narrowing.

"Yes!" said Dane with an innocent grin, realizing he now had to explain his idiotic remark. "You know, casual attire to be worn round the house. Or, in your case, castle, sire. When you're lounging alone, smoking a pipe, or having a brandy before bed, or whatever it is that great men such as yourself do in the privacy of your rooms. Because let's face it, you are great and, uh, you do have rooms. Many, many rooms."

Thidrek stared at the boy for a painfully long moment. Then, with the barest hint of a smile, he said, "I was only joking."

His royal guardsmen guffawed in laughter. What a jest! Voldar laughed as well, profoundly relieved to still have his head. Dane, too, was feeling lucky—until he caught Thidrek's baleful stare.

"So," said Thidrek, "pray who *is* this young pup?"

"Begging your lordship's pardon, sir, he meant no disrespect," said Voldar proudly. "This is my son, Dane. Dane the . . . uh . . . Defiant." Dane shot his father a look, but then caught himself and bowed to the prince in obeisance.

"Defiant, eh?" Thidrek said, eyeing Dane appraisingly. "Well, I like a boy with nerve. So long as he knows his place." He then turned to Grelf the Gratuitous, his right-hand man, who for some inexplicable reason stood to Thidrek's left. "Isn't that right, Grelf?"

"Oh, yes, sire," said Grelf, "a place for everyone and everyone in their place, I always say. Best way to run a fiefdom. And speaking of running, shan't we be moving along, sir? The games await." Thidrek agreed, and without further ado, Grelf led Thidrek away.

Voldar moved to join them, but Dane held his father back. "Dane the *Defiant*? Father, how could you? That's not the name I wanted!"

"Well, it's the name I've given you," said Voldar, "and a fine name it is. Even the prince was struck by it. It's the nature of your character, too, if you must know. Defiant, rebellious, willful, headstrong. If you're lucky, someday you might live up to all the promise it holds."

"But Father—"

"I'll hear nothing further. I bid you luck in the games, Son. Give it your all. Now if you'll excuse me, I have a tyrant to appease." Voldar turned and strode away from the scowl on his son's face.

Voldar led Prince Thidrek and his retinue to the most honored place on the field, a great wooden throne carved of oak and set atop a viewing platform. There with great fanfare Thidrek waved to the crowd and took his seat, Voldar sitting to his left and Grelf—being the right-hand man—this time sat, correctly, to his right. Thidrek again waved to those assembled and, having a fine eye for the ladies, gazed with keen interest over the girls in the fourteen-and-older section.

"I like blondes," he told Voldar. "Buxom and blond, that's how I like 'em."

Voldar nodded noncommittally. All too aware of Thidrek's mercurial moods, he knew no argument could arise from his silence.

"And redheads, if the mood strikes me," Thidrek continued.

"Yes, m'lord," said Voldar, "*rødhåres* are nice."

"I once had a beastly maggot of a woman who shaved her head and bit the heads off rabbits for fun. Hideously foul smelling she was, stank like an odious cheese, but, oh, how she danced!"

Not knowing what to say, Voldar just nodded and grinned, as if this were the most fascinating thing he'd ever been told. This upstart had the gall to call himself a prince? The barbarian in him wanted to take a knife to Thidrek's throat right then and there. But this, he knew, would only lead to more killing and, his love for family being greater than his need for blood, he stifled the urge. For now, survival for his kinsmen lay in his appeasing Thidrek's every wish and whim, and this he would do 'til such time as things were different.

Anxious to get on with it, Voldar gave a signal and the hornsman blew a ram's horn.

The crowd quieted. Voldar drew the Shield of Odin from its fur-trimmed sheath. He was about to rise with it when Thidrek himself abruptly took the Shield from his hands and held it aloft for all to see, wanting this moment all for himself. Voldar stayed seated, gazing at the Shield agleam in the sun as Thidrek moved it left to right, reflecting rays of sunlight off the disk and onto the people gathered on the field below. No sound was heard as every man, woman, and child fixed their eyes on the sacred talisman. Eldermen stood, straining to be hit with the light. Mothers raised babies into these gleaming flashes, believing that to be touched by this godly glitter—the very "light of Odin's Eye"—was to be bathed in its protective powers and blessed with good luck and good health as well.

Thidrek, it seemed to Voldar, was anxious for his own moment of glory, for he soon dropped the Shield into Voldar's lap and struck a regal pose. And, keenly attuned to the use of the dramatic pause, Thidrek gave his subjects time to gaze upon him in wonderment. When they'd been given a long enough look, he raised his arm and let his princely voice ring out.

"Let the games begin!" he cried. And so decreed, the competition commenced.

And great games they were! Archery and axe-throwing contests for both distance and accuracy. Tree-climbing and wood-chopping and spear-throwing. There were foot races and boat races and wrestling matches and rope-pulls. There were even ice-carving and cheese-sculpting contests for the less athletically inclined. The winner of each match moved on to the quarterfinals, the semifinals, and finally to the final finals.

The crowd saw amazing feats of athletic prowess. One young man could lift twice his weight in ox manure. Another could wrestle three men at once and pin them all. There was even a senior division, in which the elderly (those over forty years of age, long past their prime) were allowed to compete in contests more suited to their physical abilities, such as ale chugging and thumb wrestling.

There were also moments of lesser athletic prowess. During the river-cross—with men racing hand over hand along ropes suspended across a raging torrent of water—Drott the Dim had lifted a hand to wave to his mother on shore, fallen in, and nearly drowned. And in a tree-climb, Orm the Hairy One lost his footing and fell down onto Fulnir, who was clinging to a limb right below him, and they both went tumbling all the way to the ground, where they landed in a heap and lay moaning and writhing in pain, and had to be carried off and tended to. This, of course, drew cheers from the raucous crowd, seeing others cry out and writhe in pain being the whole reason most folk watched sporting events in the first place. The other reason being to watch people actually die.

Perhaps most popular of all was Astrid, Mistress of the Blade, as she had come to be called. Looking fine and fetching in furred vest and blond braids, she put on a dazzling display of axe throwing that had the crowd on its feet. In speed, distance, or accuracy, no one could beat her, and by midafternoon she'd swept all five axe-throwing events, winning a standing ovation. Then, as spectators chanted for more, she began juggling her axes, spinning them up in the air two, three, four at a time, until finally she was juggling five axes at once, each sharp enough to slice off a finger in one false move. And then—just as the crowd thought she could do no better—she caught and threw them one by one backward over her shoulder and *thwik! thwik! thwik! thwik! thwik!* each axe sank into the side of a tree, forming the runic symbol ᚨ, which represented her name.

The Blade Mistress had done it again! The place exploded in cheers! No one appeared more pleased than her father, Blek the Boatman, who looked on in pride, cheering a little too loudly at his daughter's prowess.

Thidrek took a keen interest too, telling Voldar that he thought Astrid possessed "remarkable poise and a pleasing shape." She would make a fine serving wench, he went on to say, to cook and clean and polish a man's armor and bring him a drink whenever he liked and work out the kinks in his back. Voldar agreed, saying the Blade Mistress's beauty was indeed a subject much talked about throughout the surrounding fjordlands, and adding that several men had already approached Blek with proposals to take her to wife, but her father had driven them off at spearpoint.

Dane gazed at Astrid with the kind of singular intensity and longing that only comes to one first in love or to a wolverine in heat. He cared dearly for the girl, and not a night went by that he didn't wish upon the stars and ask the gods to grant him the strength, charm, and musculature to win her affections and someday make her his wife.

But Astrid was no buttercup. Though she had feelings for Dane, she wasn't going to let him win her easily. Others sought her hand. Suitors from neighboring locales and even eligible young men from her own village had given her pause.

There was the good-looking Jarl the Fair, for example. And once or twice she'd entertained the notion of going with Orm the Hairy One, but the thought of all that braiding and combing had put her off. This, and his annoying habit of saving the heads of all the animals he'd killed. No, there'd be no easy way into her heart. To win her, a young man would have to prove himself worthy. She wasn't going to give in and give over to just any smooth talker who professed undying love. She knew that, for love to last, for it to grow and endure the various calamities of life, a man must be made of harder stuff than talk. And though her affections were with Dane, he still had yet to prove that he possessed the kind of inner fire her heart told her she deserved in a man.

Dane fought hard to stand out in the day's contests, and by afternoon's end, it was down to him and Jarl in the final round. They were called out to the center of the field and stood side by side in the sun.

Jarl the Fair had great hair. Gorgeously long flowing locks that shone golden in the sun. He did a thing with it—tossing back his head to flip his hair off his forehead—and when he did the hair thing, the girls would squeal in delight and Jarl's toothy grin would grow wider, his muscles would bulge a bit bigger, and his chest would puff up ever so slightly. This made girls swoon all the more, which was the very effect he hoped it would have. This kind of display of vanity was known in the village as "doing a Jarl," and no one could do it quite like him, what with his golden hair, his high cheekbones, and his high opinion of himself.

It drove Dane mad to see Jarl so full of himself. Boastful and brash and so arrogantly humorless! "What do they see in that guy?" he once asked Fulnir while out on a soul-searching walk.

"Great hair, good looks, a fine singing voice—"

"I *know* what they *see* in him! It was just a rhetorical question."

"Oh. Right." They walked on.

"What does *rhetorical* mean again?" asked Fulnir a few moments later, but Dane didn't answer.

Jarl and Dane stood side by side in the center of the field, preparing to face each other in the final round of competition.

"And now . . ." the ringmaster's voice rang out, *"the final round!"* Jarl did the hair thing. Girls went wild. Even some men cheered. Jarl did a two-fisted "victory dance," playing to the crowd and drawing more cheers. This dented Dane's confidence, until he caught sight of Astrid waving to him, and he waved right back. Jarl then threw her a wave of his own, grinning his perfect-toothed grin, and under his breath said to Dane: "She'll be my wife, y'know."

Dane eyed Jarl and, keeping a smile on his face for the crowd, said, "She'll be *mine* or I'll die trying." At that moment the ringmaster again called to the crowd.

"Jarl the Fair! . . . versus Dane the Defiant!"

Dane's friends on the sidelines cheered when they heard his name announced. Astrid did too, he noticed, as did Klint, who gave a *crawk!* of comment from high in the fir trees overlooking the field.

Jarl merely sneered. "Ooo, 'Dane the Defiant,'" he said mockingly. "I'm *so-o-o* scared."

Dane's cheeks burned in anger. He yearned to flatten Jarl right there and easily could have had the flag not been raised, signifying that the final event had begun.

They drew lots. Dane's hopes sank as he saw Jarl draw the long straw. It meant Jarl would choose archery. Dane was handy with bow and arrow, but Jarl was a master. There was no way Dane could win. Briefly, he entertained the notion that if he signaled to Klint, the bird could fly high in the air and knock Jarl's arrow off course. That would surely fix him, Dane thought, cheered by the idea of Jarl humiliated in defeat. But this, he knew, would be cheating, a thing strictly forbidden in Viking society. The Viking code of honor was a sacred bond, never to be broken. So Dane said not a word.

From his seat beside Thidrek, Voldar looked down in pride, silently imploring the gods to give his son strength for the final contest. Dane had greatly surprised him in getting this far. He'd thought the boy would surely be eliminated by now, believing him somewhat lacking in stamina. Yet there he was, his own flesh and blood, one of the last two standing. Perhaps Dane had it in him after all. The crowd went silent. The day's events would be decided by three shots: each man to let fly three arrows, and he who shot the farthest would be declared the winner. Voldar saw that Thidrek too had taken interest in the outcome; his lordship's gaze was fixed on the field.

Jarl and Dane took turns shooting arrows. And when it was over, the ringmaster pronounced it a draw: Each had shot the same distance. Now it was a free shot; each man would do the trick shot of his choice.

Jarl shot first. He pointed his bow straight up in the air over his head and, holding his arm stock-still, let it fly. *Bzing!* Up, up it flew, disappearing, it seemed, into the clouds . . . and then down, down it came, speeding straight for Jarl. He moved not a muscle. The crowd gasped. His arrow was falling directly toward him; if he didn't move, he'd surely be killed. Then, at just the last moment, he thrust his bow aloft over his head and *thwwfft!* the arrow point sank into the wooden bow itself, stopping inches from Jarl's face.

Cheers went up! The spectators could scarcely believe it, and neither could Dane. He was beaten. He knew he had no trick shot to top Jarl's stunt. He dropped his bow and walked off the field, the villagers rushing past him to crowd around and congratulate the victor, their chants of "Jar-rl! Jar-rl! Jar-rl!" making Dane feel empty and small.

Astrid felt sick. She'd dearly wanted Dane to win. Feeling his pangs of dejection as if they were her own, she tried to find the words that might ease his pain. Pushing through the throngs of commoners, she was halfway to him when the crowd abruptly parted, and a tall commanding figure moved toward her.

It was Prince Thidrek, pinning her with his coal-black stare.

"*You*, young lady," said Thidrek, "were magnificent. Allow me to congratulate you." Curtsying, she offered her hand. He kissed it and said, "Do me the honor of dining with me tonight at the feasting?"

She eyed her father, then Thidrek. What could she do but accept? And by the time Thidrek withdrew, she looked round to see Dane was nowhere to be found.

Lut the Bent felt momentarily dizzy as the crowd swarmed round him, streaming toward the feasting tables. Where was Voldar? And how would he tell him of his awful premonition with so many people around? He'd wanted to take him aside and tell him at first light that morning. But he'd overslept, and by the time he'd risen and stretched and bathed and combed his beard and breakfasted on ale and salt fish, well, Voldar had been too involved in preparation for the festivities. Then Lut had been asked to say a blessing over the athletes and Thidrek had arrived, and then the games had begun and Lut decided he'd have to wait until later. But when? The longer he waited, the harder it would be. Wearied by the long day in the sun, his belly rumbling in hunger, he looked for a place he might sit down and rest. Yes, he would get his strength back. He needed his strength.

And then the crowd parted and there was Voldar, standing right in front of him, deep in excited conversation with a half dozen elders from the outlying villages, the men all drinking with gusto and replaying favorite highlights of the day's games. Lut saw too that Thidrek himself was among them, joining in the joviality.

"Lut!" said Voldar, spotting the old one. "Great games, huh?"

Stepping forward, Lut cleared his throat and tried to speak.

"My friend—" he rasped. "I need a word."

"A word?" Voldar said, playing up to the men. "I got a word—*bacchanal*! How's *that* for a word?" The men exploded in knowing laughter. Lut felt his nerve now faltering, acutely aware this was the worst moment possible for broaching such a delicate subject.

Then, noticing Lut needed to speak, Voldar said, "What is it, Lut?"

In a blink, everyone stopped talking. They turned to stare at the seer, waiting to hear what he had to say. But Lut couldn't speak. His mind went blank. His throat went dry. His insides quaked with hunger. The sky spun overhead. His thoughts were ablur. Lifting his gaze, he found Thidrek staring at him, the dark eyes drilling into his.

"It's about—your son . . . ," Lut blurted out.

"What about him?" said Voldar.

"I—I—"

"Well, out of with it, old man!" said Thidrek, drawing a laugh from the men. Lut's nerve then evaporated altogether.

And Lut said, "He played well today."

"Yes, yes, that he did," said Voldar. "Now to the feast." And off he went with Thidrek and the others. Lut was only too relieved to see them go.

8

A Feast of Delicious Complications

The feast was a grand event. There were goats and wild boar and game birds roasting on open spits, a long buffet table laden with dish after dish of great hearty fare, such as elk steaks and rabbit stews and smoked fish, and platters piled high with various breads, nuts and cheeses. There were sauces aplenty, sugared plums, and mounds of fresh elderberries for dessert, and, as always, lots of freshly churned butter.

Inside a great circle of torches, the athletes and their families sat at long, roughhewn tables having a raucously good time, guzzling mead made of fermented honey, stuffing their faces, and pinching the bottoms of the womenfolk who served up the food.

At the head of the main table sat Thidrek and his retinue, along with Voldar, Geldrun, Blek the Boatman, and other village dignitaries. Astrid sat to Thidrek's left, as his guest of honor, or "dinner companion" as he insisted on calling her. And Jarl, as winner of the games, sat to his right.

Much to Astrid's surprise, Thidrek was thoroughly charming, engaging in witty repartee, complimenting the athletes, taking his drink in moderation—acting in every way the perfect gentleman, not at all the imperious, overbearing boor she'd heard he could be. At times he actually paused to listen to what others had to say, chuckling at jibes that proved unamusing, not once interrupting or disagreeing. And when Blek lamely blurted out that the taxes on their village were too high, instead of ordering that the man's tongue be cut out, Thidrek calmly explained that, yes, perhaps they were a bit steep, but it was all to build new roads to encourage trade between the villages, which would thus improve the economy and hasten in a highly desirable thing called "progress."

"Bah! Bring back the old days," said Jarl, with a mouthful of food and a head full of drink. "Pillage and plunder. That's what real Norsemen were made for. 'Live off the land'? Pisspots! We'll have peace in death. We, the living, should spill blood!" He gobbled another portion of boar meat, chewing with his mouth wide open, and as its juices dribbled down his chin, he thoughtlessly wiped his mouth on his sleeve, leaving a long, unsightly smear of grease.

What happened next was a revelation to Astrid and other women at the table. Thidrek drew from his pocket a soft, square piece of cloth, wiped his lips and mustache clean of gravy, and then returned it to his pocket. Astrid and the other ladies looked upon this in wonder. A man had actually cared enough to remove the unsightly food particles from his mouth! Thidrek noticed their interest.

"It's a *lommetørklæde*," he explained patiently. "A handkerchief. What a true gentleman uses at table. Part of a new idea called 'personal etiquette' that's all the rage on the continent." Not wanting Jarl to feel bad, he added, "No way for you to have known, boy—just one of the perks of upper-class life, I suppose."

Jarl issued a loud belch and laughed, unaware that the older man had just insulted his utter lack of sophistication. "Whatever," Jarl muttered, and refilled his mead cup.

Thidrek then paid a compliment to the table centerpiece, a handmade ice sculpture of a flower, its open petals aglow from the lighted candle inside. With obvious pride, Blek said his own daughter, the Mistress of the Blade, had carved it.

"I've never seen a woman so artful with an axe," Thidrek said, flashing Astrid a grin, "or so deadly with a smile." And then the sound of music filled the air. Musicians—three pipers, two lyre strummers, and a drummer—had arrived and begun to play. Stirred by the music, one by one everyone began to join in a chain dance.

"Ah, music," said Thidrek, and he turned expectantly to Astrid. But Jarl was already on his feet and saying, "Honor me, dear lady?"

She hesitated, not wanting to breach princely protocol. But Thidrek, ever the gentleman, nodded his approval, knowing that the winner of the games always had first pick of the ladies.

She rose, bowing once to the prince, and went off to join Jarl at the end of the chain of dancers.

⚡

Dane fumed. Stuck at the far end of the table, twenty seats away, he could barely eat, having to watch both Thidrek and Jarl seated beside *his* girl! They looked too cozy up there, the three of them smiling and chatting away like the best of mates. It sickened him to see it, and the longer the night went on, the worse he felt. And then seeing Astrid get up to dance next to Jarl—well, that just tore it. Taking a flagon of mead, Dane stood to walk out, but caught a reproachful look from his father at the far end of the table. Obediently, he first went to Prince Thidrek and, with all the decorum he could muster, bowed in courtly fashion and bade his lord good night.

"Turning in early, I take it?" asked Voldar.

Dane gave a sullen nod.

"Well, good job in the games, son."

Dane produced a shrug and a half smile, turned, and walked off.

"Good lad," said Thidrek to Voldar.

"Yes, my lord. Still too young to show proper respect to his elders, I fear."

Thidrek waved it off. "Shows spirit. Guts. He's his own

man." Then he added, "Could be worse. You could have *him* for a son." Thidrek nodded toward Drott the Dim, who at that very moment was crawling across the ground with a leg of roast lamb clenched in his jaws, grunting and growling like a deranged dog at no one in particular, looking every bit the village idiot.

"Yes," Voldar agreed. "Much worse."

Out on the dance floor, Astrid wasn't giving Jarl an inch. She hadn't wanted to dally with him at all, having agreed only so as to avoid dancing next to Thidrek. She felt uncomfortable under the prince's penetrating gaze. Yes, he was handsome; yes, he was charming; and, yes, he had a certain rakish appeal. But her intuition told her that his intentions were anything but honorable. Flush with the exaggerated emotions often found in girls her age, she felt a sudden hand on her shoulder. A chill shot through her when she heard Thidrek's voice, all velvet. "I believe it's my turn," he oozed.

Jarl bowed and went away wordlessly. Steeling herself, Astrid turned to Thidrek, put her hand in his, and allowed him to join in the dance next to her.

As she nervously made small talk, Thidrek's gaze never wavered. He kept his eyes fastened only on her. As she danced beside him, she felt the cold hard cut of his leather coat against her side, his steady gaze drilling into hers. The image of a scaly reptile suddenly leaped to mind. A snake, perhaps. Or one of those green four-legged crawly things with the long tail her father had brought back from one of his long sea voyages to the south. What was it called? A lizard? Yes, that was it! Thidrek reminded her of a lizard. A sly creature with cold, rough skin and eyes that seemed to pierce right through her. The words of her father came back to her now as she recalled what he'd often said while gazing at the prince's distant castle: "There is nothing colder than the heart of a tyrant."

Absorbed in this reverie, she was surprised to find Thidrek moving closer, pulling her into the shadows and putting his mouth on hers, or trying to, at least. Astrid stepped away before he could successfully complete his maneuver, careful to keep the smile on her face and conceal her revulsion.

"I'm feeling poorly, m'lord," she said quickly, clutching her belly as if ill. "Something I ate disagrees with me. I should take my leave."

"By all means," Thidrek purred. "Tend to thy health, dear girl. So that one day we may dance again."

"It shall be an honor, sire," she said, and then excused herself with a curtsy, turned, and walked off, relieved to be free of him.

Moments later, having watched this last with some concern, Grelf arrived at Thidrek's side and asked if they should save a slice of elderberry pie for him, though he really only wanted to be sure his master hadn't been rattled by the girl's rudeness. His nostrils flaring, Thidrek said nothing, fixing his gaze on the girl as she disappeared past the torchlit line of dancers and into the shadows of the village beyond. Noticing the possessiveness in Thidrek's stare, a look he'd too often seen before, Grelf issued a naughty smile.

"Caught your eye, has she, m'lord?" Grelf asked airily.

The look Thidrek gave him in return suggested that she might have caught more than that.

9

Life Is Torn Asunder

Dane couldn't sleep. He lay in his bed-straw, tossing and turning, his mind astir. No matter how hard he tried to think of other things, images of Jarl and Thidrek whirled through his head, making sleep impossible. Worse, he cursed the gods for having let him down. Odin? Thor? How foolish he'd been to have ever believed in their powers. And how dare his father force him to honor them? If they were truly powerful, they'd have helped him win that day, but clearly they cared little for him or his dreams. No one understood him, it seemed—his own father least of all.

His confidence shaken by the loss to Jarl and driven by a rebellious impulse to strike back at his father—to steal his power—Dane rose and went to take the one thing his father most revered. And, slipping it beneath his coat, Dane crept from the house, moving through the village in the moonlight, careful not to wake the sheep and goats in their pens, nor the dogs that lay asleep. The air was thick with the smell of wood smoke that rose from each of the homes' hearth fires. Soon he stood outside Astrid's home, a modest log hut built into the side of a hill. *Flik, flik, flik.* He tossed pebbles against the shutters, hoping to wake her without raising the ire of her father. As fortune would have it, Blek had drunk too much mead at the feast and was snoring soundly. But Astrid had been very much awake and heard the *tip-tap* of the stones. In a trice she slipped out the door, a fur wrapped over her underthings, and joined him in the moonlight, her pack of axes on her back. Wordlessly, he took her hand in his and disappeared with her into the woods.

A tingle ran through her as she moved under the towering firs, Dane at her side, leading her by the hand, their bodies casting moon-shadow shapes along the ground. There was a special kind of excitement in meeting him like this, away from the prying eyes of the elders.

"I think we're alone now," she heard Dane say.

They stood at the edge of the woods, the smell of the pine needles like perfume in the air, the night sky above them a dome of glittering stars. The moon, rising just over the trees, shone clear and bright. Below them lay the silver oval of a frozen lake blanketed in new-fallen snow. They watched in silence as a mother deer and her young fawns made their way across the lake, leaving a line of tiny hoofprints in the snow.

"It's beautiful," said Astrid in a hushed whisper.

"You're beautiful," he told her, squeezing her hand and drawing her closer.

"And you're a fool who'd say anything for a kiss."

"I can't deny it. I do dream of a kiss . . . and more."

They fell silent. The only sound was their breathing, which came in icy wisps of steam that gleamed in the moonlight and then were gone. Dane opened his coat and brought out the Shield of Odin, the violet-colored stone in its center—the magic Eye of Odin himself—agleam in the moonlight.

"The Shield—?" Astrid gasped. To be in the presence of such a precious object took her breath away. But Dane, eager to make an impression, held the Shield up in a sudden show of bravado, slashing left and right at imaginary foes.

"They say the Eye of Odin sees every attack and wards off every blow," Dane said, "making him who possesses it invincible."

"Can the Eye see us now?" Astrid asked. Dane laid the shield in the snow, its "eye" side down on the ground.

"No, not now," he said. Dane drew closer, near enough to kiss. And pulling his hand from his pocket, he held it out to her, his fingers closed around something inside it. "With this I thee pledge . . ." he said, and opened his hand. In his palm lay a locket, in the shape of Thor's Hammer, made of silver and turquoise. It glowed there like a drop of liquid starlight.

Astrid felt her heart stop. This was serious. A Thor's Hammer locket held a promise within it. When a boy gave it to a girl, it meant he loved her and no other. It meant he was pledging himself, for life, to her and her only. For her to take it and wear it would mean that she had accepted his pledge and returned the same love. It was the precursor to marriage and children. It was what every Viking girl dreamed of someday receiving from a young man like Dane.

She lifted it from his palm, and with Dane anxiously watching, she gently fingered open the locket. Her eyes went wide: It contained a tiny portrait of Astrid herself that Dane had asked a village artisan to etch into the silver. It took her breath away—but then she pushed the locket back into his hand, saying, "I cannot accept it."

"Why not?"

"You steal the Shield of Odin and think you're worthy to carry it. But you're not. I cannot promise myself to one who pretends to be a man."

"Pretends?" said Dane hotly. "Am I not as *strong* as any man in the village?"

"Don't you see? If I wanted only strength, Dane, I'd marry an ox."

"But as son of Voldar, someday I'll inherit the Shield and then be able to protect you from harm better than anyone."

"The Shield isn't inherited," Astrid said in rising irritation.

"Like all great things, it's something that must be *earned*. Just as one earns respect. Or love." Astrid saw that he didn't understand. She gathered her words, about to tell him that she believed Dane had the strength and skill to be a great man, and that she loved him and wished for them to be together someday as man and wife, but that she had to make sure he loved her enough to be everything she needed him to be—but then a shadow fell over them and the words caught in her throat.

Prince Thidrek stood before them, flanked by five menacing guardsmen. The iron-helmeted men brandished long, metal-tipped spears, and each had a dagger in his belt. Thidrek's only weapon was a poisonous smile.

Dane tried to pull Astrid away and dive for the Shield. But two men seized her and the Shield as the three others fell upon Dane. He fought bravely, but the guardsmen landed many more blows than he could, and soon they had him pinned to the ground, half conscious, his face bloodied and bruised.

"You call yourself Terrifying, yet you aren't man enough to fight your own battles!" Dane shouted as he fought in vain to free himself. "Lay a finger on her and I swear I'll—"

Ooof! Dane received another kick in the belly and lay there coughing, barely able to breathe.

"You'll what?" said Thidrek lightly. "*Kill* me?" Thidrek and his men laughed, voices thick with scorn. "Now *that* is amusing. The boy is jesting. *Ha!* His japery knows no bounds." The men laughed again, and Thidrek gave Dane a final look. "I'll do with her *what* I wish *when* I wish. And you? You'll never lay eyes on her again. And *that*, my 'defiant' friend, is the most amusing thing of all."

And the last thing Dane saw was the tip of Thidrek's boot as it swiftly swung down and crushed his face. The sudden pain was so sharp, it blurred his vision and rendered him helpless, and all he could do in his last few moments of consciousness was lie there, listening to the sudden galloping of horses' hooves and Astrid's cries for help dying away in the distance.

10

Where Things Go From Bad to Worse

Sometime later Dane awoke to see stars. In the sky, that is. So big and bright, it seemed he could just reach up and grab them. His body throbbed in pain from too many places to count. How long had he been out? Minutes? Hours? He didn't know. He was cold and wet. A shiver shook through him. Rolling over in the snow, he felt something hard against his cheek. Groping around, his fingers found it: the locket, caked with mud but unbroken. He squeezed it tightly in his hand, the touch of it reminding him of Astrid, the sweetness of her smile shimmering before him again. A rage rose up inside him, remembering how he'd failed her and the horror of having Thidrek steal her away.

And then something else crystallized in his head: the sound of people screaming. Cries in the distance. And all at once it hit him: the village! It must be under attack!

Pocketing the locket in his coat, he hobbled to his feet with some difficulty and stumbled through the woods, the cries growing louder as he ran.

⚡

At first he couldn't believe what he was seeing. His village was on fire. The rye-straw roofs on many homes were ablaze, the smoke and flames licking high into the sky. He staggered into the village to find that all was chaos. Homes had been looted; clothing, furniture, and personal effects lay strewn on the ground, many of them on fire too. Men lay bleeding, groaning—even dying—on the ground, Drott's grandfather Horkel and Orm's older brother, Sten, among them. Mothers ran past him in fright, bawling babies in their arms, as the hiss and crackle of the fires mixed with the wailing cries of the women and children to form a sickening, otherworldly sound. The whole of it like a bad dream from which he couldn't awake, the sight of so many dying or crying in pain too much for Dane to bear.

Then, as he rounded a corner, the nightmare got even worse: He saw on the shore that their longships were ablaze. The attackers, a horde of bloody Berserkers, were setting fire to all the warships, the sails exploding in streaks of yellow and orange, the hulls of many of the boats already engulfed in flame.

Desperate to find a weapon to help in the fight, Dane knelt beside a slain village elder and began to pry a sword from the dead man's hand. He saw it was Klunter the Good, a kindhearted sheep herder who'd never hurt a soul.

And now there he lay, his belly gory with stab wounds, stilled forever. Filled with fury and armed with the man's broadsword, Dane rose and ran with all swiftness to the water's edge, plunging in after the fleeing attackers; but, alas, he was too late. Twenty men strong, they had already reached their longship and were swiftly rowing away. The cloaked figure of Thidrek and the ship's carved dragonhead prow disappeared back into the thick fog like seaborne phantoms.

Drott then splashed up beside him, yelling and firing arrows in vain at the receding ship. Relieved to see his friend unharmed, and knowing it pointless to pursue, Dane pulled Drott over to one of their own burning longships. Gathering other men, they tipped it sideways. The seawater extinguished the burning sails, but when the hull took on water, too, the ship sank. Silently, Dane watched the burning ships of his people sink one by one into the sea. The moment seemed to him one of insurmountable sadness and loss. He was roused from his daze by Fulnir, who ran up and said, "Dane! Quick, it's your father!"

A clutch of villagers stood in a circle as Dane approached. They parted. Dane saw his mother crouched beside a figure on the ground: his father. Voldar lay mortally wounded, an arrow through his chest. Dane hurried to his father's side. His father's breath was labored, his eyes' light dimming. Dane held his father in his arms. Geldrun knelt there too, stroking her husband's hand. The villagers looked on in silence, waiting for Voldar to speak.

"The Shield, son . . . ," said Voldar in a whisper. "Where is the Shield?"

Dane could barely bring himself to look into his father's eyes now. The truth was too shameful to admit.

"It's lost, Father," Dane finally managed to say. "Lost to the invaders. And Astrid, too, has been taken." The villagers gasped, aghast at this news. Fair Astrid *and* the Shield of Odin? Now all was lost. With the magic that had protected them gone, there could be but three things in their future: *hungersnød, drepsótt,* and *mørke* (otherwise known as famine, pestilence, and darkness).

Dane knew his father was dying. There was nothing he could do to save him. Fighting back tears, Dane said, "What are we to do, Father?"

Voldar gazed up at his son, knowing this would be the last moment they shared upon this earth. The old man was seized by a fit of coughing, and Dane gripped his father's hand to give him strength. The last of his heart fire then spent, Voldar lifted his eyes to Dane and in a faint whisper said, "You must redeem yourself, my son . . . regain the Shield and the girl. . . ." Then, gasping for breath, he said, "If you fail . . . all is lost." These were the last words the great man spoke. He died in his son's arms, Dane and his beloved mother overcome with grief.

Voldar the Vile was no more.

Valhalla surely would be receiving him soon.

The villagers gathered around Dane, pointing fingers and spitting in disgust.

"It's all Dane's fault! He's to blame here!"

"Got that right."

Their voices grew louder and more threatening.

"Poor judgment is what it was."

"Stupid kid!"

"You had no business taking the Shield like that!"

"And my daughter! You let them take my daughter!" cried Blek the Boatman, who'd never thought Dane a good match for Astrid, and had only let her dally with the lad in the hopes she'd learn enough about him to see that Jarl the Fair was the wiser choice.

Jarl, for his part, just stood there, biding his time, letting the others speak.

Dane felt numb. That morning, after the funerals honoring the other dead villagers, the elders had burned his father's body, floating it out to sea on a traditional funeral pyre boat, as the crackling flames and smoke sent a signal to the gods that a great one had fallen. Lut the Bent solemnly presided over the ceremony as villagers paid their respects. Grown men wept as they spoke of their fallen friend. The elders recounted how bravely Voldar the Vile had fought the Berserkers who'd come ashore unseen in the fog, and how Thidrek himself had dealt the fatal blow.

For a moment, Dane had thought he'd seen a strange shape shoot upward amid the plumes of smoke over the water. A Valkyrie, perhaps, transporting his father to

Valhalla? It thrilled him to think it, but his sight was too blurred by tears for him to be sure it was anything at all.

Later, after Voldar's smoking remains had sunk into the sea, things had descended into chaos. With their chieftain gone and the village in ruins, their food supply pillaged and hope for the future in tatters, the villagers had turned on Dane. Despite his mother's pleas to the contrary, they blamed him for the destruction of the village, the death of Voldar, and the kidnaping of Astrid.

Then Drott spoke, his voice quivering with uncertainty. "Correct me if I'm wrong, but—"

"You're wrong!" Jarl said, drawing snickers from some of the others. But Drott continued.

"But wasn't Prince Thidrek really to blame? *He* had the Berserkers attack and burn down our huts and chase down our women and—"

"But it was Dane who made us vulnerable."

"Yeah!"

"Those Berserkers would've never felled your father if he'd had the Shield! He'd have been invincible!" This gave way then to an even louder cacophony of threats and accusations; the rising tide of acrimony was so sharp that Dane began to feel that he, too, would soon join his father as one of the dear departed.

Then Lut the Bent raised his staff high over his head, signaling for silence. Everyone stopped speaking, and for a time the only sound heard was the rustle of leaves in the trees from a light wind that blew in off the bay.

"It is time for the gods to speak," croaked Lut, his voice dry as parchment. From his cloak Lut pulled out his runebag and uncinched its leather drawstring. Dane watched intently as Lut drew out the sacred runes and held them in his palm.

Dane watched Lut bow his head and begin to chant an invocation to the gods. Suddenly, Lut stopped praying and tossed the runes into the air. All held their breath as the runes arced upward and fell to the ground. Lut opened his eyes and peered down at the runes in deep concentration, reading what was written there. He leaned his head left. He leaned it right. No one spoke. They watched as Lut began to scratch his chin. Then the top of his head. He dug a finger in his ear and pulled out a bug. There were doubting looks now among the villagers, Dane noticed, people beginning to wonder whether Lut the Bent had finally snapped his twig. Then Lut's eyes suddenly shot open, as if electrified by an inner vision, and the old man again raised his staff to make his pronouncement.

"The gods decree that we must gain three things in this order: First, wind! Second, wisdom! And third, thunder!"

The villagers looked perplexed.

"What's it mean, Lut?" said Blek. "Wind, wisdom, and thunder?" As they were simple folk who preferred having things spelled out for them, all eyes went to Lut to await his answer. But Lut's gaze was steady and unblinking. "What do *you* think it means?" he said. His question turned the group dead quiet.

A fart rang out from Fulnir's direction. Jarl said he didn't think *that* was the kind of wind they needed. There were a few chuckles.

"I think I know," said Dane, now feeling their eyes upon him. "Wind. It means we must set sail. Follow Thidrek and his Berserkers by ship across the sea before they get too far away."

There was a silence. Then Jarl spoke.

"By sea? Have you forgotten? We haven't any ships! They've all been burned!"

They had seen that Thidrek had sailed out of the bay, away from his castle. He had vanished, but to where? If given too much time to escape, they knew, he could all too easily hide amid the many hundreds of islands and fingerling bays along the coastline.

Then other elders spoke up to say they had seen Dane sink one of the boats himself. This drew even more derision.

Dane said, Yes, it was true, he'd sunk a ship to save it from burning, for he knew that at low tide the villagers would easily be able to haul it ashore and salvage it.

"Even if that's true," said Jarl with outthrust chest, "do we propose to let *you* lead us? The very man responsible for this ruin?" There were grumbles of agreement. Jarl had a point. "I say it's time to let real men come forth. I shall lead a quest of able men to hunt down and kill Thidrek the Terrifying—"

"Uh, what's a 'quest'?" interrupted Drott. "I forget exactly—"

"I shall retrieve the sacred Shield of Odin," Jarl continued, ignoring Drott. "I shall safely return Astrid to our village, where she will be my wife and give me many children and, if the gods decree it, I shall become the leader our people now lack! I shall find this wind, wisdom, and thunder, and my blade shall taste my enemy's blood!" He said this in a loud voice, flinging his golden locks back and forth over his enviably well-shaped shoulders. A cheer went up.

Dane's heart sank. Would he lose all chance of saving his family honor? Then his mother stepped out and spoke in his defense.

"My son has a duty to right his wrongs!" *Uh-oh.* Sensing things going from bad to worse, Dane tried to speak up, but Geldrun shushed him and continued. "It was my Voldar's dying wish that his boy make good. Does that mean nothing to you?"

There was an uncomfortable silence. Lut the Bent looked up from the runebones that still lay on the ground, eyeing both Jarl and Dane.

"The runes say," croaked Lut, "that two shall lead. There is strength in unity, weakness in division. You both shall join together to defeat this foe. Agreed?"

Dane held out his arm. After a moment, Jarl locked his arm in Dane's in a show of solidarity. It was agreed. They would join in a quest to avenge Voldar's death and make things right again. The villagers crowded around them, patting the two young men on the back, shouting encouragement, saying "Kill the invaders!" and "Death to Berserkers!" Amid these rallying cries, the cold thought occurred to Dane that though he might have correctly guessed what *wind* meant, he had no clue whatsoever as to the *wisdom* and *thunder* parts. Oh, well. He hoped he'd have plenty of time to figure out the other two later.

With most of the village elders injured in the attack, nursing broken bones, many unable to walk, much less hold a sword, it was soon agreed and deemed necessary that eight of the younger men of the village would join our two heroes on this voyage. Dane's friends Drott the Dim and Fulnir the Stinking both quickly volunteered, as did Dane's other friends Orm the Hairy One and Ulf the Whale. Their fathers readily gave their blessings, for this was an ideal chance for their sons to prove themselves men of stature and good standing.

There was some discussion as to whether it would actually be a good idea for Ulf the Whale to go along, he being so monumentally large that he'd take up twice as much space on the boat and consume twice as much food (not to mention four times the drink). But Dane came to his defense, making the exceedingly good point that Ulf, though oversize, was also doubly strong and could row twice as hard as anyone else, and everyone agreed this was true. Plus he had committed to memory a vast number of really good jokes.

Orm, as his name suggested, was awesomely haired. The human furball, they called him. His head and face, his chest and back, his arms and legs—even the palms of his hands! Every place there could possibly *be* hair there *was* hair, and lots of it. Long and thick and black it was, and very popular with the womenfolk, too, for though he was short and squat and given to mumbling, he was a frequent bather and would allow girls to comb and braid his hair in whatever fashion they wished, giving them countless hours of hair care practice. Oddly enough, Orm's father, Gorm the Round, was completely bald, his face and head as hairless as a stone, and many of the village wondered how this was possible, asking Lut the Bent how father and son could look so unalike. Lut had wisely shrugged and said nothing, knowing that every family had its secrets and that this one might be bigger than most.

It was no surprise to anyone when Jarl chose Vik and Rik the Vicious Brothers. Vik and Rik were like Jarl's own personal bodyguards. They followed him wherever he went and, as their names might suggest, were not known for being charming conversationalists. They were big and brutish and bearded and possessed the kind of irascible dispositions most often associated with bears disturbed during hibernation. Being twins, Vik and Rik looked a lot alike and so, to help others tell them apart, they each wore an earring, Vik in his left ear, Rik in his right. And being simple guys with simple tastes, there were really only two things Vik and Rik the Vicious Brothers liked doing: drinking and fighting. It was all they knew how to do, and so they took great pride in drinking and fighting often and well, and usually both at the same time.

It was then that Blek the Boatman emerged from the outhut. Hearing what had been decided during his absence, he gave protest. After all, it was *his* daughter who'd been snatched, and he demanded that he be taken on the journey as well, if only to help read the stars for navigation. Badly cross-eyed and gimpy-legged as he was, Blek's volunteering didn't exactly raise cheers from the group. But Dane came to his aid, vouching for Blek's bravery and his badger-paw soup, and soon it was settled.

They also got an argument from Fulnir's father, Prasarr the Quarreler, who insisted that he too should go, if only to be an oarsman and help sing the sea chanteys. "Help guzzle the grog is more like it," his wife barked in derision. And she took Prasarr by the ear and dragged him off, the two arguing all the way home.

Lut the Bent was also taken on board to act as spiritual advisor and runemaster. The final occupant onboard was Klint the raven. Ever since Dane had befriended him after the wolf fight and nursed him back to health, the two had been inseparable. Klint had proven very intelligent, helping Dane and his friends to locate prey while hunting out in the wild and to find their way when lost in the darkest of forests. He had even learned to understand sixteen different verbal commands. This was five more than Drott had ever learned, and though Drott was Dane's closest friend, Klint was the creature Dane trusted most in moments when keen instinct was needed. When it came to brains, everyone knew Drott had drawn the severely short end of the stick; in fact, some thought he hadn't drawn a stick at all. It was common knowledge that even a drunken weasel had more sense than poor old Drott. But Drott's friends didn't love him any the less. For they knew there was no more loyal a pal nor more jocular a drinking companion than Drott the Dim, and when Dane set out that day on the voyage, he was happy to have his dear friend Drotty at his side.

So the prophecy has come to pass, thought Lut. The boy had brought darkness to the village as his birth dream had long ago foretold. And now the wise one, their chieftain, was dead. So be it. What's done is done. *What the fates have writ, men shall not erase.* This bit of accepted wisdom came to him like a warm blanket on a cold night. For he'd been awash with guilt, feeling it his fault for not telling his chieftain sooner. And though benumbed by an unspeakable sadness, he found comfort in the ancient ways, and in some deep recess of his mind—or heart, he wasn't sure which—he was reassured to know that he'd been right. He hadn't lost his seer's touch; the old one still had it.

As he packed for the journey, his thoughts drifted away from the pain of recent events to that still place inside wherein each man finds tranquility. And once there, he began meditating on the idea of destiny. *What the fates have writ, men shall not erase. . . .* How many times he had uttered those words. But what exactly did they mean? That one's fate was inalterably fixed? A man's entire life? Was there no chance for redemption? Though he had never revealed this to anyone, especially not the elders, he'd long entertained the notion that perhaps not *all* of a man's life was preordained. For, if so, what was the point of living? Perhaps, just perhaps, he dared to imagine, impediments were placed in our paths by the gods, and a man was judged by how well he *dealt* with these obstacles. Did he give up? Did he give in? Did he fight to change his circumstances? Was he weak? Strong? Indolent? Indomitable? Instead of a man being wholly defined by his fate, perhaps a man's very character was defined by his *response* to the fate that was spun for him. Couldn't it at least be possible? It certainly seemed—

Craaash! His reverie broken, Lut looked down. His jar of ale lay on the floor. It had slipped from his hand while he'd been thinking. A sign if he'd ever seen one: *Stop dreaming, old man, and get aboard the ship! They're waiting for you!* He hurried to put his last few things into his rucksack, not forgetting his leather runebag, and shuffled out of the hut into the dusty light of morning.

He walked through the village, or what was left of it, past the mostly silent women and children at work rebuilding their homes. He patted the heads of the wee ones as he went, nodding at their good-byes. Bits of gray ash rose from the charred and blackened remains. There was an air of death about the place. It occurred to Lut that this might be the last time he ever laid eyes upon his home or his people. He was embarking on a journey with the same man the runes had warned him would bring trouble.

He saw the raised longship on shore, the younger men loading it for the journey ahead, its striped sailcloth billowing in the wind above its carved dragonhead prow. He saw Dane the redhead on the shoreline, hefting a cask of drinking water to his shoulder, and the old one watched him wade to the ship and lift it aboard. Lut heard a familiar *crawk!* and there flew the raven, looping high and lazy in a pale blue patch of sky, *skreek*ing every so often as if conversing with his master. And then, when Dane made answer, the bird, in instant obedience, flew down to alight on Dane's outstretched arm. Lut pondered the raven. He knew that, according to the lore of his forefathers, the ravens Hugin and Munin sat on Odin's shoulders, acting as his eyes and ears, spying on the doings of men below on earth. And he remembered the words of his own father, Lundrin the Wise, who'd taught him what the seers of yore, now long dead, had once written, "Men watch, but the raven sees. . . ."

And then Lut knew: The raven would watch over them. He would be their sentinel. Their eyes and their ears. Comforted by this notion, the old one turned his back on the village and walked on toward the redhead, the bird, and the ship—and the adventure that lay ahead.

11

Lost in the Labyrinth

A spray of seawater wet Dane's cheek as he crouched on the foredeck, anxiously poring over the maps laid out beneath him. Two hours at sea and already they were at each other's throats, he and Jarl, and Dane knew that he'd have a full-scale mutiny on his hands if he didn't soon settle on a course of action.

They'd found their wind, but now they were sorely lacking in wisdom.

Behind him, he heard the men grumbling, as seamen often do, about the quality of the food being served and the body odor of their oaring companions and general conditions on board ship. And though he knew the men well, had known them all since boyhood, Dane felt alone on the open water, without a friend in the world. Klint, his raven, gave a solicitous *crawk!* from the railing nearby. Dane peered down at his maps, pretending he knew what he was doing.

It was as Dane had said. The low tide had left the warship he'd sunk partly exposed on the beach. It had taken some doing, but the men had managed to pull it out of the water, raise a new sail, and come morning launch it. Finding it seaworthy, in the space of an hour the men had loaded stores of salt fish and meat and casks of fresh water on board, as well as maps and medicinal herbs and all the weaponry the villagers could spare: axes, arrows, broadswords, halberds, long spears, and even a few knives for hand-to-hand combat. Lut brought the runes for further guidance and Drott his own personal keg of ale notched with his own mark—this so others, especially the Vicious Brothers, would know it to be his and not drink from it.

Jarl, of course, had brought two things he valued most: the silver-handled dagger he had named Dæmonklösa, or Demon Claw, which he kept on his person at all times, and his prized collection of grooming combs and brushes. By Dane's count, Jarl had already used the grooming kit three times on his healthy mane of hair, employing an all-too-familiar routine of rigorous combing and brushing to preen and prettify what he termed his "flaxen locks," the third of his three most-prized possessions.

Soon after they'd set sail, an argument had broken out between Dane and Jarl about which direction they should go. They'd soon realized they had no idea which way Thidrek's ships had sailed or where, in the many hundred fingerlet fjords along the coastline, he might be hiding with Astrid. It was thought that like the Berserkers he had employed, he would keep constantly on the move, attacking more villages haphazardly to expand his empire, for it was fairly apparent now that he was on the warpath and therefore would keep his enemies in the dark as to his whereabouts. So, save for a stroke of blind luck, it seemed they had little chance of finding him—or Astrid—anytime soon. The men began to grumble. Despair set in. Where were they to go? What were they to do?

"Isn't it customary for the captain to have *some* idea where to point the ship?" asked Blek the Boatman testily, casting dark looks at Jarl and Dane. "My daughter's in the clutches of a madman, and you both stand there dithering!"

All eyes went to Dane and Jarl, who hovered over their maps while the men waited for one of them to make a decision, to say or do something that showed they were capably in charge. Dane felt suddenly foolish, like a little boy who'd lured his friends out onto thin ice, swearing it wouldn't crack. Then he remembered the runes.

"We've reached the first of our three goals. The gods have given us wind," he said, nodding to the wind-billowed sail. "Now we must seek wisdom."

"Oh, great," said Rik the Vicious. "So what you're saying is you've got no idea what to do! That's encouraging!"

"Hey, give him a chance, will you?" Drott said in Dane's defense. "So he doesn't know—he's doing his best."

"But he's in charge," chimed in Vik. "He's *supposed* to know."

"Oh, right," Drott said, his cheeks reddening, realizing he'd said something stupid again.

Yes, Dane thought, *I'm supposed to know. But I don't. If I'd only listened more to the seafaring stories my father had told, maybe, just maybe—*

"Wait! Look!" said Jarl, stabbing his map. "I think—yes! It's the Well of Knowledge! I've found it!" The men hurried over and gathered round Jarl, the fair one excitedly explaining that two of the ancient maps handed down by his great-great-grandfather had been stuck together, and when he'd pulled them apart, he'd spied a spot on the hand-drawn map underneath, an island marked *Visdomvatn,* meaning "wisdom water"! It had to be the lost oracle of legend! Jarl stood, lifting the vellum map for all to see, and throwing back his hair, he called out:

"Let no man doubt me! It is here we shall find the wisdom we seek!"

Vik and Rik instantly threw him their support, clapping Jarl on the back and saying of course it was the Well of Knowledge and wasn't Jarl clever for having found it. Hopes on the rise, other men chimed in, gathering round to look at the map, telling Jarl, "We knew you had it in you" and "We were behind you all the way!" Jarl beamed, drinking it in.

For the good of their cause, Dane ate his pride and congratulated Jarl for his seamanship, inwardly cursing himself. Jarl took charge then, calling out orders. The men were all too pleased, it seemed to Dane, to be taking orders from his rival.

With their sails billowing in the wind and eight men at the oars, they soon reached the island Jarl had found on his map. There, within a sheltered fjordlet, they drew up beside a high, sheer cliff that rose like a wall straight up out of the sea.

"There," Lut said, pointing to the mouth of a cave high above them halfway up the cliffs. "The entrance to the Well of Knowledge."

"Way up there? Gee. Couldn't they have made it any easier to get to?" joked Jarl, feeling his oats, drawing guffaws from his shipmates.

"That's the whole point," said Ulf the Whale. "If knowledge were too easily gained, we wouldn't value it as much. You have to work for it." Many made the mistake of believing that if you were fat, you were oafishly stupid as well. As if the two things just naturally went together, like peas and carrots or hugs and kisses or weasels and weasel bites. But in Ulf's case, it wasn't true at all; he could cipher things called "numbers" and read in foreign languages. His father's brother Snorl the Blacksmith had taught him to do this using the many things called "books" he'd brought home from his years of raiding and pillaging. These volumes were handwritten in ink on vellum sheets of thinly stretched sheepskin. Ulf the Whale hungrily absorbed these volumes, for he enjoyed reading almost as much as he enjoyed eating. Dane and his other friends could barely decipher inscriptions in their own runic alphabet.

"They say," Lut rasped, "the Well of Knowledge holds many death traps and hidden dangers. They say that to reach the Well of Knowledge and return safely requires much of a man. They say that many venture in, but few ever—"

"O-*kay*, Lut! Lots of danger. Got it," said Jarl with a nervous grin. "But *they* aren't *me*, now *are* they?" he added, regaining his bravado. "If I don't come back, you can draw lots for my things." Jarl gave a cocky wink and turned to go. Dane stopped him.

"We both lead, we both bleed," said Dane. "'Twas the oath we swore."

Dane saw a quick smirk alight on Jarl's face, a look he'd seen enough times to know it usually meant that Jarl was wishing someone ill or imagining his own glory at their expense. It made Dane ill at ease, and he wondered: Was Jarl to be trusted? Could he be counted on to help if peril befell them? But then the smirk was just as quickly replaced by a warm grin, and Jarl gripped Dane's arm in solidarity. "May the Fates be on our side," Jarl said, and slapped Dane on the back; and Dane put away his doubts, choosing to believe that Jarl was at last casting aside their differences and warming to the task at hand.

Lut gave them both a blessing, placing a palm atop each

of their foreheads and chanting an invocation for their protection. Dane felt especially comforted by the old one's prayer and the leathery feel of his hand upon his head. "May the eyes of your father guide you well," said Lut.

"And may yours," answered Dane, sharing a long look into the old one's eyes, hoping this wouldn't be their last farewell. Then, after bidding good-bye to the others, he and Jarl leaped into the sea, swam to the rocks, and began the long, arduous climb up the craggy cliff to the cave mouth. It was slow going in spots. The two had to pull each other up over a few escarpments, but at last, with aching muscles, they reached the safety of the precipice.

They stood at the mouth of the cave and stared in. A jumble of fallen rock lay near the entranceway. Beyond that, a narrow passageway disappeared into darkness. Just inside the cave, they noticed a small pile of torch sticks, each one tarred at the tip. And then, above it, chiseled in stone, they found the following runic inscriptions, which they slowly deciphered:

BEWARE ALL YE WHO ENTER
TO KNOW IS TO PRESUME
THE SAME PATHWAY TO WISDOM
OFT BRINGS ETERNAL DOOM

"They really know how to make you feel welcome, don't they," said Dane. Then, using their flint and tinder, he and Jarl each lit a torch. They stood there, staring into the cave, neither showing fear to the other, but each waiting for the other to take the first step. Then they drew their knives and, shoulder to shoulder, swords sheathed across their backs, they marched into the cave.

They moved slowly at first, raising the torches high so the light would be cast deep into the passageway. Soon, sunlight from the cave mouth behind was gone, and the flickering torchlight was all that they had.

Jarl halted.

"What is it?" asked Dane, stopping beside him.

"I heard something." They waited, listening. They heard nothing.

"Probably just a mouse," said Dane, and began to walk on when his flickering torchlight fell on the skeletal remains of a man sprawled before him in the passage. The rotted bones of the ribcage latticed with spiderwebs were sickening to see. Then the pointed head of a brown rat poked up through one of the eyeholes in the skull and scurried away.

"There's your sound," said Dane. "Rats have picked him clean." Dane waited for a response, but Jarl said nothing and Dane walked on past the bones into the darkness ahead.

Dane could feel his heart thumping as he crept down the passage, his senses sharpening. The path began to angle downward. He could see the ice-covered walls narrowing. A brisk chill came into the air and a sour smell filled his nostrils. He began to hear a faint rasping noise, repeating itself, growing louder. Any moment, he feared, something wild and vicious might spring from the darkness. He held his knife at the ready, his heart pounding faster.

His torchlight fell on two more human skeletons, and he passed them without comment. Then he slipped on a patch of ice and fell forward. His torch rolled a few feet away, and its flame flickered out.

Dane lay in darkness, hearing the rasping sound echoing back at him, louder now. And in one panicked moment he realized that he was hearing his own *breathing* echoing off the walls.

Dane stood and relit his torch off Jarl's.

They saw they had reached a fork in the path, a place where the one tunnel split into two. They stood there a moment, absorbing this new development.

"Two paths," said Dane. "We must part ways." Fully expecting a frightened Jarl to insist they stay together, Dane was surprised when Jarl quickly agreed. "May the gods be with you," Jarl said brightly, walking off into the tunnel on the right and calling over his shoulder as he disappeared into darkness. "Last one's a moldy cheese!"

Now having no choice, Dane moved down the tunnel on the left, stepping carefully to avoid any traps as he went, inching his way forward.

And then a gust of air blew out his torch. Blackness. He called out to Jarl but in response heard only the echoing emptiness of his own voice. Why couldn't Jarl hear him?

Was he in trouble too?

Dane instinctively fell on all fours and crawled forward down the ever-narrowing passageway. The ice grew slicker and colder. He heard a hammering in his ears. The rank odor again hit his nose, this time even fouler than before. He thought of his father's last words and the disappointment he'd seen in his eyes. He thought of Astrid and wondered whether he'd ever see her again.

He heard a sudden scraping noise, like the jangle of iron against ice. Perhaps Jarl had found something and was sending him a message! With his knife, Dane started stabbing the wall nearest to where he thought Jarl would be, moving down the narrow passage toward the sound. And just as suddenly the floor beneath him dropped away so steeply that Dane lost his footing and went sliding feet-first, shooting down a slick icy tube, with no time to react or stop himself.

Faster and faster he slid through the darkness, taking wild stabs with his knife at the wall to try to slow his descent. Louder and louder he screamed as he rushed down the slope to what a tiny primal voice inside warned was certain death until—*floosh!*—he shot out onto a flat sheet of watery ice and went tumbling tail over teacups. Then *wham!* He hit something hard and came to a sudden, dizzying stop facedown in a pool of muck.

A blinding pain shot through his head. There was a penetrating smell so overpowering, he thought it must be the stench of some horrific beast that lay panting nearby. Time to face his fate. He rolled over and opened his eyes, expecting to be eaten alive. The next thing he knew, he was staring into the face of what he could only describe as a blood-starved demon.

12

Dane Matches Wits with the Wellmaster

Actually, it was only a dwarf. Or troll. Dane had had too little experience with either to tell the two apart. Its stench was so fetid and foul, anybody might mistake it for a demon at first. But now Dane saw that the creature that stood before him was indeed of human form—a hairy, grime-encrusted thing about three feet tall, half clad in a tattered, sweat-darkened tunic, its face comprising two pink, bulging eyes, a large, misshapen nose, and a toothless hole of a mouth, above a tangled triangle of chin hair. And there was something odd about the eyes. They stared out, unblinking, seeming to look *past* him, not *at* him. Strange. And as the thing sniffed at the air, Dane noticed something even stranger: The thing's nose had not two nostrils but *three*. And it had a pair of pointy ears. Telltale signs that it—or he—was a troll after all!

As a child, Dane had been told by his mother that trolls were basically harmless loners who lived beneath bridges, more to be pitied than feared. But later, he had learned from Lut and his father the real truth about trolls: While some could be trusted, they said, most trollfolk were a coarse and warlike people who shunned humans and preferred to live deep in the forest among their own kind, delving into the dark arts, forging bewitched weaponry, and perfecting high-gloss ceramics. He was to avoid contact with them at all cost, they had told him. But now here he was, face-to-face with one.

Dane sat up and peered at the homunculus, wondering if he was anything of a threat, when suddenly the troll issued an animal growl and lunged at Dane. Scrambling backward over the ice, Dane saw the troll jerk to a sudden stop and fall to the floor, cursing the rusted iron chain round his ankle, the other end of which, Dane now saw, was secured to the wall. And seeing the troll so tethered made Dane feel safe.

Dane saw he was in an ice grotto inside a glacier, a great cavernous space at the base of a fissure that rose a hundred feet high. A glimmer of bluish turquoise light from above reflected off frosted ice formations, making the icicled ceiling and walls seem to glow from within, illuminating two glistening pools of water.

The troll got to his feet. "Well, who were you expecting? The evil spawn of a Saxon queen, perchance?" he asked with a demented cackle. Then Dane heard a cry. Out from another chute hole shot Jarl, sprawling to a stop at Dane's feet. Dane helped him up.

The troll arched his eyebrows in amusement. "Well, thanks for dropping in, boys," he said, his voice surprisingly deep and rasping. "If I'd known you were coming, I would have made sandwiches."

"What *is* this place?" said Jarl, getting his bearings.

"It's the world-famous Well of Knowledge, pox brain!" growled the troll. "Didn't you read the sign out front?"

"Hey, a dwarf!" said Jarl in wonder.

"Actually, I think he's a troll," said Dane.

"What kind of idiots are you?" said the exasperated troll. "No, don't answer, I already know. You're prize scut-wits in desperate trouble. Some ridiculous life-or-death situation, a marital squabble, a murder charge, a love triangle—I *hate* love triangles!—and you've traveled far and risked all to come here and find the answers you seek."

Jarl looked at Dane, dumbfounded. "How'd *he* know that?"

"I'm the Wellmaster, nimrod! Fifty winters I've been here listening to people's problems. Fifty long years! And if you think it's fun listening to people whine and worry and snivel and snerk about the many foul forms of human misery, then you don't know pisspots from periwinkles. You name it, I've heard it. Bees in the bonnet! Boils on the buttocks! Idiot sons! Wart-ugly daughters! Lost fortunes! Frostbite! Famine! Pestilence! Sick pets! I've heard it all! But the worst, the absolute worst of all, is *love*! And you know why? Because the wounds of love never heal! Love can crush a man's soul—knock him out for good—and I for one am all too weary of seeing good men cut down in their prime because they fell in love with some prissy little missy who couldn't see it in her heart to love them back!"

He now paused to catch a breath.

"Sounds like you've had it hard," said Dane. "Sorry for your plight."

"My plight? What plight is that?"

"Well, being stuck here alone, no one to talk to."

Again the troll exploded. "Who said I've no one to talk to? I have myself, don't I? I listen to every word I say. No matter *what* mood I'm in. Which is a mite more than my wife ever did, I can tell you that."

"You had a wife?"

The troll fell silent, surprised he'd let this slip. "Yeah. Long story." An awkward silence hung in the air, Dane sensing this might be something of a sore subject to the little man. They heard the steady drip, drip, drip of melting ice dropping from the ceiling. Then the troll erupted.

"You *had* to bring it up, didn't you? Just had to go poking around inside me, trying to hit my sensitive spot. Well, you *found* it, all right!"

"I didn't mean to—"

"You want the whole sad story? Yes, I had a wife. Yes, she was beautiful. Yes, I loved her with all my heart. And you want to know what she did? She ran off with the VILLAGE IDIOT, that's what she did! *Okay?* You happy now?"

Dane said he was sorry.

"Sorry?" sighed the troll. "No one knows the pain of another man's heart."

Dane listened as the wee one continued to pour out his heart, but Jarl cared little.

"Uh, I hate to interrupt the pity party here, guys," interrupted Jarl impatiently, "but can we get to the well water? Time's a-wasting."

"What?" snapped the troll. "*My* pain is a waste of *your* precious time?"

"We *are* rather in a hurry," said Dane apologetically. "You see, someone we know is in trouble and we're trying to save her, so we'd really appreciate it if—"

"Oh, so there *is* a girl in the picture," said the troll triumphantly. "Which one of you is in love with her? No, don't tell me! You're *both* in love with her. Hah! I knew it. It *is* a love triangle! Ah, ha-ha-ha. Oh, you poor raggers, will men never learn?"

"Can we just *get* to it?" Jarl said angrily.

"Okay, okay, *okay*," said the troll testily. "Here's the deal." His voice took on a bored, almost mocking tone as he launched into his memorized declamation. "You see before you two wells," he said, gesturing vaguely toward the twin wells behind him. "The water from one well will give you great wisdom and insight, but only for a very short time. The water from the other will make you lose whatever wits you have and turn you into a drooling idiot forever."

"Uh . . . could you repeat that last part again?" said Jarl.

"I *said* one gives you wisdom, and one makes you an idiot."

"But you're not going to tell us which one is which, are you?" asked Dane.

The troll gave a toothless grin. "That's right, I'm not. And do you want to know *why* I'm not?"

"Because we brought up the wife thing?" said Jarl.

"No," said the troll. "Because, in case you haven't noticed—I'm *blind*!"

The word hung there, echoing up through the cavernous fissure.

"You mean you can't see?" asked Jarl incredulously.

The troll turned his head in Dane's direction. "Is he really as dumb as he sounds?" Dane was about to nod yes but realized the imp couldn't see.

"I can't tell you," continued the troll, not waiting for an answer, "because I really don't know. As you can see, my chain has prevented me from ever getting close enough to take a drink from either well myself. And all the others who've come to drink have failed to furnish me a clue. I can only conclude that those who drink the wisdom water are too smart to utter a word and those who drink from the other well can no longer speak at all. So I'm sorry to say you're on your own. You want wisdom? There it is. Go get it."

Back on the longship, Lut the Bent was worried. Two hours and so far no sign. Moving away from the others on board, most of whom were in some state of boisterous disagreement, he knelt down and drew out the runebones. Closing his eyes to focus his mind, he threw them on deck and then braved a look. Hmmm. *A tiny trouble could turn nasty.* Not so promising a sign, Lut mused, especially given Jarl's lack of good judgment and the excessive attention he gave to his hair. But did it foretell disaster? Lut returned the runebones to their pouch and secreted them away in his coat. Fortitude. One must have fortitude. He heard a bird cry overhead. His eyes drawn upward, he spied the raven circling in the sky and the dark mouth of the cave high on the cliffs above. The mouth that had eaten his companions. But would it spit them back out? For now, all he could do was ruminate and wait.

Jarl and Dane drew out the goatskin drinking sacks they'd carried with them and approached the wells.

"So what do we do?" said Jarl. "How do we know which water is which?"

Dane said he didn't know, and the two stood there a moment, pondering what to do. Then Jarl's eyes lit up, and he picked up a pebble he found on the cavern floor. "I know. I will turn my back and throw this pebble in the air, and the pool it lands nearest to is the one the gods want us to choose."

"But," said Dane, "what if it's the wrong pool? What if it lands near the well with the water that will make us morons?"

"Then our fate has been written by the gods and our quest will fail."

Dane wasn't sure he agreed. "But what if there's no such thing as preordained destiny? I mean, what if the gods don't really decide for us at all? What if we're supposed to live or die by our own decisions? Our own judgments?"

"You can't be serious," said Jarl, shocked by these blaspheming words. "That's crazy talk."

"But the gods wouldn't have given us reason if they didn't want us to use it, right?" Dane pointed over to the far left, where a dozen skeletons of men long dead lay strewn about. Didn't it seem possible, he asked Jarl, that those who drank the idiot water—since its effects were permanent—probably didn't have the brains to even find their way out of the cave? "Many skeletons lie near the well on the left, but no bones by the well on the right. So I think it correct to conclude that the well on the left is the idiot water and we shouldn't drink it."

"But all you're going on is what your own mind tells you. That's nonsense," said Jarl in exasperation. "You do what you want. I'd rather trust in the gods." He tossed the pebble over his shoulder. He turned to see it bounce twice and come to rest beside the pool of water on the left. "Aha, you see? It *is* the left. The gods have guided us well."

Jarl went over and filled his goatskin bag with the water from that well.

Dane, following his reason, filled his goatskin with water from the *other* well, the one on the right. The water felt cool to the touch and smelled faintly of roses, and this made Dane instantly wary. Was it a trick? Making the idiot water smell nice so he would mistake it for the good stuff? It was certainly possible, but with no way to tell for sure, he went on filling his skin, worried he might have chosen wrong.

Dane thanked the troll for his hospitality and asked how they could find a way out. The wee one walked them over to one of the ice tunnels and took hold of a long, ropelike vine that disappeared up inside it.

"Our pulley system," said the troll. "Just hold on and it'll pull you all the way up." Dane felt bad, leaving the troll behind; he was beginning to like the little guy. They said their good-byes, and when the wee one put out his hand, Dane didn't hesitate to shake it warmly, though it was a tad diminutive and hairy.

"Farewell," said the troll. "And thanks for listening." As Dane turned to leave, the troll added, "My name's Skogul. Skogul the Gloomy."

"I'm Dane the Defiant," Dane said, nodding to Jarl, "and his name is—"

"Jarl the Impatient," Jarl said hastily, "and if we ever run into your former wife, we'll be sure to say hello for you." Then to Dane he said, "Can we go now?" And as Jarl and Dane took hold of the viney rope, it suddenly jerked forward. The two had to hold on tightly as it dragged them upward into the tunnel. The last thing Dane saw before disappearing up into darkness was Skogul's grinning face as he waved good-bye and called out a final warning: "Whatever you do, don't let go!" Then the troll exploded in laughter, his echoing cackles reverberating up the tunnel, making Dane wonder if they were really out of danger yet.

Jarl prattled on about how they'd gotten the better of the imp and how the gods were on their side and how he couldn't wait to find Thidrek so he could cleave him in twain and watch his blood run and see his face turn pale and his eyes go white and how Astrid would be so thankful she'd hug and kiss him and agree to marry him at once. Jarl always talked a lot and never really cared if the person he was talking to talked back because mostly it was just the sound of his own voice he liked to hear.

Dane let him drone on, happy to be with his own thoughts as he held tight to the frayed vine pulling him up the steep incline in the freezing darkness. His mother's face suddenly came to him, her sweet smile and the grit in her voice as she'd growl curses coarser than his father's whenever the hearth fire went out or someone forgot to put smudgie wipes in the outhut. His mind was so busy with memories of home and of Astrid that when he looked up and saw the round circle of daylight ahead, it took several moments for him to realize that there was also a big round shadow blocking out a good portion of that light. And once they reached the top and let go of the rope and could stand up in the tunnel itself—he finally saw what it was that was blocking the passage ahead. His blood ran cold.

Because now, he realized, what he'd thought was a vine he'd been holding on to wasn't a vine at all—but rather the hairy tail of a giant ice rat! Or *ísrotte,* as it was called.

Some pulley! And now the monstrous thing, having reached the top, had moved round to face them. The ice rat looked to be at least four feet high and twice as long, with thick bristles of shiny white fur covering its body. Its long pearl-gray whiskers quivered as its pointed dirty-pink snout sniffed at the air. Its breath smelled of rotting flesh and its eyes glowed a dull green. When its jaws broke open, Dane could see jagged rows of fanglike teeth and—to his horror—a wriggling mass of maggots crawling among those teeth and over its glistening gray tongue. The maggots were apparently feeding on the remains of something *else* the ice rat had eaten some time ago.

Jarl and Dane stood trembling.

"The troll tricked us," said Dane, trying to stay calm and keep his wits about him. Jarl asked Dane under his breath if those were maggots he'd seen in the ice rat's mouth, and Dane said, yes, he thought they were.

"So that means," Jarl half whispered, "we get eaten twice, then, eh?"

"Yeah. First by the ice rat, then by the maggots."

"Well, first it'll have to get past this," said Jarl,

unsheathing his sword, brandishing it at the monstrous thing. The ice rat flared its nostrils. Its eyes glistened at the sight of the weapon. It gave a dismissive snort and drew nearer, its eyes narrowing to two gleaming pinpoints. Soon they'd be devoured. Swords would be useless, Dane saw. In desperation, he searched his mind for an idea. *What* could they do? And then he had it. A story he'd once heard about rats aboard a sinking ship.

"Slash its whiskers!" cried Dane. Jarl shot him an are-you-kidding? look, and Dane said, "Just do it!" Dane's sword flashed, slicing through the rat's protruding whiskers on the left of its snout. Enraged, the rat lunged at Dane, who leaped back, barely escaping the snap of its daggerlike teeth. Jarl then slashed the whiskers off the other side of its snout. Suddenly shorn, the ice rat gave a sharp, ear-piercing squeal and pawed its snout in alarm.

"Run!" shouted Dane. And run they did, dashing toward the circle of light at the end of the tunnel. Throwing a look over his shoulder, Dane saw to his horror the two green eyes advancing with inhuman speed. He felt the hot, fetid breath on his neck.

And then, just as he burst into the daylight, something hit him from behind. The next thing he knew, Dane was falling through the air, plunging toward the sea, a panicked scream filling his ears. The scream, he quickly realized, was his own. Plummeting beside him was Jarl, his long golden hair whipping in the wind.

But worse, falling just above them was the ice rat!

It hissed, and its horrid fangs snapped at Dane's head—once! twice!—but it caught only air. Dane spun, and again the rat came, this time its teeth finding the flesh of his upper thigh. Dane felt a stab of pain, then—*kuh-flooosh!*—he hit the water, the weight of the monstrous ice rat crushing him senseless as they both went plunging deep into the sea, the rat's manic churning finally throwing Dane free. He struggled his way to the surface, gasping for air and coughing up water, Jarl, he saw, a short distance away, doing the same.

And the ice rat? It came out of the water half a ship's length away, thrashing to stay afloat, its paws flailing and tail churning behind it, a flash of raw panic in its eyes. Once, twice, it went under, each time rising again, gasping and spitting water. And then at last, unable to propel itself or stay buoyant, the ice rat sank beneath the waves for good, leaving only a few last bubbles floating on the waves.

For a moment Dane marveled at this sight, which proved the truth of the story his father had told. Once in his youth, Voldar had said, after setting fire to an enemy warship, he'd seen rats, many on fire themselves—a few with their whiskers singed off—fleeing the ship as it sank. Voldar had sworn that as the rats abandoned the burning ship, some swam to safety, but those who'd lost their whiskers soon sank like stones. Perhaps a rat's whiskers, his father had surmised, were like a ship's rudder; without them the creature's navigational skills are gone and it drowns.

Even though he was ice cold, Dane felt happy in the water: He was going to live. Until he felt something coil and tighten around his legs—and looked down to see it was the tail of the ice rat. If *it* was to drown, it seemed bent on taking Dane with him! Dane tried to pry loose, but no, the rat's tail held him fast. He felt for the sword he'd worn slung across his back, but it was gone, no doubt jarred loose in the fall. And now he was pulled under by the weight of the rat, and the harder Dane fought, the tighter seemed the grip of the tail.

Desperate to free himself, he opened his eyes and saw, through the murky water, the creature's face staring up at him as it sank belly-side up into the blackness of the deep, its own imminent death made easier by the knowledge that Dane too would die. The rat's grin gave Dane a final surge of anger; he reached down into his boot, and finding his dagger, he slashed the creature's tail repeatedly, until he'd cut clean through it and slowly its grip gave way and Dane floated again to the surface, back to friends and freedom.

13

The Mistress of the Blade Tries to Bury the Hatchet

For what seemed days, Astrid had lost all track of time. Behind the oarsmen, at the aft end of the ship, on a bed of dried grass and goose down, she'd lain in a kind of delirious fever, coming in and out of consciousness. In her few lucid moments, she'd formed the idea that she'd been drugged—with oleander leaf or some other sedative—and suspected it was in the herbal concoction the so-called healer had been forcing her to drink. But soon she'd grown wise to it—realizing that the healer was no man of medicine at all but merely Thidrek's sly man-in-waiting—and then only pretended to drink the brew, spitting it out when no one was looking. And sure enough, in the last few hours her head had sufficiently cleared to give her a better idea of exactly where she was and what was going on, though she still pretended to be in the grip of the potion.

She'd been kidnaped, that much she knew, and was on board a longship bound for she knew not, as yet, where. The woolen sail amidships billowed sideways across the vessel, where she lay screened from view at the aft end of the ship, giving her a modicum of privacy. Berserker guardsmen came and went, as did the one who'd masqueraded as the ship's physician. Was it Gerulf? Galf? She couldn't remember his name.

Every so often Thidrek would come to inquire about her condition. At times he seemed genuinely solicitous, almost affectionate. The more she'd feigned a fever, the more attentive he became, sponging her brow and caressing her hair, whispering assurances that all would be well. There'd even been a moment when she felt faint stirrings of regard for him, but it was only the kind of stifled warmth a prisoner feels for her jailer when asked if an extra pillow might make her solitary confinement more comfortable. No, Thidrek was up to no good, of that she was certain.

Now she lay there, very much awake, very much afraid, alert to the fact that the guards were soon to change and that this would be her chance to escape. The past few hours she'd kept track of when her sentries had come and gone and knew that one guardsmen in particular—Blackhelmet, she'd named him, for his war helmet was painted as black as his heart—was quite fond of his drink and so drunken a sot that he always sank into a stuporous snooze soon after coming on duty. It was her plan to wait for Blackhelmet to fall unconscious and then slip past him.

She lay debating what to do. If she were to get free and dive overboard, she'd have a real chance of slipping away undetected *if* she were close enough to shore. But if they were too far out to sea, or if she were caught . . . well, she pushed all thoughts of failure from her mind. She'd mastered many a blade; surely she could surmount this situation.

After a time, she heard the shuffling of feet and the exchanging of oaths too crude to repeat. Peering through half-opened eyes, she saw to her excitement that Blackhelmet had indeed relieved the former guard and now sat slumped against the bulwark, benumbed and belching as he mumbled, the odor of liquor so strong on his breath that even from these few feet away she had no doubt of his intoxication. Never had a man's drunkenness so pleased her. She lay motionless, feigning sleep, anxiously awaiting her moment. She heard him mumble a few epithets regarding the prior guard's manliness, and then a long stretch of silence.

She opened her eyes wide. Blackhelmet was at last snoring away, dead to the world. She was alone at the aft of the ship. From voices carried on the chill night air, the others, she could tell, were all amidships, dicing, drinking, and guffawing at what she imagined could only be rudenesses of the lowest kind. With their view of her blocked by the sail that stretched between them, Astrid set to work trying to free herself.

All she had to work with, she realized, were her legs,

since both wrists were lashed to the railing above. She stretched her left leg toward Blackhelmet's knife, the wooden handle of which protruded from his belt. Arching her back and straining to reach it, she managed, with the tips of her toes, to nudge the blade's handle a tiny bit closer toward her, away from the folds of his tunic. Then, with keen concentration, gripping the handle between her toes, she lifted it up. The blade slid free of its scabbard—there! She'd done it! Now to bring it toward her . . . and with a deft flick of her foot, she flung the knife backward . . . the blade spinning end over end in the air and embedding itself—*thwack!*—in the wooden deck inches from her ear.

Then voices! Closer now. Thidrek, it seemed, murmuring to—what was his name? Grulf? *Grelf?* Yes, that was it. Something about colder winds in the northlands . . . a half day's journey . . . and the power just within their grasp. . . .

Only half listening, straining in silence, she stretched out the fingers of her left hand and yanked the knife free. Then, slipping the knife blade between her teeth, she transferred it to her other hand and worked to cut through the bindings. In moments she had them severed and now, half freed, she made short work of the corded rope round her left wrist, cutting clean through. Unbound, she leaped from the bed and looked for her pack of axes, the ones taken from her the night she'd been seized. They were nowhere to be found, of course. Thidrek had been careful to keep her clear of any weapons. But they must be somewhere on the ship, she reasoned.

She peeked out, seeing a knot of guardsmen at the far end of the ship, their bodies draped in various angles of repose over the deck and ale casks. The cloaked figure of Thidrek stood at the bow, towering over the diminutive Grelf, who, rabbitlike, was bobbing his head in assent at whatever his master was saying, a quill pen poised above a scroll. Between Astrid and Thidrek were some twenty trunks, upon which the oarsmen usually sat. The oars themselves were neatly laid in horizontal rows, with each oar shaft poking through its individual oar hole on either side of the ship, the blades of the oars a good six feet above the water line. For a brief moment she considered just jumping overboard, without her precious axes. But leave them behind? How could she? Without them, the Blade Mistress would be powerless.

Peering again through a small tear in the sail, she spied the pack. It hung upon a peg on the mast, between where she stood and Thidrek. Getting to it would be difficult, but not impossible. She slipped over the bulwark and crawled out onto the outstretched oars, crouching and moving on her knees from shaft to shaft, careful to keep them from creaking. Thidrek's murmuring, like the voice of death calling from the depths of black seawater beneath her, spurred her on.

Once amidships, Astrid lifted her head and peeked over the bulwark. Her pack of axes hung just a few steps away. Hungry for the power they would impart, she drew a quick breath and nimbly climbed aboard. Hiding first behind a stack of ale casks lashed to the deck, she crept shadowlike to the mast and pulled down the pack, its familiar heft renewing hope that freedom would soon be hers. But no sooner had she reached inside to find her favorite blade, when a voice rang out.

"The girl! She's gone!"

It was Blackhelmet, now awoken, bellowing in alarm from aft. Then all seemed to flash by at once. Thidrek whirled, eyes blazing as he caught sight of Astrid there on deck. Cries. Chaos. Thidrek roaring, "There! Get her!" Pushing beneath the sail, Blackhelmet tore toward her. Astrid drew back and let fly her axe—*whoosha-whoosha-thwack!* Its razor-sharp blade caught the drunkard's tunic, pinning him to the mast as he grunted in pain. She spun round, but another man lunged. Her swift kick to his groin crumpled him in a heap. Surrounded now, with more men advancing upon her, in one smooth move she vaulted over the bulwark and dove overboard. Except she'd forgotten one thing: the oars. And instead of hitting water, she went sprawling over the oar shafts. Before she could roll off and disappear into the sea, the Berserkers were upon her.

14

Our Tale Takes a Stupidly Melodramatic Turn

Jarl the Fair stood on the prow of the ship, his goatskin bag of well water held aloft as he addressed the men, his long golden curls aflutter in the wind. "I have braved the labyrinth! You see before you water from the Well of Knowledge!" The men sent up a *Huzzah!*

Dane finished taking a leak off the side of the ship, pulled up his trousers, and turned back to the men. In between gulps of ale, Jarl had excitedly related the high points of their adventure, enlarging and embellishing, naturally, the part he had played in the ice cave proceedings. Dane had then explained about there being two different wells, one that would make you wise, the other an idiot, but that they didn't know for sure which was which. Jarl was making his case before the men.

"The gods have chosen my water," Jarl proclaimed. "And because we are on a just quest, *my* water brings wisdom, Dane's idiocy." The men began talking at once, trying to figure out what this all meant and what they should do. Perched upon the rail, Klint too seemed to be listening intently, following the proceedings with keen concentration.

"I shall drink my water and gain ultimate wisdom—and shall know in which direction Thidrek and his Berserkers have gone so that we may hunt them down and kill them like dogs!"

"Like dogs?" said Drott. "But I don't like killing dogs. It's not right to kill a poor, defenseless—"

"Drott! It's a *figure of speech*, okay?"

"Oh."

"But what if you're wrong?" asked Vik the Vicious. The men fell silent, for Vik had voiced what they were all thinking. "What if—I'm just riffing here—but what if, you know, the troll tricked you or something and you just happened to get the idiot water by mistake. You drink that, you'll lose all your wits forever, right?" The men absorbed this for a moment.

"Not that we'd care, mind ya," said Rik with a sly wink. "You're a little too smart for your own good anyway." The men roared in laughter, enjoying this little dig at Jarl's vanity. Jarl beamed, their laughter like a gust of fresh air to him, too vain to think the joke had any grain of truth.

Then Ulf spoke. "So what do we do? We need what's in that water. But who's going to take the risk? Who among us is stupid enough to . . ." His voice trailed off. Everyone had the same idea simultaneously. The men swiveled to look at Drott the Dim. Drott stopped picking his nose and looked back at them, as it slowly dawned on him—*really* slowly—what their looks meant. He was *already* an idiot: He had little to lose.

"No, not doing it, no way," said Drott, shaking his head. "You heard what the man said. If I drink the wrong water, I could lose the few brains I have left. Forever! Pick one of the smarter guys!" Seeing that his words had no effect, he backed away as the men slowly advanced and he continued to protest. "My family! My brothers and sisters! My pet pig! They depend on me! They need me at the peak of my mental powers—for food! shelter! entertainment! It isn't fair, I tell ya! It isn't fair!"

Fair or not, the men fell upon him, elbowing Dane away, Vik and Rik holding his arms and legs down on deck as Jarl pried open Drott's mouth. He looked up at them, utter terror in his eyes. "Bloody pirates! At least let me pick which water I have to drink!"

Dane thrust himself into the fray, stopping Jarl from pouring his water into poor Drott's mouth. "He's right! I say let him choose."

Ulf the Whale's prodigious brow furrowed again. "But if he *does* pick the idiot water, how will we *know*? I mean, his name *is* Drott the Dim, right? How much stupider could he get? The change could be imperceptible."

"It's a chance we'll have to take," said Dane. "The man's volunteering for dangerous duty. We use him as a test subject, he gets to pick." No one argued. Dane lifted the goatskin bag holding his well water. Jarl brandished *his* goatskin. Drott looked from one to the other, thinking hard, unable to decide. He counted eenie-meenie-minie-mo. He flipped a silver piece. The men waited, giving him time to make up what mind he had. Finally . . .

"I pick Dane's water," said Drott. "He's my friend. I trust him."

Dane smiled, knelt, and uncorked his goatskin. He looked at his friend, a man he'd known all his life. "Don't worry, Drotty. If this goes south and you lose your marbles, I promise I'll take care of your family for you. They won't go hungry."

"Thanks, Dane," said Drott. "You're a pal."

Dane slowly brought the goatskin to Drott's lips. Drott stared up at it, steeling himself. Then he shut his eyes and opened his mouth, and Dane gave Drott a tiny swallow. Drott blinked once. Twice. Then . . . nothing. He still looked as stupid as ever to Dane. The men began to grumble. Dane wondered whether the Well of Knowledge was all just hogwash, whether they'd been had, given false hope by the cunning little imp guarding the well.

Then Drott's eyes abruptly shot open. Seizing the wineskin from Dane, Drott put it to his lips, sucking down the liquid in great gasping gulps. Some of it spilled over his chin and down his chest, but most went down his gullet. Afraid of what too much of the stuff might do to Drott's meager mind, Dane tried to wrench the goatskin away. But

Drott held on, guzzling down all the contents until, just as suddenly, he fell backward to the deck, stuttering and sputtering so violently, he couldn't get out a single word. He grabbed his neck with both hands, tearing at himself as if something were stuck in his throat that he couldn't get out. His body went into spasms, great heaving convulsions, his limbs jerking this way and that as he rolled back and forth across the deck, the men all recoiling, shrinking back, no one wanting to catch whatever Drott had caught.

"Somebody do something!" cried Fulnir, worried for his friend.

"I ain't touching him!" said Vik.

"Nor me," said Rik.

"Must be the idiot water draining the last bit of brains from his head."

"Maybe he's turning into a beast!"

"Or maybe he's possessed by a demon! Throw 'im overboard!" shouted Jarl, suddenly concerned for his own safety. "Serves him right, not picking my water."

"Nobody touches him!" said Dane, stepping in front of the twitching figure of Drott, daring anyone to step up. No one did. Jarl gave Dane a hard look but did nothing.

At last, the conniptions stopped. Drott's eyes fell shut, his tremors ceased. He lay still for a long moment. Dane's heart sank for his friend, feeling at fault.

"Is he breathing?" somebody asked.

"Can't tell," said Fulnir, and carefully leaned over

Drott's motionless body to look for signs of life. "Drotty, you in there?" No answer. Fulnir's eyes met Dane's, tears welling up. Their dear friend gone? It was too horrible to think of. Then all of a sudden Drott's eyes popped open, and he looked up alertly into the faces of his friends.

"What are you ox brains staring at? Have you never seen a man in a postcataleptic state before?"

Speechless, the men watched as Drott got to his feet. The man wasn't dead at all. In fact, he was so full of vigor and vitality, he seemed like an entirely new person, nothing at all like the slow, slack-jawed Drott they'd known before. His voice boomed with new baritone authority and brightness. His eyes sparkled and seemed to dance. He seemed absolutely electrified with a new kind of energy and intelligence. And now he began in the most animated way to strut about the deck, spouting all kinds of strange and wonderful information that seemed to burst forth from his mind with unstoppable force.

"Let there be no disambiguation! Two plus two is four! Four plus four is eight! Eight hundred plus eight hundred is one thousand six hundred! Ha! I don't believe it! The square root of sixty-four is eight. Euclidean postulate number four states that all right angles are equal. I love this! Wood floats because it has air inside it, stones sink because they don't! And—oh my god—the earth revolves around the sun!"

"The earth *what*?" said Orm the Hairy One. "Around the *sun*? He's daft, Dane! Did you hear what he said?"

Drott ran to Dane and wrapped him in a bear hug. "Dane! Thank you thank you thank you!"

"Drott! Is it really you?"

"Of course it's me! Isn't it wonderful! The wisdom water worked! I actually *know* stuff! My head is literally bursting with—I don't know what to call it! Information! Insights! Ideas! Facts! Figures! Data! Knowledge! I'm smart, Dane, I'm actually smart! Did you know that a hummingbird beats his wings eighty times a second? And that geologically speaking our earth is over four thousand million years old? And that any theorem stated but left untested could be true in the Aristotelian sense but not in the Pythagorean? I'm speaking empirically, of course. *Ad hoc ipso post facto erratum et cetera ad nauseum*. That's Latin, in case you guys were wondering."

Now he really had the men scratching their heads.

"Does the earth really revolve around the sun?" asked Fulnir.

"Absolutely!" And now he really started laying it on thick, the men standing there agape as he cavorted about, describing how many million square miles of ocean covered the earth, exactly how many days it took the moon to orbit the earth each month, and why it was that some wildflowers bloomed in the spring and some in the fall, and why water flowed downhill and not up. Then the men began shouting questions at him, and Drott swelled with pride: Finally, for the first time in his life, *he* was the one they looked to for the answers.

"Where does the sun go at night?" asked Vik the Vicious.

"It doesn't go anywhere. We just move round to where the sun can't see us."

"When's the next ice age coming?"

"Not for another ten thousand years at least."

"How come women change their mind so much?"

Drott wasn't thrown in the least. "Because, like the swells of the sea, their moods are ever changing. You see, in the bearing of children—"

Then a hand grabbed him from behind and wrenched him around. It was Jarl.

"If you're so smart," said Jarl, "tell us where Thidrek is."

"Yeah, yeah, I'll get to that in a minute," said Drott, breezily waving him away. "But first I want to take you through the basics of Euclidean geometry. It's really a beautiful system of—"

"TELL me!" cried Jarl, grabbing Drott by the shirtfront and pushing him up against the mast of the ship. The others gathered round now, anxious to know the answer too.

"Okay, okay, *okay*! Don't be so pushy." Drott put his finger to his temple and looked upward into the air, squinching his face, concentrating intently for a few moments. Then a sly smile appeared on his face, and his brilliance burst forth.

"Ah, yes, this is so simple, I'm surprised I hadn't surmised this before. Thidrek, if you may recall, just happened to attack on the night of a full moon. Why?

Coincidence? I think not. Because of the *tides*, my friends. He knew, as do all enlightened men, that tides are highest when the moon is fullest. And high tides meant his Berserker ships could roll in closer to shore, giving them the element of surprise. Okay. He attacks. He withdraws. Where does he go? If he doesn't retreat to his castle, he only has two choices. Sail south along the coast or sail north? Yes, the south is nice this time of year. Warmer. Balmier breezes. Friendlier women. But—going south gives him fewer defenses. Seas are calmer there. Less fog. Nothing but clear sailing all the way south. Fewer sheltered fjords, hence fewer places for him to hide. But north, you say? He'd have to make it through the Extremely Narrow and Shallow Shoals of Peril and Almost Certain Death—which we all know is impossible. Unless—what?"

He waited to see if anyone else knew the answer. No one did, and this gave him just the tiniest bit of satisfaction. He turned and cast a superior look at Jarl.

"Jarl? No idea at all?"

"No, ya nimrod, just tell us!"

"Uh, I believe *you* are the nimrod now."

Jarl made a threatening move toward him and Drott quickly spat out the answer:

"Again—the tides! The only way to safely navigate over the Shallow Shoals of Peril is to go at the highest of high tides. Given the fact that they lie roughly twelve hours north of our village, if he left our shores at high tide, he could have easily reached the deadly shoals in question precisely a half day later, just in time for another unseasonably high tide to carry him safely over the rocks and on to any inlet of his choosing, knowing, of course, that as the tides receded, anyone trying to follow him would be dashed upon the rocks and destroyed. The tides gave him the perfect entry and exit, and thus concluding, I rest my case."

Drott crossed his arms and looked back at the men, rather satisfied with his explanation. Dane and Jarl traded looks, all the others knowing that they were in charge and waiting for them to decide whether what Drott had just said was bunk or worth believing.

"But why?" Jarl asked. "To what purpose? What's he after?"

"I don't know *why* he's going north, I just instinctively know that he is. Plus, I kinda heard one of his guardsmen say it last night in the attack."

"Why didn't you say so before, then?"

"'Cause I just thought of it now. The wisdom water made me remember!"

The men traded questioning looks and then looked to Lut for his opinion. The Bent One merely smiled and raised his drinking horn in salute.

"Well, Drott," said Dane. "How's it feel to be the wisest man on this ship?" Dane broke into a grin and knocked fists with Drott. The other men clapped Drott on the back and thanked him for risking his life for the good of all on board.

"Set a course due north northeast!" Dane called out to Blek the Boatman, who was manning the rudder. "That bastard Thidrek's gonna get his just rewards after all!" A cheer went up. Then Fulnir began pouring grog for the men and proposed a toast.

"To the man what brought us wisdom!" The men cheered *Huzzah!* and drank to Dane. It felt good to have been right, to have the men with him at last. Drott began lecturing the Vicious Brothers about the differences among mead, ale, and grog . . . mead being a drink of fermented honey, made mostly for special occasions, ale a hearty beer brewed from malted grain, and grog being just a gallimaufry of alcoholic beverages all thrown together. Rik and Vik the Vicious brothers looked confused by this new information.

"But mead, ale, and grog," said Vik, trying to comprehend what Drott was saying, "they all have the same kick, right?"

"Yes," said Drott, "all produce the same state of euphoria."

"And last just as long?" asked Rik, now getting what his brother was driving at.

"Yes, yes," answered Drott, finding this line of questioning tiresome. "All will make you equally drunk."

The brothers beamed and turned to each other.

"Grog me!" said Vik.

"Ale me!" said Rik.

They bumped chests and began guzzling from their goatskins, chugging their inebriant of choice, racing each other to the comforting arms of drunken euphoria.

Jarl stood there uncomfortably, holding his wineskin of idiot water, feeling every bit the twit. He felt the eyes of the men upon him.

"Whaddaya keeping *that* for?" he heard Fulnir ask. "To make you smarter?" This made the men guffaw and Jarl feel worse. That he'd been wrong, that he'd chosen the idiot water, was bad enough. But to be bested by his rival and made a fool by the others, this was sheer humiliation. Suddenly wanting to be rid of all that had shamed him, he moved to empty the goatskin over the port side bow. But Dane grabbed his arm and stopped him.

"'Tis nothing to those who know of its danger," said Dane, "but perhaps a weapon against those who don't." The sullen Jarl thrust the bag at Dane and walked off, though still in the range of their laughter, which further darkened his mood. Perhaps the gods weren't on his side after all, he mused morosely. Perhaps he was doomed to die, and the best he could hope for would be to die bravely and heroically in battle. As he watched the others busily prepare to set sail on their new course, the men gave Jarl not a single look. The ship was now clearly under Dane's command.

15

Astrid Lights a Fire in Thidrek's Icy Heart

The girl lay asleep in the moonlight at the rear of the longship, tied at the wrists and ankles and secured to the bulwark to prevent her escape. Thidrek sat on a cask nearby and gazed upon her lovely form, the sight of her bare shoulder and the wisps of her golden hair taken by the breeze awaking in him some long-buried tenderness. The Mistress of the Blade, they called her; the sound of this pleased Thidrek still more. He might have to torture the poor girl if she chose not to accede to his wishes, and for the first time in his life, he felt something akin to—what was it? Discomfort? Regret? He wasn't sure. This must be what others talk of, he mused, when they speak of having "feelings of affection." But oh, how weak he felt! Horribly, horridly weak! And visions of grisly torture again flooded his mind, comforting him, and soon his moment of weakness passed.

Thidrek turned his gaze to his clothier, Hrolf the Finicky, who had finished taking the girl's measurements and now sat nearby, sketching designs on sheets of vellum with a stick of charcoal. Though barrel-chested and balding, he cut quite a stylish figure in his silver-studded black-leather vest and matching boots. In his youth, when known as Hrolf the Ripper, he had dutifully burned, looted, and maimed, all the while secretly harboring a desire to work with fabric. At last he gave in to his urge to create and, working nights, fashioned a line of smart warrior attire, ensembles of chain mail, dyed leather, and ermine that won him wide acclaim. When the designs caught Thidrek's eye, Hrolf was put on retainer as his personal clothier and ever after known as Hrolf the Finicky.

"May I see it *now*?" Thidrek asked, eager to see what Hrolf was dreaming up for him.

"When I *finish*!" Hrolf snapped, his voice a reed-thin rasp due to an old knife wound on his throat. Thidrek said nothing, knowing it best not to push the man. He was a temperamental artist, rumored to have killed a former patron for daring to criticize his color scheme.

With the girl asleep, Thidrek turned his gaze to the Shield of Odin that lay gleaming in his lap. He stared in distraction, mesmerized by its opalescent Eye, lost in the glints of starlight it reflected. It was funny. He felt most alive when taking life. The power he felt when killing things—the swell of strength that swept through him—these were the moments he lived for, taking him to heights of pleasure his weak-willed father hadn't had the character to grasp, much less emulate. Yes, Thidrek had far outstripped his father's own pathetic accomplishments, and now the prince was on the verge of possessing the ultimate prize. When he thought of the exalted powers that might soon be his, the possibilities were so thrilling, he could scarce contain himself.

"Did you know, Hrolf," Thidrek intoned, "that some men are fated to rise above mere mortal status? To stand eye to eye with"—he drew in a breath and eyed the heavens—"the gods themselves?"

"I shan't be surprised," Hrolf rasped, "to someday see *you* in that vaunted company." Then, finally finished, he presented his drawing to His Lordship, who eyed it with interest.

"Snow white and teal," said Hrolf, "that's the color scheme I recommend, m'lord. With ruffles here, here, and here." He then handed Thidrek something he called a "fabric swatch."

Taking the swatch, Thidrek gave it a brief glance and began buffing the Shield with it, polishing it to a high sheen. "You're my clothier—I leave that to you," he said distractedly. "So long as it says 'Ice Queen,' Hrolf. That's all that matters."

"She'll be the picture of icy reserve," Hrolf said.

Only feigning sleep, Astrid had lain awake the whole time and heard it all. They'd roughed her up a bit after her capture and lashed her again to the aft deck, this time tightly binding her wrists and ankles with long straps of sealskin leather. Though the ties had cut into her flesh, she'd borne the discomfort with stoic strength. This was made all the more difficult as the fur she lay beneath was infested with fleas, and she had to lie still and not scratch at the beastly little things.

She'd heard Thidrek's footsteps recede and after a few moments of silence had cracked open an eye to see that she was now alone. Her mind sharpened by the pain in her leg and her primal need to escape, her thoughts raced, piecing things together.

They were fitting her for a garment of some kind. But what was it? What kind of sick scheme did he have? A nuptial dress? No, it couldn't be. But she'd heard him say "queen." He must be thinking of a royal wedding. But how *could* he? After the way he'd treated her? She was so steamed that when Thidrek returned, kneeling over her, offering a plate of food, she blew up in anger, blowing off all pretense of being cooperative.

"Are you *that* deluded to think that after all you've done—the kidnaping, the poison, the hard bed—I'd actually agree to *marry* you? Of all the colossal gall! I'd rather die by my own hand than have you touch me!"

A light of desire came into Thidrek's eyes. "I so like your fire," he said with an oily smile. "But who said we're to be wed?"

"Oh, so I'm just a gutter wench, is that it?" Astrid shot

back. "I'm fine for a good time but nowhere near worthy to be a queen?"

Thidrek grinned, further aroused by her outburst. "Woman, you stir me!" Enflamed, he bent to kiss her—and Astrid used the only means of self-defense at her disposal. She spat a gob of spit in his eye.

His cheeks flamed red. He quietly drew out his handkerchief and wiped away the saliva. His voice went cold.

"This time tomorrow," he said, "you'll wish you hadn't done that." And he swept away, leaving Astrid lying there alone, shivering in the chill wind, further pained by the knowledge she had only one more sundown to effect an escape.

16

Our Hero's Moment of Truth Gets Him All Wet

Strutting back and forth before the men at the aft end of the ship, the wisdom water still firing his mind, Drott was alive with insights. Enthralling his friends, Drott pontificated on matters great and small, enjoying each moment of his newfound brilliance, telling Rik and Vik and Orm and the others he wanted to explain as much as he could before its magical effects faded once and for all and he went back to being Drott the Dim again.

The men asked why the effects of the wisdom water had to fade at all. Why couldn't they last forever, like the effects of the idiot water did? Drott admitted that, on the face of it, it did seem unfair. Since there was already a seemingly endless supply of idiocy in the world, you'd think the gods would be a bit more generous with the wisdom. But, no, he said, wisdom had to remain a rare and precious thing or else men wouldn't value it as much—

which would make life a lot harder than it already was—and so it was only fitting that the gods would dole out wisdom in such minuscule amounts, if only for our own good. Some of the men, slow to accept Drott's mental superiority, threw searching looks to Lut to see what *he* thought of this explanation. Lut just nodded and smiled, and the men eagerly returned to peppering Drott with questions.

Orm wanted to know why it was that in their land both snow *and* rain fell from the sky, whereas in other lands his father had visited there was only rain. Drott explained that snow was merely frozen rain and that in warmer climes it rained all the time and never snowed and people were always wet and miserable and never able go sledding or throw snowballs and that's why the Norsefolk were lucky to live where they did. Orm seemed satisfied by this answer.

Ulf the Whale wanted to know if the Romans had really thrown people to the lions. Drott said, yes, they had. Ulf then wondered aloud how many people a lion would have to eat before it was full, and Drott said he wasn't sure but guessed a dozen at least, maybe more, and Ulf the Whale observed that once his grandsire Zander the Remarkably Tall had eaten an entire ox at one sitting, *with* dipping sauce, and Blek said, "Yeah, and fell over dead the following day."

After the laughter died, Rik and Vik had an astonishing array of questions on the many intoxicating aspects of ale and grog and other alcoholic potions and which drink would keep you drunk the longest and which would make you pee the farthest. Drott described how grapes were used to make wine and how to get rid of hiccups, deftly avoiding having to answer the urination-distance question at all.

Asked about the origin of the runes, Drott said it was the god Odin himself who, in ancient times, had given their ancestors the original runic alphabet carved on a magic staff. Using this "language of the gods," men had learned to communicate with the deities, carving runic symbols on bones and pieces of tree bark, which they then read to know the future.

Years later, he said, men made the language their own, using runes to communicate with *each other*, inscribing in wood men's names, dreams, and, at times, grocery lists. And to preserve for future generations the exploits of the most heroic among them, they carved tales of their selfless deeds on giant slabs of granite they called rune stones. And these rarest of heroes so memorialized came to be known as Rune Warriors, men who would live on, in stone, for ages. "And thus it was," Drott said, "that men used language to stop time."

Fulnir showed great interest in the causes of body odor, and Drott had patiently explained that "we are what we eat," and that perhaps a modified diet would change the odors his body expelled. Blek had asked about the many moods of the sea and the faces of the moon, and Drott answered his questions as best he could.

Jarl seemed particularly preoccupied with the Shield of

Odin. What gave it its powers? How had their forefathers come to possess it? And what secret scrubbing agent had Voldar used to keep it so clean and shiny all these years? Drott told of the time before they were born when Voldar, in the full flower of youth, while in the service of a Gottlander king, had been given the Shield in gratitude for having saved the king's twin sons who'd nearly drowned when their trading ship had been attacked by pirates. The Shield, the king had told Voldar, had been crafted generations before by trollfolk who dwelled in a far northern realm and were known to employ the bewitchments of sorceresses—known as *vølvas*—in the forging of their weaponry, and thus had the Shield gained its powers. And when Jarl asked how he knew all this, Drott said that his suddenly sharpened faculties had helped him recall long-forgotten tales his uncle Hakon the Rude used to tell when Drott was an infant.

Finally there came questions about the nature of death and whether he knew how each of them was to meet his demise. This Drott could not answer. He patiently explained that he only had wisdom. Intelligence. This was not the same as foreknowledge; only the gods could see the future, he said, for they were all-powerful and all-knowing.

"But if the gods are all-knowing," asked Ulf the Whale, "how could Thor lose his Hammer?" He was referring to the prophecy they'd heard since childhood, the one Voldar had so often told them round the fire.

"Hhmm," said Drott with a frown, appearing to be stumped. "It does seem rather unlikely, doesn't it?"

"So the prophecy isn't true?" Some of the men seemed alarmed.

"Well, think about it," said Ulf. "How could the great and powerful Thor lose his Hammer? What? In a fit of drunkenness he drops the Hammer and can't remember where he left it? It's fifty feet long! He'd always know where he left it."

"You're right," said Drott. "I don't think a god of his stature would ever lose the greatest power in the heavens by accident." A small look of pride then spread over Ulf's big ruddy face, pleased his own mental prowess was now on display.

"Unless," Drott paused for emphasis, "he were to lose it on *purpose*."

"On purpose?" Ulf asked. "Why?"

"Yes!" Drott answered, his excited mind seeing a new possibility. "What if he let it fall to earth deliberately? As a *test*?"

A test? Now he had Ulf's attention. The others, too, traded quizzical looks, wondering where Drott was going with this, Drott himself not altogether sure.

"Yes, you know—maybe he knows *exactly* where it is and is just testing us, to see what we mortals will *do* with it. To see whether we'll use it for good or for evil—or for some nuanced and multifaceted mixture of the two." He looked at them expectantly, awaiting a reaction, wondering himself if his notion indeed had any truth to it.

The men considered it a long moment. Then Ulf said, "Naaah!" and dismissed it with a wave. The others chimed in, saying Drott had stopped making sense and he ought to stick to things he really knew about, like which herbal remedies were best for frostbite and why flint rock could be used to spark a fire and other stones could not.

Knowing that their situation was dire, Dane stood alone at the bow, staring into the misty darkness, trying to quiet his mind and forget what Drott had told him. His stout friend had taken him aside earlier, eager to share his newfound literacy.

"Listen, Dane," he'd said, "I know what you're feeling. You're anxious. Uneasy. In an apprehensive muddlement." Dane had just stared at him uncomprehendingly. "Or maybe it's more like a jittery disquietude? A kind of distress edging toward despair? Or perhaps a dark foreboding, a fretful trepidation bordering on full-scale panic and—"

Dane had silenced his friend with an oath, but Drott had continued, explaining that he was just having a "crisis of confidence," wherein a man whose true nature is yet untested feels overwhelmed by problems he faces and fears he hasn't strength to carry on.

Dane hadn't felt very encouraged by these words. But he'd thanked Drott all the same and bidden him go back to the men at the stern of the ship, where he'd continued his speechifying. And though Dane, overhearing it all, had

had his doubts about the whole Thor's Hammer business, he'd been glad the men had the distraction, for it gave him time to think.

They'd traveled north with no problem, entering the narrow passageway known as the Shallow Shoals of Peril—which Drott said had once been called "The Extremely Narrow and Shallow Shoals of Peril and Almost Certain Death" but then shortened to make it less cumbersome in conversation. Dane had confidently sailed into these dangerous straits, believing the tide high enough to carry them safely through the rock-plagued waters.

He'd been wrong. Soon after they'd entered, the tide receded, revealing the first few massive rocks rising up out of the sea. But he hadn't panicked. He'd calmly guided the ship himself, calling from the bow back to Blek at the rudder, telling him how to maneuver safely through the deadly straits.

But the tide sank further. More rocks appeared. Night fell and it grew dark. And then, worse, a blinding fog had set in, and even after lighting all the ship's torches, they could see but a few yards in any direction. The choppy seas heaved the ship in unexpected ways, making it harder to steer clear of the rocks that would suddenly appear out of nowhere.

And *that's* when Dane panicked. He could hear the mutinous grumblings of the men behind him and knew that one way or another they'd soon be sunk, no matter how smart Drott was. Lost and alone, he drew his coat tighter around him for warmth and peered out into the misty fog, searching for answers.

They'd found their wind, all right. And the wisdom they'd gained had only led to this deadly pass. But what of the thunder they sought? What form would it take, and where and when would they find it? And even if they found it, how exactly were they to employ its powers to defeat their foe? Maybe the gods had forsaken him altogether, just as they had abandoned his father. What good were the gods, anyway? They never were there when you needed them. Perhaps, as Dane had often secretly believed, they existed only in the imagination of mortal men, as a kind of ideal of perfection men themselves created in order that they might strive to attain it.

Further troubled by these thoughts, his mind sought comfort in the past. He remembered something his mother had told him on the night of his father's death. After the funeral at sea and Lut's reading of the runes, everyone had gone back to what was left of their huts. It was then, alone with his dear mother, that Dane had broken down and wept. He'd told his mother he was afraid, that he didn't think he was up to the task of being a leader, and that Jarl was a more able man than he. He even confessed his urge to run away and live alone in the woods for the rest of his days, so he wouldn't have to bear the dagger stares from the rest of the men and women of the village. Moved by her son's vulnerability, his mother had grabbed him by the hair and given him an iron look.

"Now you listen to me. Your father, may he rest, was one flinty son of a weasel. There were days I'd've sooner bashed his head in than look at him. But he had a fire inside him. You warmed yourself by that fire, Son, and whether you feel it yet or not, you have it within you too. Forget about trying to become your father. Just become the man he knew *you* could be. Feel the fire, Son. Believe in yourself. That's all a boy really has to do to become a man."

Dane looked at her. "Is that it, Ma? That's the speech?"

"Pretty much," she said. "Oh, and eat your vegetables and take it easy on the grog and remember to change your underthings once or twice a month."

"Can you let go of my hair now, Mother?"

"Of course, Son," she said. She let go. Then she'd kissed him and started to build a fire in the hearth. Dane had lain awake all night in his father's old cedar chair, unable to sleep, staring up at the empty spot on the wall where the Shield of Odin had once hung, brooding about the other things now missing from his life and what he could do to get them back.

Alone now at the bow of the ship, Dane remembered his mother's words. Believe in himself? How could he? They were in this fix all because of him. Jarl was right. Dane had no business piloting a warship. Other than his good luck in picking the wisdom water, all he'd done was make bad judgments and wrong decisions.

Dane peered up at the cloud-enshrouded moon. The mists that rose from the sea were as thick and impenetrable as the obstacles he faced. Could he lead the men to safety? Was Astrid lost to him forever? Could he ever be as fearless and brave as his father had been? *Of course not*, he thought. *I'm just a stupid kid who thought he was hot stuff. Dane the Defiant? They might as well call me Dane the Ridiculous!* And forget ever becoming a celebrated Rune Warrior! *Ha!* There was about as much chance of that happening as there was of Dane growing a second nose!

He looked to Lut the Bent, who lay asnore beneath his furs. The old one had taken sick a few hours before, complaining of fever ache, and though Lut had tried to shrug it off, saying it was nothing to bother about, Dane had insisted he take to his bed and rest. Lut had done so, spending much of their sea journey asleep. Dane felt acutely the absence of his counsel. And when twice Dane had shaken Lut awake to give him more mead and ask how he was feeling, all Lut had said was "A man can fool his fate," and gone back to sleep. Was this an important dream truth, Dane had wondered, or just the mumblings of a feeble old man?

The southern skies were clotted with clouds, but to the north two stars shone clear and bright. For a moment Dane thought of them as two eyes looking down upon him, the eyes of his father. Staring up into these star eyes, he felt the presence of his father's spirit, and forming words from the feelings in his heart, he sent out a silent prayer, asking for strength and guidance and, yes, wisdom, for he knew he'd need these to succeed. He told his father he felt responsible for all that had happened and if it were possible he would give his own life to reverse all that had gone wrong. He waited, hoping for some kind of answer, a comforting sign.

None came. The ship drifted on. Dane peered into the fog, feeling more alone and scared than ever. He wished he could just go back to being the fun-loving boy he once was and let someone else bear this terrible burden.

Then all at once, as if on divine cue, the curtain of fog parted and the men saw a spectacular sight in the northern sky. Shimmering arcs of light, glowing yellow, green, and blue, moved across the starry firmament, great swirls of glitter alive and vibrating like a million sparklers marching in unison.

The men were gobsmacked. They stopped rowing and fell silent, gazing in wonder at this glorious sight.

Well, I'll be dipped in weasel spit, thought Dane.

Drott let loose a mighty belch, *bbbru-u-up!* This awoke Lut from his slumber, and now he, too, saw the sight.

Rik and Vik the Vicious Brothers glanced up, shrugged, and continued drinking.

"What is it?" asked Jarl, no lover of nature.

"By the gods!" cried Lut, transfixed by the sight. "'Tis the Valkyries themselves! Reflections off their very shields!"

Even the Vicious Brothers now ceased their revelry and

stared at the dancing lights in the sky. *The Valkyries?* They were the breastplated warrior-maidens believed to ride across the sky on horseback and choose which of the fallen warriors were to be taken up to Valhalla.

"The Valkyries?" said Fulnir. "If they're here, then they must know we're soon to be in battle with our enemy. It means we're going in the right direction; Thidrek must be within our grasp!"

The men traded looks, absorbing this. Dane felt especially encouraged.

"They watch us and wait," croaked Lut. "For only the most worthy of warriors will be taken up to sit at the right hand of Odin and the gods who gaze down upon our deeds." There passed a silence, each man alone with his thoughts.

Jarl, ever the vain one, could think only of what it meant for his fate.

"Take me, dear Valkyries!" he cried to the heavens. "I'm no coward!"

"You're not even dead yet, ya ninny," cracked Dane, and this drew laughs from the others. All the men, even Rik and Vik, found it amusing because they knew full well that Jarl's biggest fear was of not being taken to Valhalla after he died—being left behind and deemed unworthy by the gods.

"Go ahead and laugh," snarled Jarl in disdain. "But mark my words. The gods see all. Only the best and bravest are chosen—only they who fight with fearless hearts!" He shot a burning look at Dane. "And we know which of us best fits *that* description!"

Struck to the quick, for a moment Dane couldn't speak. But when Jarl smirked and flicked his hair, this smug display of vanity made Dane want to strike back and say the one thing that would hurt him most.

"But what if you're wrong, Jarl?" said Dane. "What if there *is* no warriors-only heaven? What if it's a *lie*?"

Jarl's eyes went wide. "What?"

"What if everyone who dies goes to the same heaven? Whether they died bravely or died cowardly or just died of old age? What if Valhalla is for *everyone*, Jarl? Not just big-headed pretty boys like you?" It was a notion Dane had been toying with for some time, but this was the first time he was giving voice to it.

"Didja hear that?" Jarl asked of the others on board. "Blaspheming, he was! The man's crazy!"

"Oh, Jarl, get over yourself. You think you're god's gift."

"See? There he goes again!" cried Jarl. "Blaspheming against the gods!"

And with that Jarl grabbed him, trying to start a scrap, but Dane, wanting no fight, shoved Jarl away.

"I'm here to take vengeance on my foes," huffed Jarl. "Not to bow to your commands!"

"You're just mad," said Dane, "that Astrid was with *me* that night and not you!"

"And look what happened! You couldn't even protect

her! Even if we do save her, you really think she'll want anything to do with a *girl* like you?"

That did it. Dane tackled Jarl, and the two went tearing into each other full tilt, rolling on the deck, landing blows and swearing oaths, erupting in a full-out fight. And as the men gathered round to watch and wager on which man would win, no one noticed the sky clouding up nor the biting wind that began to blow.

The fight grew heated as Dane and Jarl hurled curses and blows at each other, each trying to wrestle the other into submission.

"They will smite you, Dane!" growled Jarl. "The gods will smite the unbeliever!"

And smite they did. That moment—*ka-REEECH!*—the ship hit a rock and the hull scraped across it, the screech of granite against wood so earsplittingly loud, it seemed to tear the night in half. And the next instant—as if sent by Thor himself—a storm blew in, and in what seemed only moments, gale-force winds were whipping across the deck. Objects that weren't lashed down went flying overboard. Their wooden shields and iron war helmets went bouncing away, along with some weaponry.

Even Dane's raven, Klint, trying to fly to safety, was caught by the horrific force of the wind and blown sideways out to sea, gone in the blink of an eye.

Waves, now ten feet high, rose and crashed into the hull of the ship, tipping the ship nearly sideways, threatening to sink her altogether. The wind howled so loudly, the men could barely hear one another's cries as they fought to grab the mast or other parts of the ship to keep from falling overboard.

Dane's mind went first to the weakest of his crew. Taking a line already tied to the mast, he lurched over to where Lut lay huddled and swiftly looped it between the old one's legs and round his waist. This way, even if a man were washed overboard, he could be easily hauled back on deck and saved, something Dane had learned from his father years before. Doing it came as naturally as the instinct to save himself.

"My time is nigh," he heard Lut rasp as he met the old one's frightened eyes. The sheeting rain made it hard to see, much less knot, the rope. Dane shouted reassurance over the wind-howl, working frantically to knot the rain-slippery rope. Then he felt a poke in his ribs. It was the runebag. Lut had it tight in his hand and was urging Dane to take it. Lut entrusting the runes to him? For a moment, Dane was tempted. But how could he take them? To do so would mean he no longer expected Lut to live, and this was the last thing he wanted the old man to believe, especially now, when he needed all his strength to hold on.

Dane pushed the runebag back under Lut's cloak, giving him a final look of reassurance, and finished knotting the rope. And just as he'd secured it, another wave crashed over him, knocking Dane to the deck so hard, it jarred his vision. Fighting wind and waves, saltwater stinging his eyes, he crawled to the ship's railing and clung there, holding on for dear life. Jarl and the Vicious Brothers clutched the railing a few feet away, as did Fulnir and Ulf. He held their panicked looks as again and again giant walls of water washed over them all, tossing their ship about as if it were but a tiny bit of tree bark. The crushing weight of each crashing wave pounded the deck planks like resounding thunder.

And the frothy crests of the waves, milky white in the moonlight, now appeared to him as the talons of some wicked beast as they broke over the deck, the curved arcs of water like long-fingered claws grasping at his men and trying to pull them into the sea. But then, in horror, Dane realized these *were* claws—the covetous claws of the Ægirdóttir—the Nine Daughters of the sea god, Ægir, waterborne spirits who, ever lonely for love, lurked beneath the waves and snatched men from ships, pulling them down to their undersea lair, where the drowned corpses were forever the daughters' companions.

Dane looked up and saw a massive water-claw rise high over the deck. It paused, as if selecting its prey, then plunged down, ensnaring both Fulnir and Lut in its foamy grip, pulling them toward the railing. Grabbing his sword, Dane leaped at the daughter's water-claws dragging his kinsmen overboard. His blade sliced through the talons, severing their grip, freeing Fulnir and Lut. The severed water-claws fell to the deck, writhed as if in pain for a moment, then, losing their long-fingered form, dissolved into ordinary seawater again and washed away. More foamy talons rose up, now seizing the starboard side of the ship, trying to capsize it. "Off! Hack them off!" Dane yelled, and Orm and Fulnir rose to the challenge and swung their swords, quickly slicing through the water-claws, releasing their hold on the ship, and the men watched in relief as the befrothed stumps withdrew and disappeared back into the sea.

"Look!" Vik cried, pointing portside. A flash of moonlight revealed a new horror. A jagged rock twice the size of their ship hove into view dead ahead. If the ship were to strike it, they'd all be dashed to bits.

"The *rock*!"

"We're finished!"

Jarl, his rain-lashed hair now matted across his face, turned to the others huddled nearby. Ruled as he was by fear, he could think only of his own survival. "Throw Dane overboard!" he shouted in desperation. "The gods will be appeased and spare the rest of us!"

Vik and Rik traded looks with each other, then with Fulnir and Ulf the Whale. As they hesitated, Jarl tried to push them into action. "He's a blasphemer—it's our only chance! The gods are smiting us because of him!"

Still, no man moved. Taking matters into his own hands, Jarl leaped to his feet and grappled with Dane, trying to throw him over the side.

"We must stay together!" Dane shouted over the wind. "We're stronger as one!" But Jarl wouldn't let go. The next instant Fulnir was at his side, trying to pull Jarl away, and then the Vicious Brothers were there, too, all five men in a death struggle, Rik and Vik and Jarl trying to throw Dane overboard and Fulnir and Ulf the Whale trying to stop them. Jarl's hands gripped Dane's coat so tightly that when the ship suddenly lurched, tipping the ship sharply forward, it tossed both Dane and Jarl together over the side and into the roiling sea. And by the time the others had risen to their feet and looked over the side, their two friends were gone.

For the longest moment of time it seemed to Dane that the world had stopped. He felt disconnected from his body. All was nothingness. And then—chaos. The raging force of the wind and rain felt like a hammer in his face as suddenly his head popped out of the water and he caught—in a moonlit flash—a look at the ship, which seemed about to topple sideways off a towering wall of water. A churning, thrashing panic. Then blackness again. And a stinging cold so bone chilling, he felt too shocked to move.

He kept swallowing water and coughing it back up as best he could. But some inner drive, the need to see and save the people he loved, drove him. He fought against the force of the sea, thrashing toward a dark object that seemed within reach. He felt something hard and grabbed it—it was something from the ship that had been swept overboard, an empty ale cask that he clung to, trying to catch his breath and regain his wits. He was alive! And this knowledge gave him new fortitude. He glanced down and saw the marking on the side of the cask and realized it was one from Drott's own personal supply. *Aha!* he thought, *Ale literally saved my life*—a notion he knew Drott would find greatly amusing.

And then, through the sheeting rain, he saw something thrashing in the foamy swells a distance away. He glimpsed a white face, a wet mop of blond hair. It was Jarl, flailing around and looking as though he couldn't stay afloat much longer. Dane tried to call to him, to yell over the deafening winds. It was no use. Dane started to kick his way toward his friend, for even the worst of enemies can find kinship when fighting for their lives. And then a giant wave rose up, carrying Jarl toward him, and holding on to his floating cask with one arm, Dane reached out with his other, snagged Jarl's sleeve, and pulled him to safety.

Dane sputtered a greeting over the banshee wail of the storm, happy to see him. Jarl didn't answer. Dane looked down and saw that Jarl seemed not to be breathing. His face was as pale as the moon.

Then, from out of the spray, Dane spied a new figure athrash in the sea. It was Fulnir swimming toward them, with a coil of rope over his shoulder, the other end of which—Dane now saw—led back to the prow of the ship, which suddenly hove into view. Hit by a wave, Fulnir went under for a time, and Dane's heart sank when he lost sight of his friend. Had he drowned? Had he been snatched by the sea demons? But Fulnir popped up again and kept on coming, like a loyal dog, paddling onward. Dane spent his last fiber of strength hanging on to the cask to keep himself and Jarl afloat a few more moments. And as Fulnir finally reached him and began to tie the rope around his waist, Dane felt lightheaded and sank into blackness. . . .

He awakened again as he was being hoisted up out of the sea, passing the big, pudgy face of Ulf the Whale as he came over the bulwark and flopped onto the deck like a sack of grain. He lay there, grateful to be alive, with the hard rain pounding down and into his eyes as he watched the others pull Jarl and Fulnir over the side and safely back on board. Relieved to see his fellow shipmates still alive, he let a wave of exhaustion overtake him and sank again into darkness.

17

A Heroic Rescue

A cool breeze brushed Dane's cheek. He opened his eyes to see the night sky aglitter with stars, the moon big and round as if hung from a string by one of the gods above. Still weak and achy, he stretched his arms and slowly got to his feet. He saw the silvered shapes of other shipmates lying asleep on deck, seawater from the storm still pooled beside them, and surmised that it was yet a good hour 'til dawnlight. The sea itself was calm once more, smooth as a baby seal's belly. Dane cocked an ear and listened, scanning the skies for any sign of Klint, but the bird was gone. He felt a pang of sorrow at the thought of never seeing his feathered friend again.

Others on deck now saw Dane awake and came over to welcome him back to the land of the living. Fulnir was the first to greet him.

"Welcome back, mate. Thought you were history."

"Would've been, if not for you," said Dane, embracing his friends.

Blek and Ulf the Whale clapped Dane on the back, glad to see him alive. Drott came and hugged him, saying, "The breath of life becomes thee." Not understanding, Dane looked to Fulnir for translation.

"You didn't drown," he said.

"Oh, right," said Dane.

Then Fulnir told him the good news. Once the storm had abated, they'd realized they had made it through the Shallow Shoals of Peril and were now lying to in one of the many inlets, far, far to the north. They were so far north, Fulnir said, they were now in sight of wondrous Mount Neverest, and he pointed to its snowy peaks agleam in the moonlight, the distant mountaintop so high it disappeared into cloud fluff.

Could this be Thidrek's ultimate destination? Dane knew that Mount Neverest was said to be near the Land of the Frost Giants, but why would Thidrek venture there? And then another thought struck him: the storm. Strangely, there'd been no thunder or lightning! Not a jot. In fact, he realized, it had been some time since he'd seen any signs of Thor's power. Could it be that the prophecy was true? That Thor's Hammer had indeed been lost? Or stolen? And if so . . .

His eyes rose again to Mount Neverest, while his thoughts were beset by the perils that might lie ahead, and to wishes that he'd never boarded this ship of fools, much less agreed to be in charge of it all. Then an old familiar voice broke his reverie: "They're gone, son." Dane turned to see Lut the Bent standing stoop-shouldered beside him, staring out to sea, his eyes silvered in the moonlight.

"Gone?" asked Dane, glad to see the old one up and around again.

"The runes," Lut explained. "Swept overboard. Taken by the storm. Gone." No runes? This was yet another blow, and Dane's face must have shown his dismay. "You really needed a reading, didn't you?" Lut said. "For Odin's god-sight to give you guidance?" Dane nodded, though his disappointment at this setback was softened by his relief to see Lut feeling better. The sound of one of Drott's mad cackles then reached their ears from the other end of the ship.

"I guess now we have only our wits to guide us," Dane said, sharing a rueful grin with Lut. "However meager they might be."

"Not so bad a thing, perhaps," said Lut, staring out again over the water, his eyes narrowing, as if seeing deep into the truth of things. "Sometimes I think the gods designed this life to break men's hearts." Then, issuing a defeated sigh, he said, "But now with the runes lost, I guess this old bag of bones is no good to you anymore."

"Don't say that," said Dane, putting a hand on his shoulder. "You're a father to us all, Lut. It's not just your rune sight we value, it's all the other things you teach us. Everyone looks up to you. *And* you roll a mean game of dice." This put a smile in Lut's eyes again, and their eyes met for a moment.

"You have a lot of your father in you, son," Lut said.

"Nothing I can do will ever bring him back," Dane said bitterly.

"Oh, son, didn't you know? We never lose touch with those we truly love."

Dane didn't look too certain of this.

"He sees you now," said Lut. "And he *loves* you still. You don't believe it, just ask him."

"I did. He never answered."

"Well, keep trying. Maybe he was busy."

Dane thought on this. And then said, "That thing you said last night. 'A man can fool his fate.' What exactly did you mean?"

Lut chewed his lip and stared up at the stars, trying to form a reply. "They say a man's life is a tale already told, a story already written, and that he is but playing out his part with no choice as to its end or even its many chapters. But perhaps, just perhaps, by listening to the voice inside himself, a wise man can craft a surprise or two." Then the old one looked at Dane, and off he hobbled unsteadily, leaving Dane to ponder what it all meant.

A short time later, Dane sat with Fulnir sharing a meal of salt fish and ale. Counting heads, Dane saw that two men were missing. Rik and Vik the Vicious Brothers. Were they lost at sea? Two *more* dead because of him?

"The brothers . . . ?" he asked. Fulnir quickly assured

him they hadn't come to any harm. After the storm had abated, they'd been sent out to scout for signs of Thidrek and his Berserker marauders. Hearing this, Dane felt a rush of relief sweep over him. His men had lived! Thank the gods! Then, again on solid ground and in control of the ship, Dane felt his sense of authority return as well.

"And who gave *that* order?" he asked in annoyance.

"I did," said a voice. Blek was pushed aside and Jarl the Fair presented himself. His hair now combed out and blown dry by the winds, his high cheekbones shining in the moonlight, he seemed fully recovered, save for a small scratch above his right eye, and as full of himself as ever.

"You were unconscious," said Jarl with a hint of defensive bluster, holding Dane's gaze, the tension still thick between them, neither wanting to back down or show weakness to the other.

Catching a cautioning look from Fulnir, Dane said, "Well, you are my co-captain. I'd expect nothing less."

A brittle moment passed. Finally, Jarl spoke the words they all awaited. "I owe you my life. I was wrong."

"Hey, choosing the water was just luck—"

"No," said Jarl, "I meant about wanting to throw you overboard. I was wrong."

Dane absorbed this. "You were afraid," said Dane. "We all were."

Jarl thrust out his arm. Dane reached out and locked his arm in Jarl's.

"We are stronger together," said Dane.

"As friends always are," Jarl replied.

A sigh of relief went through the men as they chimed their approval. The quarrel was now past, a peace of sorts had been brokered, and the men were cheered by the sight of the two joined in friendship, believing this a good omen.

The peace didn't last. The voices of Rik and Vik the Vicious Brothers suddenly rang out from off the starboard bow. Dane saw them oaring up in the small launch that was kept aboard for going ashore. Vik and Rik pulled up alongside the longship and clambered aboard, and the men anxiously gathered round to hear their report.

Rik opened his mouth to speak, but breathless from his furious rowing, he could only make his words come in spasmodic bursts between gasps for air. "Just round"—*pant, pant*—"the next bend"—*pant, pant*—"a mile"—*pant, pant*—"and a half"—*pant, pant*—"good cover—"

Tired of waiting, everyone turned to Vik for translation. He drew a breath and said, "We found Thidrek and his bloody Berserks camped onshore—all asleep, save two sentries on watch. We can set ashore to the west of 'em and use a thicket of woods for cover all the way to his camp. Just the surprise attack we hoped for."

"Well, brother," said Jarl, clasping Dane's shoulder. "Seems we got some killin' to do." There were satisfied grunts from the men. Jarl began barking orders as he set to arming himself with sword and dagger and other implements of war. But Dane could only stand there as a shiver of dread shot through him; all too soon he'd know what he was really made of.

The rich scent of pine needles filled Dane's nose as he and his men crept through the forest of firs, their feet crunching over the thick crust of old snow. Dane felt the blood thundering in his head, and it was all he could do to stay calm. To his left, led by Jarl, were Rick and Vik, their swords at the ready; Orm and Blek, both carrying knives; Jarl with his bow in one hand and trusted Demon Claw in the other. To Dane's right, and under his command, were Fulnir, Drott, and Ulf. Fulnir and Drott were armed with axes and two daggers each, Ulf and Dane with their broadswords. The storm had taken most of their helmets, chest armor, and other protective gear, and this loss made Dane feel all the more vulnerable.

It had been agreed they'd split into two raiding parties and attack Thidrek's encampment from both sides. Whichever group found Astrid first would make it their business to save her while the others formed a defensive shield behind them to help spirit her safely away. The plan had been Jarl's, and though Dane wished he'd been the one to hatch it, he knew it was a sound and solid plan. He'd even told Jarl this in front of the others, and hearing this had given the men confidence. Dane knew they dearly needed to feel confident if they were to succeed, for if any man failed his task, it would mean injury or even death to them all.

The idea, of course, was to surprise the enemy and not to have to kill anyone. Dane had in fact told his men that when engaging an enemy, they should first try to strike a blow to knock him unconscious, so that they could slip in and out with minimum bloodshed and lessen the chance of Astrid's being harmed. But Dane had listened well enough at his father's knee to know that no rescue raid such as this would be without peril. The Berserkers, even if slowed by drink, were merciless and would fight to the death. Worse, they had the Shield of Odin, and whichever man wielded it would be impossible to beat.

His mind filled again with thoughts of his father, of his raucous laugh and the big grin he so easily flashed. Dane remembered with sudden clarity that day as a boy when he'd first held his father's battle sword. What joy to see the pride in his father's eyes! Dane felt a sudden need for his father—and then a jolt of alarm. Did this yearning for his father mean he wasn't man enough to do this alone? Did it mean he lacked the fire? His mother had told him he had the strength of his father within him, yet now, miles from home, tramping toward who knew what, he felt his insides turn to jelly. Cold and afraid, he prayed his men couldn't see his fear or hear how loudly his heart was pounding.

Nearing the edge of the forest, Dane signaled the others to stop. He pulled aside a dewy tree branch and peered out into the predawn mist. All was quiet in Thidrek's encampment. A dozen or so tents made of stitched-together animal hides were set in a half circle round the smoking embers of a fading fire. Two figures lay asleep, their snoring easily heard through the mist. Only two sentries stood watch, and they were deep into their drink and on their knees playing dice, their attention fully diverted.

Dane scanned the tents for signs of Astrid, or clues as to where she might be held. There were none. Memories flashed: the girlish way she giggled while spearing fish in a stream; how she bit her lip when sharpening her axes; the smile agleam in her eyes as she spoke his name. His yearning to find her safe and unharmed made his insides quiver. Dane looked back to meet the eyes of his men. He saw a tense excitement on their faces, each awaiting his command. Dane drew a breath. It was time.

On his nod, they all moved at once. They broke out of the trees and into the open, rushing raven-swift over the hard snow and into camp. Dane struck first, he and Drott dispatching the two asnore by the fire with hard blows to the head, while moments later, Fulnir and Ulf crept from behind and knocked the two sentries cold. They had the camp surrounded. All was still quiet.

Dane signaled to Jarl, and the search of the tents commenced. Jarl, Rik, and Vik started at one end of camp, Dane, Fulnir, and Drott at the other. Dane crept to the door of the first tent, pulled open the flap, and peered in. Three Berserkers lay fast asleep under their furs, their heads unhelmeted. No sign of Astrid.

He shut the tent flap and moved on. So far, all was proceeding as planned.

At the next tent, he drew a breath and peeked inside. It appeared unoccupied. He moved in further to make sure and—*donk!*—took a hard blow on the head. Falling to his knees, he quickly drew his sword and turned to find—Astrid! Recognizing Dane, she gasped his name and fell into his arms, saying she'd never have hit him if she'd known it was he. He kissed her hair, her cheeks, the very sight of her too lovely to bear.

"You're all right!"

"I'm still alive, if that's what you mean, but far from all right."

"Have they hurt you?"

"No, but I haven't had a bath in days. And food! Their idea of a good meal is cold rabbit stew once a day, if *that*—and no vegetable side dish. Where were you, anyway? What took you so long?"

"So long?" She had him flummoxed. "We've been—well, we've been working very hard to find you!"

"Well, not hard enough, apparently," she huffed.

Dane said there'd be time enough to talk later, but now they had to steal back the Shield of Odin and get away. Astrid said she could use a weapon if he had a spare one, and Dane drew a dagger from his belt and gave it to her, watching as she drew its blade across her fingertip, testing its sharpness, and then slid it into her boot for safekeeping.

He peeked out of the tent flap. The two sentries lay motionless by the dwindling fire. All clear. He helped gather Astrid's things and whisked her out of the tent, coming face to face with Drott, who blurted, "They're awake!" And the camp erupted.

The sentries were up and shouting to their brethren that intruders were among them. Dane heard the clang of swords and spied through the mists—on the far edge of camp—that Jarl and the Vicious Brothers had engaged a trio of enemy fighters and, thus far, were holding their own.

A flaming arrow whistled past and struck the tent Dane had just left. It exploded into flames. *Bzing! Bzang!* Two more tents went ablaze. Dane knew it must be the work of Blek and Orm, who'd been told to stay hidden in the woods to provide cover if discovered.

In moments the encampment was in tumult. Berserkers awoke and found their tents in flames, choking on the smoke as they crawled along the ground, groping for their weapons, some with their tunics afire. Through the smoky haze, Dane could see that Jarl and the Vicious Brothers were now joining Ulf and Fulnir in fighting off a new group of attackers who'd appeared, the men in full fury though only half dressed. Seeing an opening, Dane and Astrid began to make a run for the trees, when right in front of him a helmeted Berserker crawled out of a burning tent, coughing. Instinctively, Dane raised his sword to lop off the man's head—then saw it wasn't a man at all, but just a boy no more than ten!

The boy looked up at Dane, trembling, knowing he was about to die. Dane too knew the boy should die. It was war. Survival. Dane had him cold and so should quickly dispatch him without pause and get on to killing whoever else stood in his way. But he didn't. He couldn't. And in that hair's-breadth moment of hesitation—of Dane not doing what he knew any other right-thinking Viking would—the boy rolled away and ran off.

Astrid threw him a puzzled look. "What are you doing?"

"Trying to save your life!" he said, and yanking her by the hand, he hurried them both out of the camp.

It flashed through his mind, as he stumbled over the snow crust, that perhaps the gods would look kindly upon his act of mercy and reward him now with an easy escape and a happily-ever-after with his fair maiden. Marriage. Kids. A nice home. Dogs and cats and maybe even a pet rabbit and—

But, sadly, 'twas not to be. For moments after he'd let the boy go free—in what any hardbitten Norseman would agree was an especially cruel twist of fate—that very lad decided to take Dane's life.

It was no easy decision. For failure would carry a rather high price. But it was time for the boy to prove himself, and prove himself in blood he must.

Crouched behind a rock, the boy drew back his bow, taking aim at the redheaded one running beside the escaping female, caring not a whit that he was preparing to take the life of the very man who'd just spared his. For, whether he liked it or not, the boy was a thrall, a slave, to Thidrek the Terrifying. And though just ten years of age, he knew that coldblooded killing wasn't only expected. It was an art that any stripling lad his age must master to earn his manhood and avoid incurring Thidrek's wrath.

And so, as the redhaired one and his girl neared the safety of the trees, the boy took aim at the center of the man's back and, after the tiniest moment of hesitation, the thoughts of which were known only to him and the gods, he let fly his arrow and—*zzfffftttt!*—saw the figure suddenly stiffen and fall face forward.

Astrid heard the arrow's whisper, then a thump in the snow. She turned, shocked to see Dane lying motionless a few paces behind her. Hearing death calls from camp, she hurried back to the fallen Dane and tried to lift him, anxious to carry him to safety. But just as she was hefting him to her shoulder, two Berserkers appeared, one armed with a spear, the other with a broadsword. Astrid let Dane's body slide to the snow as they slowly advanced.

"Well, aren't you a pretty," said Spear, giving her an I-can't-wait-to-kill-you grin. She drew out the dagger from her boot and brandished it.

"Ooh, *now* I'm affrighted!" Spear said in mock fear, throwing an amused look at Broadsword. "What you gonna do, eh? Give us a shave?" And without waiting for an answer, he ran straight at her with his spearpoint aimed at her heart. But then, suddenly stricken, he clutched his chest and sank to his knees, shocked to find her dagger's blade sunk into *his* heart. In a blink, Astrid had flung the dagger airborne and it had found its target. With dispatch she then seized the spear from his hands and put a foot to his chest, and he went crumpling over onto the crusted snow.

Broadsword then raised his mighty blade and came at her with a war cry. *Swoosh, swoosh.* Jumping left and right, she deftly evaded each swipe of his sword. With great practiced speed, using the butt of the spear, she poked him hard in the belly, then jabbed him right in the eye. Her favorite one-two combination. He dropped his sword and reached for his eye, howling in pain. And for a moment Astrid thought she might get away. But then she heard the crunch of boots on the snow behind her, and before she could even turn round, they were upon her, two more iron-helmeted Berserkers, bashing the spear from her hands and brutally batting her around. She fought them off as best she could, landing a few kicks and bare-knuckle punches, but soon they'd shoved her to the ground, her cheek crunching into the cold crystalline snow. And then Broadsword, angry about his now swollen eye, came and stepped on her neck, crushing her windpipe with his boot.

Choking and gasping for air, Astrid gave a strangled cry of anguish as she caught sight of her beloved lying still beside her. The toothless grins of Broadsword and the other Berserker men were obscene to her. The young man to whom she'd given her heart was now gone forever; her pain was near unbearable. She felt hot tears streaming down her cheeks and heard the cold laughter of the men, and when the boot was lifted from her throat, she heard her own voice cry Dane's name.

Her vision hazed with tears and the acrid smoke of the fires, she now saw that, back in the encampment, Drott and Fulnir and the others had been captured and were being led to a small rise. And her mind was so filled with thoughts of death and other dreary unpleasantries that when first she glanced back at Dane and saw his eyes flutter open, she gave it scant notice. Then he issued a groan and a grimace of pain . . . and *this* she noticed.

Her heart soared. He was alive! She saw his hand move up his leg to his right hip, where she now saw blood seeping from a gash on one of his buttocks. The Berserkers began to drag them roughly back to the camp. And now, her vision clearing, Astrid glimpsed—behind them, embedded knee-high in the bark of a tree—the shaft of an arrow, the one that no doubt had been meant for Dane but had left only a gash in his rear.

His mind ablur and backside throbbing in pain, Dane was dragged through the snow and dropped at the feet of Prince Thidrek. Still in his night robe, the prince stood there complacently, sipping from a mead horn, regarding Dane with mild amusement. A young boy stood before him, his eyes on the ground. The same boy, it seemed to Dane, whose life he'd just saved.

"This your work, boy?" Thidrek asked, a bit of brightness in his voice.

"Aye, sir," said the boy softly, still eyeing the ground.

"Nicked him, eh?" said Thidrek with fatherly pride, tousling the boy's hair. "Almost a kill."

"Almost, sir," said the boy, relieved to have the great man's approval.

"But 'almost' isn't good enough, is it?" Thidrek snapped, his tone abruptly darkening, eyes flashing in anger. "We aren't hunting hares, boy! Never give a man the chance to return fire! Shoot once and shoot to kill! Learn it quick or you're a danger to the rest of us, and then I've no use for you. Is that clear?"

The boy said it was clear, quite clear indeed, it wouldn't happen again, and then quickly excused himself. A few guardsmen chuckled and jeered as the boy walked away.

Thidrek smiled at their taunts, looked again at Dane, and said, "Perhaps I made the same mistake with him that your village made with you." Then he leaned down and whispered, "Never send a *boy* to do a *man's* job." Thidrek issued a self-satisfied chuckle, for he delighted in rubbing the noses of his victims in their failure and defeat.

Dane's eyes found the boy as he stopped and looked back. The boy's face showed not a trace of remorse, nor did it reveal that he had deliberately saved Dane's life.

18

Our Hero's Life Hangs by a Thread

Dane disliked being upside down. The world not only looked topsy-turvy but the blood had rushed to his head and put such pressure on his brain that he'd gotten a blinding headache. And each time he caught sight of Thidrek's face, due to his peculiar point of view, the prince's inverted features appeared all the more malevolent. No, the situation wasn't good, whichever way you looked at it.

Thidrek had captured them all—even Lut left aboard the ship—trussed them up in a large fishing net, and hung the net full of men on the limb of a tree, so that now they were precariously suspended over a pristine mountain lake, with Mount Neverest itself visible far away in the distance.

This fact alone wouldn't have been much cause for alarm. After all, it was only water they were suspended over, and rather shallow water at that. But there just happened to be one small, rather significant *other* fact they were soon to learn that would put things in a far more dangerous light.

Thidrek stood on the muddy shore, amused and delighted. The sight of Dane and his men hung there like so many herring, so helpless and terrified, tickled him no end.

"Well, look what we have here," he said. "It's the catch of the day! Suckerfish!" His men snickered, save for three who'd been wounded in the fracas at the encampment and were off moaning and dressing their wounds.

"Let's see," Thidrek said, rubbing his chin. "What shall I do with them? I suppose we could fry them up and have them for supper." His men made frowns and throwing-up gestures with their fingers down their throats. "But we're not *that* desperate, are we? No, these ruffians would be far too unappetizing. Well, perhaps we could just kill them and let them hang and rot 'til their carcasses are picked clean by the crows!"

This drew guffaws of approval from his men. Dane, less amused, with Jarl's odoriferous feet jammed in his face and Orm's elbow digging at his ribs, had an awful ache in his head.

"No, we can't just kill them," continued Thidrek. "That would be too easy. A quick, clean death is too good for these rogues. They must suffer. Feel pain. Lots and lots of pain." Then, so prompted, One-Eye, the Berserker leader, poked the net with his spear, causing it to swing to and fro over the water.

"C'mon now, men," moaned Thidrek. "What are we missing here?"

Then from behind Thidrek, the ten-year-old slowly put up his hand and tentatively said, "Torture, sir?"

Thidrek whirled round to face the boy, eyes ablaze. The boy flinched, fearing he'd spoken out of turn and would feel the sharp slap of Thidrek's hand. But a huge grin broke over Thidrek's face. "Good *show*!" he cried, fairly crowing with pleasure, going over to the boy and tousling his hair, aglow with fatherly pride. "Yes, of course! Torture!" Then turning to his men, he said, "You ought to be ashamed of yourselves, shown up by a mere ten-year-old boy!" Men hung their heads. A mischievous twinkle then came into Thidrek's eye. "But not just any torture, no! Something spectacularly—what's the word, lad?"

Again, a timorous look came over the boy, afraid he'd blurt out the wrong answer.

"Come, come, now," said Thidrek. "Don't disappoint me."

Having had little education, the boy had little command of language. Only one word came to him, and he hoped it was the right one. "Gruesome?" he said.

"The *very* word I was thinking of!" Thidrek ecstatically hugged the boy to his chest, pleased he was showing such promise. He then let go of him and, stepping to the water's edge, pulled off one of his leather gloves. Grelf saw him flick a look at the placid water lapping the shore, knowing now what his master had up his sleeve.

"Oh, sire—stroke of *genius*, sir! Hideously perfect."

Thidrek threw a sly look at Grelf. Then, archly eyeing Dane and his men, he said, "This should clear things up for you," and tossed the glove in the lake. It stayed afloat there; for a moment, nothing happened. Then . . . a stirring. Dane saw fins break the surface, shadowy shapes darting and circling. The water round the glove began to thrash and foam. Then, with blinding speed, a writhing mass of dark shapes attacked and tore into the glove, and in a frenzy of feeding, the thing was torn to itty-bitty shreds in seconds. Just as fast, the thrashing and splashing subsided, and the creatures—a dozen or more, at Dane's count, slick, gray, flat-snouted things, with long, pointed tails and each an arm's-length wide—disappeared under the glassy surface of the lake, and all was calm.

All save Dane and his men. They were understandably agitated by this upsetting turn of events.

"What in Odin's name was *that*?" said Fulnir.

"One of nature's more charming creations, gentlemen," said Thidrek in answer. "The giant flesh-eating, poison-tailed doomfish. Talk about killing efficiency! First it hunts you down with lightning speed. Then it stings you with its tail, delivering a dose of poison so potent, it paralyzes you in seconds. Unable to swim, you sink underwater, and *then*—hah, wait'll you hear!—as you begin to drown, its teeth—" Thidrek stopped, his grin growing even bigger. "But hey, why spoil the surprise? Better you find out for yourselves!"

Dane couldn't have felt sicker. *Doomfish?* They were the most dreaded of all aquatic creatures, and definite meat eaters! With their single-finned, triangular, wing-shaped bodies, and propelled by their whiplike tails, they could cut through water ten times faster than any man could swim. And once they had stung, their fast-acting poison would render a man helpless, and all he could do was bid good-bye to this world as their rows of razor-sharp teeth sank into his flesh and tore him limb from . . . Dane tried not to think of it.

"How bad you must feel, boy," he heard Thidrek say with an air of mock fatherly concern. "To have failed in your quest to save your beloved and retain your honor. A pity. But we can't all be winners, can we? No, the world needs losers, son, if only to make men like me feel smug and self-righteous in our superiority. Kill or be killed. Eat or be eaten. These are the laws of nature. Laws I'm afraid none of you are smart enough or strong enough to beat."

"Enjoy your head while you still have it, Thidrek," Dane coolly replied. "For I shall use your skull as a cup to drink your blood." Words he'd heard his father often say when recounting his glory moments in battle. Words that made Jarl and the others issue oaths of hearty approval.

Thidrek merely chuckled, spat an obscenity, and said, "Dinner is served."

But Astrid broke free of her guards and ran to Thidrek, crying, "Free them, please, I beg you! You can't do this—you just can't!" She was seized again by the guards but kept yelling, getting right into Thidrek's face. "A man who can't show mercy is nothing but a—a—" So upset, she couldn't find the word.

"A what?" coaxed Thidrek. "A tyrant?"

"A mean little *child*!" she blurted. Thidrek didn't blink. He calmly drew off his other glove and whipped it back and forth across her face. The sting of the leather was so sharp, it drew blood on her lip. She gave an anguished cry as the men dragged her off, while Dane and Jarl shouted out how despicable Thidrek was, and how, if given a chance, they'd tear him limb from limb.

"You can marry her," Dane bellowed, "but she'll never love you!"

Thidrek stopped walking. He turned.

"*Love?* Is *that* what you think this is all about?" Thidrek threw back his head and erupted in dark laughter. "Sorry to disappoint you, but marriage was the last thing on my mind. No, she's not to be my wife. She's to be traded. For something infinitely more valuable than love. I'm trading her for the ultimate power on earth. And once I possess that, it will not only make me the richest, most feared of kings. It will make me—dare I even utter it?" His voice fell to a whisper. "A *god*." He paused, luxuriating in his earth-shattering pronouncement. "And I have all you gentlemen to thank."

Thidrek tipped his head good-bye, drew his cape around him, and marched off up the snowy mountain. In minutes, he and his men were gone.

“The doomfish look hungry!”

“Maybe they’ll just go after Ulf and be too full to eat anyone else.”

“Ballocks! We’re dead for sure!”

“The gods are against us, I say!”

“Nay, it’s yer arse against me—get off!”

They’d hung there for over an hour, the sun now high overhead, the doomfish aswarm below, fins cutting back and forth, their long black pointed tails whipping out of the water, straining to reach the net full of live bait.

Knowing they were soon to be unceremoniously devoured, their nerves had begun to fray. The weight of ten men had also begun to fray the length of rope that rubbed against the rough bark of the tree branch above. Still, Dane and his men strained to break free. In a bestial frenzy, Ulf the Whale had tried to chew through the netting with his teeth, and Jarl had tried to cut through it with a knife—the one weapon Thidrek hadn’t confiscated because he’d hidden it down his backside, a near heroic feat in itself. But Dane had warned them against escaping, for if the net broke, most would fall into the water and be fed upon, which wouldn’t be good.

The more the men struggled, the more the rope frayed. It looked bleak. Their spirits had never been lower. Jarl had changed his tune and turned on Dane again, predictably blaming him for their predicament, and complaining that this kind of death certainly would *not* gain him admission to Odin's mead hall in Valhalla. He'd also lost his collection of grooming combs during the storm, and this irked him sorely.

Unnerved, Fulnir kept blasting odoriferous fumes—unfortunately for Lut, whose face was stuck inches from Fulnir's rear. And Drott, having lost most of the wits he'd miraculously gained, now babbled on, repeating the names of all the girls he'd ever kissed or held hands with and the many ways to cook goat. It saddened Dane and the others to hear Drott's dimness returning. All of them felt that something precious had been lost. So when Jarl told Drott to shut up, the others shouted him down, saying Drott should be allowed to say anything and everything he felt like saying. Everyone seemed anxious to have Drott's precious light last as long as possible.

Thus encouraged, Drott felt a final potency surge through him, and for some reason he found himself repeating over and over the words, "Fight with Thidrek, find the thunder . . . fight with Thidrek, find the thunder . . . fight with Thidrek, find Thor's thunder," as if the words held a key to their predicament.

Jarl was about to again interrupt when Dane said, "That's it!"

"That's what?" said Jarl.

"Thor's thunder! That's what Thidrek's after—Thor's *Hammer*!" Perhaps it *had* fallen to earth, as the prophecy foretold. Dane realized Thidrek was intending to find the frost giant who'd stolen it and was going to trade Astrid for the Hammer. Once he possessed it, he would have the ultimate weapon in the land and would, indeed, be all-powerful—the dream of all tyrants.

"Drotty, you must have some wits left," said Dane. "How can we get out of this?"

Drott thought real hard. "We need more wisdom water."

"Idiot!" screamed Jarl. *"We haven't any more wisdom water!"*

"Actually, we do. It's in my pocket." Drott explained that when they were on ship, he picked up the goatskin and saw there was just a tiny bit left. So he stowed the bag in his pocket in case of emergency.

"You could've told us this before!" said Fulnir.

Since Fulnir's hands were closest to Drott's pocket, he managed to locate the bag. There was just one swallow left. But who should take it? The men began to argue, each volunteering to drink what was left. But then, with the last bit of fading intelligence still within him, Drott spoke. "There is so little water, perhaps enough for one good idea. Since Dane is the smartest of us all, if he drinks it, his idea will be the greatest." All save Jarl agreed, he being unable to concede that his intelligence was second-rate. The goatskin was passed hand to hand until it reached Drott, who squirted the last little bit of water into Dane's mouth. Everyone waited for the one great idea that was going to save them.

"Everyone take a whiz!"

The men reacted. What? Go pee? Was he daft?

Dane's mind, suddenly alight with a vision he couldn't find words to explain, said, "Yes, yes, take a leak! Now! The doomfish! Their acute sense of smell! If we all pee at once, the sudden concentration of uric acid in the water might be enough to temporarily drive them away!"

"Uric what—?" said Jarl, perplexed. "He's babbling nonsense!"

"Don't question him, Jarl! Just do it."

And sure enough, with the men having no other viable means of escape, ten streams of urine soon shot forth, arcing outward like a Roman fountain in all directions, hitting the water at the same time. And wouldn't you know, just as Dane had predicted, the doomfish drew back in alarm and immediately swam away from the immense slick of pee, moving as far away from it as they could.

"Well? What are you waiting for?" said Dane. "Let's go!"

Jarl dutifully sliced open the rope netting. The net gave way and Dane fell into the water with the others, splashing and thrashing around as they made a mad scramble for shore. One by one they reached land and climbed up on the muddy bank, relieved to be out of the pee-filled water and free of danger.

All but Ulf. His rotundity being especially monumental, it took him longer to swim the distance. Gathered onshore, the men called for him to hurry—they could see the doomfish plowing across the lake straight for him. The sight of Ulf's well-fattened rump in the water doubtless spurred the ravenous creatures on to what they could only imagine would be a smorgasbord of epic proportions.

"Hurry, Ulf!" Dane shouted. But the doomfish were gaining. Twenty yards . . . ten . . . they were closing fast. It looked as if Ulf the Whale's mother might be receiving a sympathy visit.

And then, with two of the giant man-eaters mere feet away from mealtime, two arrows came whizzing through the air—*ffffttt! ffffttt!*—and made direct hits, killing the doomfish in an instant. This gave three other men time to rush into the water and pull Ulf up onto shore. And once he caught his breath, he pumped Jarl's hand and thanked him for saving his life. For indeed it had been Jarl who'd shot the arrows; while everyone else had been yelling, he'd found the bow and arrow he'd stashed and shot the dreaded predators with ease.

Dane noticed Lut looking weak and haggard and, knowing the ordeal that lay before them, suggested that it might be best if he returned to their ship and stay aboard, if only to guard it from interlopers. Lut protested, saying he was certainly up to the task, and if there was any chance of seeing a frost giant, he was certainly going to do it. But then he was seized with another coughing fit, and seeing a firmness in Dane's demeanor he hadn't seen before, he agreed it might be best. Dane embraced the old one, realizing how parchment thin Lut was, and it sent a new worry through the young man.

"The thunder," Lut said, putting his leathered hand on Dane's shoulder, "is just within your grasp. Take it, son." Dane bade him good-bye and watched as Blek and Orm the Hairy One guided Lut through the woods toward the ship. Dane had a notion this might be the last he'd ever see of the old one, but he banished the thought from his mind, turning it toward making preparations for the arduous journey ahead.

Blek and Orm soon returned. Keen on revenge, the men gathered round Dane, looking to him for guidance. Dane gazed up at the snow-capped peaks of Mount Neverest far in the distance. Then he gazed at his men and said, "We know now what we must do to defeat Thidrek. We must journey to Mount Neverest. It is there in the Land of the Frost Giants that we shall find the thunder we seek. Thor's Hammer."

A sober resolve settled over the men.

"And if we can't find it before he does, all hope for our lands—and Astrid—is lost." That said, Dane began to trudge up the snowy slope toward the impossibly high mountain. One by one, his men silently followed, the snow falling heavier about them as they plodded on, each step drawing them closer to their fate.

19

The Fair Maiden Meets Her Fate

Astrid was numb. For the first time in her life, she felt too cold to be afraid. They'd been toiling for hours in a blinding blizzard up the side of Mount Neverest, the snowfall so heavy at times, she could barely see a foot in front of her. The blistering winds had blown so bone-chillingly cold that she could no longer feel her hands or feet. Her mind was crowded with visions of giant bears and ice wolves and other ravenous beasts that they would no doubt soon encounter. Tethered to a pair of Thidrek's guardsmen, she'd dragged herself onward despite the despair in her heart and growing certainty that something bad was about to befall her. She'd lost hope of living much longer.

Now the howl of the wind subsided and the daylight darkened. She lifted her eyes from the ground to see that they were entering an ice cave, a narrow crevasse of blue glacial ice that soon opened into a large cavernous chamber. It was Thidrek's plan to take shelter here until the storm lifted and then to move on to higher elevations.

Grateful to be out of the freezing wind, Astrid sank to her knees and fell back against a wall, weak and aching with hunger. The flickering light from the Berserker guards' torches seemed to waver and go blurry. She closed her eyes for what seemed only a moment and sank into a dream of a big, silvery moon spilling out stars onto a black velvet sky. The stars began falling, turning into snowflakes, each flake uniquely crystalline and perfect. And then the snowflakes sprouted wings and turned into lovely white birds that flew toward the sun and—

She awoke to the clamor of voices.

"We've found it, sire!" said Grelf, his eyes alight with excitement. "The Hammer! Just up the mountain on the next ridge. It had been buried in snow, but the winds must have uncovered it. It's there for the taking, sir. It's . . . magnificent!"

Thidrek's face took on a look of such rare intensity that, to a passing stranger, he would have appeared to be in a state of religious ecstasy or the rapture of true love. But Astrid saw it was merely his raw lust for power, unmasked.

"This is good," said Thidrek. "This is very, *very* good. You've done well, Grelf. And you'll be rewarded."

"Thank you, sire, thank you!" said Grelf, his eyes shining with avarice. Grelf bowed to Thidrek, more obsequiously than ever before, and then turned to escort him out of the passage. Abruptly they stopped, Thidrek, Grelf, the dozen or so Berserkers who accompanied them all frozen in their footsteps. It seemed that something, or some*one*, was blocking their path. Instead of moving forward, they began to backpedal, their heads tilting upward, eyes bulging. And then Astrid saw what the men all saw as the creature moved into the cave: An enormous *frostkjempe,* a frost giant!

So the legends were true! Amazing! She'd heard the stories as a child, tales of giant men made of ice who strode the tops of mountains, their thunderous footsteps causing deadly avalanches that often wiped out whole villages, fearsome creatures who could gobble up a child in one bite. As a girl she'd loved the stories and believed in them wholeheartedly. But as she'd grown older, she'd stopped believing the fantastic tales her father told. While other girls of the village talked of jewelry and makeup and boys, Astrid had happily busied herself learning to hunt and fish with her father. She grew into a levelheaded, practical-minded girl who had stopped believing in giants.

Now the frost giant stood before her, very much alive. He was so huge—well over twenty feet tall—that he had to bend over to enter the cave. And he was made entirely of ice! His shape was every bit that of a man's—he had arms, legs, feet, and hands; but instead of flesh and bone his entire body was formed of tiny frozen crystals and covered in a thick, bluish-white frost. His limbs creaked when he walked, and when his arm brushed against his side, tiny flakes of ice were scraped off and fell to the floor. His face Astrid found particularly striking. He had a broad, flat forehead and a large frosted ridge of a brow above his tiny ice-blue eyes—eyes, Astrid saw, that missed nothing. From his chin hung a beard of frosted icicles, and each time he exhaled, he puffed out a cloud of cold air that iced over his beard, making his beard icicles grow longer. He was a breathtaking sight to behold, otherworldly and magnificent.

The men shrank away, cowering in fear. The giant bent over them, peering curiously at their gleaming armor. And as he did so, a guardsman lashed out with a sword and hacked off the first two fingers of the giant's left hand. The ice fingers fell and shattered on the floor. Instead of reacting in pain, the giant merely stared blankly at his missing fingers. Astrid was still too numb to feel anything but fascination.

"I implore your forgiveness," said Thidrek, stepping forward to address the giant. "His rashness will be *severely* punished." He glared at the offending guardsman, then raised the Shield of Odin to his chest in caution. "We come in peace. I am Prince Thidrek, son of Mirvik the Mild, ruler of the northern fjordlands. I am deeply honored to make your acquaintance." He gave a low bow, a gesture of respect he'd never shown anyone.

A small, encouraging smile formed on the giant's face, and Thidrek continued.

"I believe you're in possession of an item I desire. Thor's

Hammer. I would like to buy it from you."

The frost giant's face clouded with concern. He gave a frosty snort and lowered his gaze to the floor. Noting the great creature's dismay, Thidrek took a new tack.

"I'm prepared to pay handsomely."

Still the giant frowned.

"Try to see it my way," Thidrek said in a honeyed tone. "I'm a benevolent ruler who wants to keep peace. With the Hammer in my possession, all the tribes would cease their stupid warring, and the killing would end." The giant was silent, unswayed by Thidrek's words, his simple mind sensing them to be untrue. Feeling he was losing control, Thidrek shot a look at Grelf. "This was *your* idea, Grelf! A little help here?" And then, whispered so that only Grelf could hear: "If I don't get the Hammer, I'll have your head!"

Grelf gulped and approached the creature, feeling dwarfed by his vast size. Weeks earlier, when he'd learned from his spies that the Hammer had indeed fallen to earth and was believed to be in the possession of a frost giant, Thidrek had wanted to employ his usual method: to forcibly destroy the creature and simply steal the Hammer. But Grelf had counseled that they try a less violent, more cunning strategy, and he'd immediately begun to hatch a plan. The only way to beat a force you could never overpower, he reasoned, was not to fight it, but to give it exactly what it wanted. To find its greatest weakness. To feed its deepest need. And so he read. He called in experts. He even interviewed a troll or two. Finally he hit on the answer: Frost giants, he learned, had been formed by the very tears of the gods. This made them extraordinarily sensitive and caring creatures, easily prone to tears themselves, great appreciators of poetry, song, and, most of all, beauty, in all its manifold forms. Therefore, he would appeal not to the giant's head but to his heart. Ah, emotional vulnerability! How Grelf enjoyed taking advantage of it in others!

Now Grelf looked up at the ice-crusted thing, praying that his words would not be his last, knowing it was either the Hammer or his head.

"Sir . . . I mean, Your Frostship," Grelf sputtered, "surely the Hammer is a possession to be prized. But mightn't there be something of even greater value?" The giant furrowed his brow. Grelf forged on. "What I mean is, you dwell here alone, I see. No friends. No fellow giants. No pets. Nothing but freezing cold winds and a wasteland of ice to keep you company. The only voice you hear . . . is your own. That must be unspeakably hard." The giant's face fell, and Grelf saw he'd struck just the nerve he'd been hoping for.

"You deserve more, don't you?" asked Grelf, and the giant nodded, seeming about to burst into tears. "Well, of course you do," said Grelf. "That's why we've brought *her*"—Astrid felt herself pushed from the shadows into the center of the cave—"a lovely lady to be your bride. To brighten your days and give you the companionship you've so sorely missed."

The frost giant took one look and his face lit up. Beaming rapturously, he bent toward her in charmed fascination. The soft blue-and-white frills of her dress made her look gift wrapped in ribbons and bows, just the effect Grelf had sought Hrolf to conjure.

"Uh, I don't think so," said Astrid, who wanted no part of this trade, trying to hide behind Thidrek. But Thidrek, seeing the giant so smitten, quickly clamped a hand over her mouth, anxious to seal the deal.

"So it's settled. You take the girl and, and—" He looked to Grelf for help.

"An uplifted heart e'er after," cooed Grelf.

"Right, all that. And in exchange, I take the Hammer. Oh, and if you don't mind, could you sign for it? Just to make it legal?" Thidrek nodded to Grelf, who then unrolled on the floor a small scroll of vellum marked BILL OF SALE. Grelf handed the giant a stick of charcoal and indicated where to sign. The giant took the stick and went to sign, but then stopped. And in a voice remarkably soft, the frost giant spoke.

"You promise peace?" the frost giant said. The force of his icy exhalation was so strong, it frosted Thidrek's face and hair. But the prince didn't flinch.

"Peace forever," he said. "You have my word."

Satisfied, the giant scrawled an *X* on the bill of sale and swung his gaze back to Astrid. With a single finger, he gently stroked the top of her head. An icy chill ran through her, giving her such violent shivers, she couldn't speak.

She saw Thidrek and his men begin to back out of the cave and heard the prince bid good-bye to the giant. "Don't bother showing us out," Thidrek said. "We know the way."

In a moment the men were gone and Astrid was alone with the brutish thing. She felt too weak to run, too scared to scream. With escape unlikely, faced with who knew what horrors, she did the only thing she possibly could in these impossible circumstances. She fainted.

The storm on Mount Neverest had spread downward to where the mountain met the sea, and now it had enveloped the ship. Lut lay on deck beneath a bundle of furs, dimly aware of his own heartbeat and the patter of raindrops on his furs. The distant howl of the wind was high and shrill, like the spirits of long-dead ancestors calling to him in song. Though he felt the heat of his own heart fire fading, his mind was alive with pictures. The flinty grin of Voldar the Vile, his lost chieftain. The boyish laugh of Dane the Defiant, the son he'd gained. And the new face that had invaded his dreams. Some kind of bearded, ice-crusted creature that seemed to Lut no mere man but something far more . . . threatening. He prayed for the safety of Dane and the others, knowing that the higher up the mountain they went, the closer they'd come to the thing that could kill them all.

20

Hearts Grow Heated in a Prison of Ice

Astrid awoke to the sound of someone happily humming. She lay on a soft bed of fir twigs, the flickering glow of a nearby fire for a moment making her feel warm and safe. But again she heard the humming, and remembering she'd been sold to a brutish beast whose breath alone was enough to give a girl serious frostbite, she realized her prospects looked none too promising.

Presently the frost giant lumbered into view. Seeing Astrid awake, he grinned a giant grin. She waited, expecting the worst. She might be forced to cook and clean for him, or wash his back, or even be eaten perhaps. But he seemed so happy in her presence, she didn't have the heart to do what she normally would have done in this situation, which would be to yell and scream and kick until she'd fought her way free. The tender way he looked at her, the way he had fashioned her comfortable bed—these softened her heart and made her think maybe he wasn't going to hurt her after all.

Still, she couldn't be sure. The best course of action, she decided, was to engage him in conversation, to draw him out so she could get to know him. Only then could she tell if he was truly dangerous or not.

Astrid smiled. The giant gave a shy smile of his own, then quickly looked away. He seemed afraid to look directly at her.

"You live here . . . alone?" she asked.

"Yes," he said. The soft sound of his voice was surprisingly soothing, as if he were speaking through a flute, turning his words magically to music. "But now I have you," he said.

"Yes, you do."

There was an uncomfortable silence. Then the giant said, "My heart is glad you are here."

Astrid nodded and smiled, pretending to be as comfortable as if she were in her very own home. Inhaling deeply, he took in her scent, pleased by it. He asked if she was hungry. She nodded. Following him into the next room, she saw it was a kind of makeshift kitchen, with a giant-size table and chairs. He had made a crackling fire in the corner, explaining he used fire only for the light it cast, saying that heat was his enemy.

"Humans," said Astrid, "need fire for warmth."

The frost giant nodded, understanding. Astrid was

touched he'd gone to such trouble just for her. And when the giant added another huge log to the fire, she saw that the blaze of heat melted his hand a bit, making little droplets of water roll down his fingers and onto the floor, where they quickly froze again. She then watched in amazement as he plunged his left hand—the one with the missing fingers—into a huge pot of ice-cold water. And as he pulled it out again, Astrid saw that the water had caused frost crystals to begin growing where his old fingers had been, and soon, after another dip back in the chilled water, the missing fingers had completely re-formed themselves and grown back. The giant made a fist with his left hand, seeing that his new fingers worked just fine.

"Good as new?" Astrid asked.

The giant nodded and smiled. Then he set down what looked like a huge wooden porridge bowl, over six paces in diameter. "Join me," he said, nodding to the bowl. The wooden spoon he'd set inside was as tall as Astrid herself. Ravenous, she leaned over the rim of the bowl. It was filled with blue snow! And leaning over further, she fell all the way in. As she peeked up over the rim of the bowl, the giant saw she had a slushy gob of the blue snow on her head, as if she were wearing it as a hat. She carefully scooped a little bit off her head and tasted it. How delicious! What was it?

Snow flavored with fresh blueberries, the frost giant said, which grew on lower elevations of the mountain. He gently lifted her out and gave her a rag to wipe herself with. Then he broke a tiny icicle from his beard and, scratching an indentation into one end, gave it to her to use as a spoon. And to her surprise, it worked just fine.

"It's good," she said between bites, and the giant smiled. As she spooned up her slushie, he explained that, since he was a frost giant, ice was all he could eat. Snow, hailstones, icicles, pack ice, sheet ice—any form of frozen water at all. The hoarfrost that formed on tree limbs after a light rain was particularly light and crunchy. And the flavored bowls of slush, like the one she was eating, were refreshing. But most delectable of all, he said, was the ancient blue ice that could be found deep in the hearts of glaciers. "The older, the better," he murmured.

The more she ate the sweet concoction, the better she felt, and the easier it became to talk with the giant. She asked questions about his life, and he answered shyly at first. But soon he warmed to her and began to tell her many things.

He told her his name was Thrym. He had lived alone in the cave for some years, having been sent away a long time ago by the other frost giants and told never to return. When she asked why he'd been ostracized, at first he wouldn't say. After some coaxing, he told her it was because he'd been "blamed for the death of another." He had killed one of his own kind.

Astrid said nothing and waited for him to continue. Haltingly, he explained that he had had a girlfriend, a frost giantess, and against her father's wishes he had taken her for a midnight walk. And being a playful sort, he had started to chase her around, trying to kiss her, and she had coyly played along, trying to run from him. It had been fun for a time, but the game had gotten out of hand. They had strayed too far down the mountain, and she had slipped and fallen and rolled down past the snow line. And she'd melted to death.

"Melted to . . . ?" Astrid said. It sounded so awful.

"Yes," he said. And he told her that frost giants can survive only in the coldest climes, up on snowbound mountaintops where the freezing air and icy winds keep them frozen solid and healthy. And if he or his kind venture down too far below the snow line, where the air is much warmer, they will quickly melt and be destroyed. "You have your world," he said, "we have ours," explaining that this was the gods' way of keeping humans and giants apart. There was a silence, and then he said, "Never go below the snow." That's what he'd always been told. But he'd been foolish and irresponsible and had been banished forever from his world. And would live here alone for the rest of his days.

To lift his mood, she changed subjects, asking about Thor's Hammer. How had he come to possess it?

He said that one day after he'd been cast out, during a particularly lonely stretch of time, there'd been a raging storm. A gale-force wind had blown, with iceballs the size of sheep's heads. Lightning blazed and thunder boomed for three long days and nights, during which he'd had to take shelter inside the ice cave.

When the storm had abated and the skies had cleared, he'd gone out to play on the slopes, and that's when he'd come upon the Hammer lying half buried in the new-fallen snow. Its energies somewhat depleted, it glowed and sparked, melting the ice around it, giving off a bright halo of light. At first amazed, Thrym had danced about it in delight, further gladdened to see the shadow of himself that the Hammer's halo of light threw over the snow, a shadow so lifelike, it mirrored his every move, and this he came to call his *shadowfriend*.

Thrym soon realized that Thor most probably had lost his prized weapon in an ill-advised marathon of drinking or carelessly thrown it in a fit of anger, and it had fallen from the sky and landed on Thrym's mountaintop. He'd kept it as a kind of toy or companion, often talking to it out loud, unburdening his troubles, expecting any day that Thor would be down to retrieve it, and he would be rewarded for having looked after it with such devotion. (Thor's impulsive rages and drinking bouts were widely excused, if not altogether celebrated, since they were thought to be the by-product of an unhappy childhood. Though he was among the greatest of all the gods, Thor still needed to blow off steam every now and then.)

For a whole year Thrym had lived alone on the mountain, the Hammer his only companion. But Thor had never showed. Thrym had grown tired of waiting, his heart hardening in disappointment. He felt that not only had his own kind rejected him, but the gods had as well. And so, when Thidrek had arrived, being a peaceable fellow, he had gladly given the Hammer away for the pleasure of Astrid's company. When he admitted this to Astrid, he smiled a little-boy smile that made Astrid fear him less and feel that, despite his huge bulk, he perhaps was far less a threat than she had first imagined. All Thrym wanted, she sensed, was someone to love—and someone to love him in return—and that made him like everybody else inside.

On their journey up the mountain, Astrid had overheard Grelf tell Thidrek how frost giants had been formed by the tears of the gods. When gazing down from Valhalla and profoundly moved by human events, whether it was mothers dying in childbirth or true love torn asunder by envy and ignorance, they shed their godly tears. These fell from the heavens onto the highest, coldest mountaintops, and when the teardrops touched the icebound earth, like seeds of life, they crystallized and grew and, alive with the spirit energy of that god's emotion, formed giant-size creatures made entirely of ice. This was why, as Grelf had said, though brutish in appearance, most frost giants were known to be sensitive creatures much given to shows of emotion.

After their meal, Thrym picked the wayward blueberry skins from his teeth with an old knife he'd found on the mountain long ago. Astrid asked if she could use it. "You want to pick your teeth too?" he asked.

She laughed and said, "It's a little big for *my* mouth. No,

I want to do some ice sculpting. It relaxes me." The giant asked what she was going to make, and Astrid said she'd show him later, and he mustn't peek. So, as Astrid set about cutting and shaping a block of ice, Thrym did everything he could to entertain her and make her feel at home.

He did a little show with handpuppets that he'd sewn himself out of bits of cloth and goatskin. He made funny faces. He juggled snowballs. He performed feats of strength, hefting five huge tree trunks over his head at once. He danced a jig while playing a tune on a finely carved wooden flute and sang a song he composed on the spot just for her.

Oh, you of smiles
And golden hair,
Girl so glowing
And so fair,
'Tis no wonder
That I stare.

Oh, how lovely
You must be
To make me sing
This melody.

Might you stay
And warm my heart?
Might you play

The partner part?
I can't abide
A life apart.

Oh, how lovely
You must be
To make me sing
This melody.

Astrid was touched. But the more he tried to please her, the more Astrid realized the sad truth. Since he was covered in frost, his touch kind of left her cold. Not to mention that he was four times taller than Dane or any other man she'd ever known. She felt even worse when Thrym began to talk of wanting to marry someday and have children. Well, it just wasn't going to work, no matter how many layers of protective clothing he agreed to wear. She tried to let him down easy.

"Listen, I have to be honest," she said, easing her way into it. "I'm sure you're a kind and gentle giant, and I so appreciate everything you've done for me, Thrym, really I do. But the simple truth is it'll never work, you and me."

At first he didn't understand. "What? You don't like me with a beard?" He quickly raked his hand across the icicles that hung from his chin and broke them all off. He struck a grinning pose, hoping she'd like his new look.

"It's not that. You look fine, Thrym . . . it's just . . ."

Thrym's face fell. "My height, eh?" he said. "But see,

I'm not so tall when I slouch." He tried to lean over farther, but still he towered over her, and even he could see it wasn't working. "I'm too cold for you, is that it? The whole frost thing puts you off?"

"Thrym, please, it's not you. It's *me*."

"You? But I think . . . I think you're beautiful."

Astrid blushed to hear it, even from a frost giant.

"No, I mean . . ." Here she paused, amazed at what she realized she was about to say. "I mean, I love . . . someone else." There. She'd said it. It was the first time she'd actually said it aloud. The first time she'd publicly admitted to anyone that she loved Dane. The boy she'd always dreamed of having one day. The boy who'd grown into a man right before her eyes the day he had nearly died trying to save her life.

"You love . . . another?" Thrym's gaze fell to the floor, and for a long moment he said nothing, remaining silent and morose. Astrid felt awful. She knew she'd hurt his feelings and wanted to say something to ease his pain.

"Listen, Thrym, just because *we* aren't right for each other doesn't mean you should give up on love. You'll find someone. I know you will." She reached out to touch his arm, but struck by the sudden chill, she instantly withdrew it.

The giant pounded the tabletop with his fist. *Bam!* The cave shook. "*Find* someone? Fat chance!" He stomped about, his heavy footfalls shaking loose shards of ice from the ceiling and walls. "Do you know what it's like for me?

Of course you don't! You take your beauty for granted. Look at me! I'm made of *ice.* And ice is *cold*! Do you want to feel a deadly chill when touched? No! Humans want warmth! Well, I don't have what you want and I never will!" He slumped to the floor, put his head in his hands, and actually started to cry, the tears freezing the moment they landed on his cheeks.

"See? Even my tears freeze up . . . ," he blubbered.

Astrid tried to comfort him, hating to see him so upset. "You'll find someone—someone of your own kind, someday—and you'll find love, too, I'm sure."

This was impossible, he said. All the frost giantesses wanted nothing to do with him. He was an outcast. A pariah. He was fated to a miserable life alone. Then he erupted in fury again and began throwing things, kicking the furniture, until huge, jagged chunks of ice came raining down from above.

"You! It's all *your* fault!" he thundered. "Why did you have to come here, anyway? I was doing just fine until you showed up!"

Cowering in the corner, Astrid feared for her life. If she weren't crushed by the falling shards of ice, the ranting giant might soon turn his rage on her. She had to escape. And while Thrym's back was turned, she saw her chance. She ran for the passageway, hoping to slip away, but Thrym caught sight of her out the corner of his eye. His arm shot out and swept her back into the cave, his overpowering force roughly knocking her backward onto the floor.

"And where do you think *you're* going?" He lumbered over to where she lay quivering, glaring down at her, the look of affection that had once been on his face now replaced with an overpowering fury. "Out for a little walk, eh?"

"I—I—was afraid," she said, deciding that telling the truth was the only way to stay alive. But it did little to quell his anger.

"*Afraid?* Don't forget, I own you! So whether you like it or not—whether you like *me* or not—you won't ever be leaving. 'Cause no matter what"—he lowered his face just inches from hers—"you're *mine*!" And as he breathed this last word, he sent forth a blast of air so cold, it covered her with a thick layer of frost that froze her to the spot. She tried to move, but her whole body was fastened to the ice floor beneath her. Seeing her so tethered, the giant grunted in satisfaction and soon took up his club and left the cave, too overcome with emotion to care what might happen to her.

Unable to move a muscle, her teeth chattering from the freezing cold, Astrid searched her mind for some way to survive. If Thrym intended to leave her this way, she couldn't last even a few hours. Her only chance was finding a way to get free. If only she had her axes, she thought, she could chop herself free and be gone. But her axes, she recalled, had been confiscated by Thidrek's men. And thinking of Thidrek brought back thoughts of her dear father and Dane and Jarl and all the others who'd come so far and risked so much to try to save her. And now it had all come to this. Freezing to death in a mountaintop cave hundreds of miles from home. Images of Dane came to her, memory flashes of when they were children, laughing and playing in the snow at twilight, the night he kissed her and tried to give her the Thor's Hammer locket. . . .

She closed her eyes and tried to warm herself with thoughts of Dane, wondering where he was and if she would ever see him again.

21

Dane Makes a Chilling Discovery

At that very moment Dane was freezing too. The progress he and his men had been making up the mountain had been halted by the blizzard. Lost and unable to move through the howling, punishing winds, they had taken shelter for the night huddled together on a wind-shielded ledge. The storm raged well into the next day, and when it finally abated the following afternoon, the men resumed their climb, albeit with great difficulty, the winds still blowing too hard to make progress easy.

When at last they reached the upper slopes of Mount Neverest, instead of splitting up, Dane and his men had decided to stay together. If they did find Thor's Hammer, Dane had reasoned, they might need every bit of manpower they could muster to help carry it. And if they met Thidrek and his men again, they'd need every hand they had to work their revenge and free Astrid.

Though a raw haze of sunlight had begun to burn through the high mountain mist, a powerful wind still blew from the north, making progress slow and arduous.

All at once the men came to a halt, struck by the sight of footprints in the snow. But these were not just the footprints of Thidrek and his men. These were *massive*, at least three feet long and two feet across, outsize impressions so deep, they had not yet been covered over in snow. The line of prints led from an upper ridge down to a stand of fir trees in a ravine a half mile below. Dane and Jarl traded disbelieving looks, for a moment both too overcome to speak.

"Are you thinking what *I'm* thinking?" said Dane.

"I think so," said Jarl.

"Maybe we're closer than we thought," said Dane. He began to walk on, eagerly following the footsteps, when Jarl grabbed his sleeve.

"Wait, wait," said Jarl, having a rare moment of clarity. "If there *is* a . . . giant one, he could be down there foraging for food. Better to go the other way. Find his lair while he's not there. Maybe there we'll find Astrid and the Hammer, and be gone before he even knows it." Dane saw the wisdom in Jarl's words and told him so. He changed direction and started to follow the tracks in reverse, climbing up toward some ice formations around a rocky peak on an upper ridge.

Minutes later, as they came round a high wall of ice, Dane stopped cold in his tracks. The giant's footsteps had come from an opening in the wall of ice, a tall, narrow crevice just high enough for a giant to call home.

Astrid was deep in a delirious dream . . . amid thick wispy clouds, sunbeams warming her cheeks. . . . The clouds parted and she spied, far below her, the seas and forests of the earth itself, large patches of green and blue . . . and she abruptly realized she was flying just like a bird through the sky. Oh, what freedom, like nothing she'd ever felt . . . but how was this possible? She felt a horse beneath her and looked down and saw that she wore a silver breastplate . . . and it was then that she fully knew the wonder of her dream: She was a Valkyrie, a warrior-maiden in the service of the gods of Valhalla, in search of the most deserving man among the many brave hearts of the northlands . . . and it was then she saw it—the face of Dane floating before her . . . his bright blue eyes and warm smile seeming so real, like she could almost reach out and touch him. She saw his lips move and heard the comforting sound of his voice . . . "Astrid! I'm here." Ahhh, what a dream, she thought, what bliss . . . and then a new face appeared—one with big, bulbous cheeks. Ulf the *Whale*? What was *he* doing in her dream?

And abruptly she opened her eyes to see faces all around her: Jarl, Fulnir, Drott, Orm, and her father too! They were using Jarl's knife and Thrym's rusty toothpick knife to chop her free from the ice, and all at once a great rush of feeling swept back into her heart, and she realized it was the thrill of having hope again. Perhaps she would live—and, yes, even love!

After they'd cut her free and hugged and kissed her—Dane's kiss the sweetest and longest of them all—she'd hurriedly told them what had happened with Thrym the frost giant and all about how Thidrek had taken the Hammer. Jarl and Dane knew what Thidrek's possession of this weapon would mean to their world. They argued about how best to escape down the mountain and back to the ship and how to stop Thidrek once they'd caught up with him on the sea.

They were just starting to get tiresome when Astrid said to quit wasting time, that she had been lying there for hours thinking it all out, and that she had a plan that would work far better than anything they could think of, so why didn't they both just shut up and do what she said? Everybody just kind of looked at her, then at Dane and Jarl, and Jarl shrugged and said, "If you say so." Astrid hurried back to a far corner of the cave. And when Dane asked what she was doing, she simply said, "Saying good-bye."

22

Things Go Downhill

Thrym trudged up the icy ridge, a huge sack of cloudberries slung over his back. He'd trekked far and found a rare patch of particularly red and well-ripened ones, thinly covered with snow and flash frozen the previous fall. He'd had to go to a far lower elevation, and the warmer air had weakened him somewhat. Now, on his way back after picking the berries, he found himself whistling as he walked.

He'd thought a lot about the girl, about the way he'd treated her, and he felt bad. He had hated losing his temper and hoped she wasn't still mad at him or, worse, still frightened of him. Hurting her was the farthest thing from his mind. As he walked, he rehearsed what he was going to say to her, how he would apologize and say he didn't mean to have frozen her to the floor but it was the only way of knowing for certain she wouldn't leave while he went to fetch food. And now that he'd found the cloudberries, he was going to whip up the tastiest treat she'd ever had, a blue cloud slushie! Fresh snow flavored with blueberries *and* cloudberries, with perhaps some icicle bits thrown in to give it crunch! And once she had eaten, Thrym imagined she would allow him to kiss her on the cheek and then he'd dance and sing another song for her, one straight from the heart.

I'm so sorry,
Astrid dear.
Hurting you is
My worst fear.
Forgive me, please,
My clumsy ways.
For how I feel
There is no phrase.

And being so caught in his own thoughts, he at first didn't see, upon entering his lair, that Astrid was conspicuously absent, nor did he notice the present she had left him on the table by the hearth fire. He continued whistling in his lighthearted way as he busied himself with preparing the berries, calling out to her from the other room.

"Boy, are *you* in for a treat! A blue cloud slushie! My own recipe! Two kinds of berries *and* a crunchy surprise inside!" He was then visited by the notion that, instead of adding only icicles, he could throw in chunks of glacier ice as well to make it even crunchier. He could call it "Blue Cloud *Double-Crunch*!"

Excited, he came out to the cavernous main room to tell Astrid of his new idea, and was surprised to find her gone. He didn't understand at first, his simple mind trying to make sense of what he was seeing—or not seeing. He lumbered over and looked down, toeing the ice where she'd been.

"Astrid!" he called out. "Astrid, where are you? Sorry about before! I won't hurt you!" When he got no response, he began to check the side tunnels to see if she was hiding somewhere. No Astrid. As he reentered the kitchen, he spied the new object that had been set upon the table. He leaned down to take a closer look.

It was a small Valkyrie's horse, carved of ice, its wings spread and mane flowing back as if it were flying. It was something she'd quickly carved while he'd been off making dinner earlier, before their fight, and she'd hidden it in a corner of the cave, intending to give it to him when the time was right. In a word, it was beautiful, and Thrym was charmed by it. He carefully picked it up, marveling at the artistry and intricacy of it. And turning it round, on one side of the horse he found engraved a small heart. Although he'd never before seen this symbol, in his own heart he knew what it meant. It took a long moment for him to realize it also meant that she was gone. He gently set the ice carving on a shelf for safekeeping, taking care not to breathe on it for fear his frosty breath might ruin this wonderful memento. And then he turned and went out.

Outside, he craned his neck and squinted, gazing in every direction, trying to see where she might have gone. He saw nothing. It was then he thought to look down, and that's when he spotted the many small footprints heading down the mountain the other way. He bounded after them. His legs being so long, in twenty bounding steps he reached the next ridge and peered down the mountainside. There, just a speck on the slope far below, he spied something he was surprised to see. It was his porridge bowl, and it was moving fast.

⚡

Dane was amazed. Astrid's plan had actually worked. Well, so far, at least.

They'd rolled the porridge bowl out of the cave and carried it to the ridgeline. As instructed, they'd piled into the bowl, which was just big enough to carry them all, even Ulf the Whale. They'd pushed off, and just as Astrid had surmised, the smooth bottom of the bowl had made for good sledding. Down they slid, gaining speed as they went.

"Wheeee!" shouted Drott gleefully, the wind in his hair. Now they were whooshing down the slope at quite a clip, believing that they'd escaped danger once more and that much-deserved freedom at last lay ahead. Dane, too, was relieved that maybe the gods were on his side after all—if there were such things as the gods; he still wasn't sure.

And then, as thoughts of the still-elusive thunder in the hands of his enemy filled his mind, he worried about when and how they might meet again when—*Kuh-bloom! Kuh-bloom!* The earth shook. *We're under attack!* Dane thought. *It's Thidrek!* Then, catching a look from Fulnir, he spun round and saw the real cause: The frost giant was in hot pursuit!

By the gods! The legends were true! Dane reacted to the sight of the creature with fear and fascination. Fearful—for the thing was gaining fast, and it was abundantly clear he didn't mean to just shake hands when they met—and fascinated by the very existence of this magical being! Oh, glory, what a sight! A living, breathing man of ice! Just as his father, Lut, and other elders had so often told of in their tales but had never seen themselves. And now he beheld it with his very own eyes!

But the magic of the moment was soon obliterated. *Ka-blomm!* A giant-size snowball landed nearby, exploding into sharp bits of ice that spattered and shook the bowl, nearly capsizing it. Dane looked again. The giant had an armload of snowballs and was lobbing them as he bounded down the mountainside, drawing nearer with every stride.

"Snowbombs!" yelled Dane. He strained his brain to think of something—*any*thing—that could save them. Astrid caught his helpless look.

"He can't go below the snow line or he'll melt!" he heard her cry. And Dane, seeing that the brute would easily overtake them before that, yelled, "We need more speed to outrun him!"

Ka-blomm! Another snowbomb hit.

"But how?" shouted Fulnir. "We can't even steer!"

Before Dane could think, Astrid had the answer. She whipped off her cape and swiftly fashioned a makeshift sail, tying the ends of it to one of the spears as a mast. Catching the idea, Jarl and Vik helped to hoist it up and held the mast steady while Dane took hold of the cape's free end to act as a kind of guiding bowsprit. And instantly the "sail" caught wind, and away they went over the ice-slickened snow, Drott wild with glee as they rocketed downward.

Astrid was exhilarated. Her idea had worked. With Dane now beside her at the "bow," maneuvering left and right, dodging snowbombs as they fell around them, Astrid had never felt so alive.

"A new sport for the games!" she said to Dane, thrilled at the idea.

"Yeah," he said, grinning. "We'll call it 'snowbowling'!"

The farther down the mountain they flew, the warmer it got. But then, as the edge of the snow line drew nearer, she recalled Thrym's words: "Never go below the snow." But maybe, in the excitement of the chase, he'd forgotten or didn't care. Maybe he was so angry at Astrid's having abandoned him, he didn't care if he lived or died, or whether she did either.

The porridge bowl left the last of the snow behind and

hit the lower slope, where sharp, flat granite soon gave way to patches of high grasses and even a welcome warm breeze. The terrible moment was at hand. Would the giant follow? She dared a backward look and—in the flash of a moment—her eyes met his. Something in the pale blue of his gaze softened. And just before he ran out of snow, Thrym leaped up, dug his heels deep into the iced-over snow, and skidded to a long, slow stop.

Astrid was about to rejoice, when she was alarmed to see that his sudden braking had dislodged a small avalanche of ice chunks, which was advancing on *them*. She cried out to the others. They braced themselves. And soon the mini avalanche caught up and smashed right into the porridge bowl. Astrid, Dane, and the others held on for dear life as the bowl rode atop the tumbling, churning snow right over a cliff . . .

. . . and splashed into the sea!

For a moment, no one breathed. A cloud of sea spray and broken bits of ice showered down around their heads. Soon the mist of debris lifted. The porridge bowl was afloat on the water. All members of the crew were still present and accounted for, astonished they'd been saved.

"And there's the ship!" shouted Fulnir, pointing farther out to sea. All eyes gazed upon their swan-breasted long-ship, adrift just where they'd left her anchored in the fjord. Drott and Ulf the Whale began to paddle toward the ship with their hands as Astrid checked on Dane and the others, happy to find them unhurt. And then, after giving

Dane a warm smile, she found her gaze traveling back to shore, up the slope to the white expanse of snow, searching for signs of Thrym the frost giant.

"Did he hurt you?" she heard Dane say.

"No more than I hurt him," she answered, her eyes still scanning the mountainside. She saw nothing, and turning away, she slipped her arm through Dane's, pressing herself against him, feeling the warmth of his cheek on hers, the very thing she'd been yearning for and feared she'd never feel again.

Dane said nothing; he was too busy smiling. He had his fair maiden back, his ship, and the respect of his men. Now it was time to think about the thunder they still sought, and he gazed out to sea, his mind awhir with intrepid notions of how they might intercept Thidrek and seize the Hammer.

He was further cheered to see Lut the Bent frantically waving and shouting from on deck. Dane couldn't make out the words, but it sure looked like Lut was glad to have them back. Their spirits lifting, the men began humming a sea chantey, feeling a little closer to home and to kinsmen most dear. Soon, the wee bowl of a boat reached the longship. One by one, everyone clambered aboard the mothership, calling for Lut. The old one, however, was now nowhere to be seen. Dane heard muffled sounds at the aft end of the ship, and as he went to look, a one-eyed Berserker jumped up from behind some ale casks and, in an instant, was holding a blade at Dane's throat. A second Berserker sprang up, holding Lut, one hand clamped around the old one's mouth.

"Easy, boy," One-Eye grunted. And all at once, before Dane could give warning, the rest of his crew were overtaken by a dozen more of Thidrek's brutes who came leaping over the side onto the deck, having been hidden from view in a small skinboat normally kept lashed on the starboard side. Dane realized that Lut had been frantically trying to alert them to the danger before he was overcome.

And now Dane was further sickened to see the figure of Grelf step forth, a broken oar shaft over his shoulder, an insidious grin on his grotesque little face.

"Well, won't the prince be pleased at *this* turn of events. Now he'll have everything his heart desires—the Hammer *and* the girl!" said Grelf, his eyes roving hungrily over Astrid's shapely form. "And I'll be even closer to that Cutthroat of the Month Award I've been coveting." Grelf went on to explain rather rudely that Thidrek's Berserker troops and horde of guardsmen had successfully carried the Hammer down the mountain and loaded it onto a warship. They were, at that very moment, sailing southward toward Thidrek's castle, where, once there ensconced, his lordship would have no trouble in greatly expanding his lands into a full-fledged kingdom and exterminating anyone who stood in his way—Dane and his entire village topping the list, of course.

"We spotted you up on the mountain, and I deduced

you were going to the frost giant's lair to rescue the girl," said Grelf. "Knowing you'd soon be returning, I decided it would be more fun to wait and seize you right here." Grelf gave a malicious grin, showing his yellowed teeth.

Dane burned in anger as Astrid and his men were roughly trussed up. As his hands were tightly tied behind him and the rough rope cut into his wrists, Dane was overtaken with an even greater rage. He spat an oath at Grelf. "You're scum, Grelf! Ugly, cretinous scum. Actually, *less* than scum, because scum doesn't kill just for the fun of it—"

Whaaack! With whiplike speed the oar blade slammed into Dane's forehead, and all went black as he crumpled to the deck.

From high up on the mountainside, hidden in a thick stand of fir trees, a pair of watchful blue eyes followed the longship as her sail was raised and the wind began to blow her southward from the harbor. The eyes, of course, belonged to Thrym, one very sad and forlorn frost giant. Being far too distant to see the details of what was happening onboard the ship, he did not know that Astrid was again in danger, only that his beloved was leaving, no doubt lost to him forever. He waited until the sail of her warship was but a white speck on the distant southern horizon, and then he turned and trudged slowly up the slope back to his snowbound home and a cold life all alone.

23

The Beginning of the End

Of all the deaths Dane had imagined possible, this was the worst. He'd always dreamed of dying on a battlefield somewhere, or being torn apart by wild animals while trying to protect his kin, or drowning at sea during a punishing storm. Once he'd even entertained the notion that it was possible to die from the suffocating stench of one of Fulnir's meat-pie farts. But to be locked away in a dark, damp dungeon, soon to be put on public display and summarily executed? To die without a fight? That was a death fit for a rat, not a man. And most rats were wily enough to claw their way free.

But this, it seemed, would be his fate, despite all that he had endured and all the confidence that had been placed in him by others. He had failed in his quest to save Astrid and retrieve the Shield of Odin. Failed miserably, in fact—and this knowledge weighed heavily upon him.

Now that Thidrek had the Hammer, he was more powerful than ever.

They were locked in the dungeon of Thidrek's castle, a dark cell built in the basement of the outer walls of the stone fortress. They'd received word of what Thidrek was planning, and it wasn't pretty. They were all to be executed at noon the following day, beheaded one by one, each forced to watch the deaths of the ones who went before. In front of a live audience, no less! Their deaths would be merely an appetizer for the wedding to follow, a mere sideshow for the Saturday matinee, the union of Thidrek and Astrid.

In one fell swoop Thidrek had increased his power ten thousandfold. Word had spread like wildfire through the villages that he was now in possession of a new kind of fearsome weapon. To further trumpet this fact, he had sent the ruthless Berserkers on horseback to the north, east and south through the farthest-flung villages, rousting commonfolk as they slept, informing them that Thidrek was their new ruler. If anyone resisted, their huts were burned and livestock slaughtered. If that didn't convince them, they were drawn and quartered.

Needless to say, before long, each of the outlying tribes that had once lain beyond the prince's official domain swore fealty to Thidrek. He and he alone now ruled all the northern fjordlands, nearly doubling the size of his realm in a matter of days, no doubt doubling the taxes he would receive as well. A darkness was descending over the land, and Dane envisioned the horrors yet to come, hoping the death of his own dear mother would be swift and painless.

"'Tisn't your fault," said a voice. Dane looked up to see Jarl crouched beside him, his handsome face dimly visible in the moonlight that shone through the one tiny barred window that looked out over a grove of trees growing on the rocky cliffs below.

"You did your best, mate. Even I could've done no better." It was amusing, Dane thought, how even in giving what he thought was a compliment, Jarl was still paying tribute to himself. But Dane knew Jarl's heart was in the right place, and he nodded and knocked fists with his friend. They sat a time, listening to the snores of their brethren who lay asleep in the darkness beyond. Dane asked Jarl how he thought the others were doing.

"Well, Lut's on his last legs, poor spiker, Orm's been blubbering for his mother, and Ulf's so starved he's gobbling cockroaches. Twenty-nine at last count." A silence passed between them.

"She forgives you too," said Jarl, Dane knowing full well whom he meant.

"Strange, eh?" said Dane, who felt closer than ever before to the young man he'd once hated and hoped would die. "Us both loving the same girl."

"She's worth it," came the reply.

"That she is," said Dane. He feared he'd never see her again. He had but one seed of hope: the weapon he'd covertly slipped to Astrid while captive on the ship sailing to Thidrek's castle. If she could find a way to use it, perhaps all was not lost.

Astrid's place of confinement gave far more comfort than did Dane's dungeon. For a country girl who knew only the confines of smoky, dirt-floored huts, her opulent castle chamber was something from a fairy tale. There were plush carpets to walk on, a luxurious canopied bed to lie in, and artful tapestries on the walls to entertain and entice her. And though at first she resisted and tried to fight the servants sent to fuss over her, she eventually gave in and let them do their work.

They bathed her and scrubbed her clean. Then they brushed back her golden hair and trussed it atop her head in silver ribbons. They rouged her cheeks and painted her lips red. And at last, for the crowning touch, they dressed her in a gown of scarlet Oriental silk, long and flowing, its ruffled bodice bedecked with golden threadwork and a jeweled brooch.

Now, alone in her locked chamber, she gazed in wonder at herself in a large mirror made of beaten and polished silver. She looked so . . . *beautiful*. Before, she'd seen her face and figure reflected only in the still waters of a pond. In her brief life she'd pursued only the rough-and-tumble activities of men: hunting, fighting, flinging her axes. But now, admiring her image in the mirror, resplendent in her finery, she saw a wholly different Astrid. *Is this indeed the look of a queen*? she wondered, utterly enchanted. And for a moment the thought of a whole new life stretched before her. One of leisure and refinement, of power and privilege and—

She caught sight of her smile in the mirror. Pompous, smug, imperious—all the things she hated. *No, no, no!* she told herself, disgusted. This wasn't her at all. No, she would either slit Thidrek's throat or take less direct means to bring him down.

Thidrek rose from the table as Astrid was led into his chamber. "Ah, Astrid, my sweet! You look ravishing!"

She did a girlish twirl, presenting herself.

"You," he oozed, "are the fairest in all my domain."

"Truly? You're sure? It's a big domain."

"And getting bigger all the time!" Thidrek gave her a caught-little-boy look. "I hope you've forgiven me for leaving you with that ugly frosted fellow. An unfortunate lapse of judgment, I'm afraid."

"That *was* rather rude," Astrid purred, caressing his cheek with the back of her hand. She shot him a pouty, playful look.

Thidrek felt his blood begin to boil. His plan was working! He knew if she got a taste of the lavish life he could provide, she'd be his. What woman wouldn't be? He had wealth and, most of all, *power.* Women loved power. They couldn't resist it. She'd hated him before because he hadn't proven himself. He'd been but a man grasping for control and authority. Unworthy. But now—*now* he possessed the ultimate power of the land, and she was helplessly drawn to it. To *him*. In her eyes, he'd become a kind of magnetic force, pulling her closer, ever closer into his web of dominion. Aah, women. Such simple creatures. So easy to control when you got right down to it. Thidrek moved closer, gently entwining his arm in hers.

"I suppose you know why I summoned you."

". . . a girl does get ideas."

"It would greatly gladden my heart if you'd agree"—here he lowered his voice to a suggestive whisper—"to *marry* me."

Astrid batted her eyelashes and gave him her most bewitching smile. *Her* plan was working. Thidrek was proposing! She had him on the hook. "I'd certainly consider it," she purred, "but let's be honest, you *are* Thidrek the Terrifying. Known for acts of cruelty and, some might say, crimes against humanity. . . ."

His face abruptly darkened. Oops. She tried to recover.

"On the other hand," she continued coyly, "you're rich, handsome, and so very, *very* virile. Certain aspects of your character could be overlooked." This made him brighten, and Astrid, feeling back in control of things, in full command of her charms, stretched languorously, affecting a kind of feline self-absorption. "And I imagine marriage to a man of your position would come with certain . . . fringe benefits?"

"Why of course!" Thidrek crowed. She'd have unlimited

visits to the castle physicians, he explained. Her own private sauna, imported from Finland. And, if so desired, she could get all the beauty treatments she wished without ever having to make an appointment.

She cooed in response, and his head began to spin. She *wanted* him! Being a bloodthirsty barbarian at heart, he'd usually never think to ask. He'd merely take the girl by force. And once he'd had his fun, he'd keep her in servitude forever, as a serving wench or foot masseuse or some other minimum-wage employee. But this—*this* stirred him even more. A queenly lass who'd actually consent to wed! Her perfume had him dizzy with desire. He bent to kiss her—but she abruptly pulled away, and he nearly fell over.

"Wine!" she cried. "We must have wine to toast our union!" Hiding his annoyance with a smile, Thidrek snapped his fingers, and in came a servant with two goblets and a pitcher of wine.

"No, allow *me*, m'lord," she said, taking the wine from the servant and beginning to pour it herself into the goblets. "If I'm to be your wife, I must learn to serve you myself. As only befits a *king*." Ah, Thidrek thought, alluring *and* submissive. How could he resist? Eager to be alone now with his intended, he shooed away the servant, turning his back on Astrid to usher the lowly one to the door.

With Thidrek's back momentarily turned, Astrid made her move. She quickly drew out the goatskin of idiot water from the folds of her gown, the item Dane had slipped her back on the ship—and poured a prodigious amount into Thidrek's goblet. Was it enough, she worried? It would have to be! She frantically slid the bag back into her gown, and just as Thidrek turned round and returned to the table, he found her filling his goblet with burgundy. He took it up and held it aloft.

"To love everlasting," he said, eyes filled with desire.

Astrid returned his smile and raised her own glass. She watched the prince lift the goblet to his lips. He tilted it up. The liquid touched his tongue—and then just as quickly he lowered the drink.

"How silly of me," he said, shaking his head. "My taster! Nothing against you, m'love, but a king-to-be mustn't take chances." He tinkled a bell at his right hand, and in trundled a porcine, broad-bellied ball of corpulence with a look of utter terror on his face. "This is Bodvir the Unlucky," Thidrek explained, "my personal food taster. We men of power are prone to be poisoned, you know, and I must take every precaution. The eleventh taster this year, I'm afraid." He glanced up at Bodvir, completely oblivious to his taster's discomfort. "Not to worry, eh, Bodvir? A stomach of iron, they say."

"Y-yes, sire," said Bodvir, nodding and wiping the sweat from his brow. Astrid blanched. She couldn't let *him* drink the idiot water! It wasn't right. But how? How could she stop him without drawing Thidrek's suspicion? Bodvir raised the goblet to his lips. He shut his eyes, about to drink.

"No!" cried Astrid.

Bodvir lowered the goblet, relieved to have some reason not to drink.

Thidrek frowned. "What *is* it?"

Astrid searched for the right thing to say. "Uh, the wine! It's corked!"

"Corked?" Thidrek said, looking perturbed.

"Gone bad. Can't you smell that?" She put the wine to her nose and made a face. And then, seeing Thidrek staring in suspicion, she took a large gulp of the burgundy wine, swirling it round her mouth—as if having a tasting expertise of her own—and then, eyes bulging in sudden disgust, she spat the wine to floor, spraying some on the table. "Can't you *taste* that? It's pisswater!"

Thidrek drew back as if slapped by her words. She poured the rest of her drink out on the floor, hoping he would do the same. He didn't. He reached up and grabbed the goblet from Bodvir, putting it under his nose to smell it himself. He crinkled his nostrils. He flicked his gaze to Astrid, giving her a long, searching look. And then, flashing a conciliatory smile, Thidrek rose from his chair, goblet in hand, and told Bodvir he was excused.

"Yes, sire! Thank you!" Never had Astrid seen a look of such relief on a person's face as Bodvir showed as he bowed and backed out of the room, acting as if he'd just escaped the executioner's axe.

Thidrek grinned and set his goblet in front of her. "Astrid, *you* seem to know a lot more about wine than I do.

Tell me, is mine corked too? I can't tell." He stared down at her and gave a chilling grin.

Uh-oh. He was going to *make* her drink it. Astrid fiddled nervously with her brooch, stalling for time. "Well, of course it must be, sire," she said, thinking quickly. "Both goblets were poured from the same bottle. Here, let's throw this out and open a new one—"

But as she reached for the goblet to empty its contents, Thidrek suddenly thrust his hand down onto the base of the goblet, holding it firm, fixing his eyes then on hers, and saying, "*Drink* it. I really want your opinion." Astrid paled. There was no way to avoid it. With Thidrek's fingers held fast to the stem of the goblet, she took his hand in hers and slowly drew the glass halfway up toward her lips. Her eyes met his, where she saw a mixture of contempt and regret burning in his gaze. She looked down into the goblet itself, eyeing the red liquid, knowing all too well what lay therein. And then, in one smooth movement she pulled the goblet to her chin, making sure to scrape Thidrek's forearm against her brooch pin. Thidrek yowled in sudden pain and jerked his arm away, upturning the goblet and splashing wine all down her gown.

"By the gods—!" Thidrek cried, grabbing his arm.

"Oh, sire! My brooch pin must've come loose and stabbed you. I'm so sorry—"

Thidrek whirled, now in high dudgeon. "*Sorry*? You don't know the meaning of the word!" He advanced on her, pushing her backward and pinning her against the wall.

"You tried to *poison* me!" With one hand tightened round her throat and his body pressed against hers, he rifled her skirts with his other hand until he found the goatskin bag. He wrenched it free and threw it to the floor. From beneath her belt she drew a dagger and swiftly brought it up to thrust into Thidrek's chest, intending to kill him before he even knew it. But his hand caught hers, stopping the knife inches from his heart.

Thidrek yanked the knife away and slapped her hard across the face—once! twice!—and before she could flee, two guards rushed in and seized her. Thidrek's face was black with fury.

"Lock her up in the tower, the filthy wench! No food! No water! No visitors! And no honeymoon!"

Dane tried to sleep, but his mind wouldn't rest. If Astrid had succeeded in slipping the idiot water to Thidrek, wouldn't he have heard something by now? Panicked whispers from the guards? A wild rumor? But nothing had changed. Nothing at all. And now worries of what would happen to Astrid after the wedding went spinning through his head. Sleep was made even more impossible by the fact that Ulf was snoring like an inebriated walrus.

Dane sat at the window, staring through the bars at the stars in the night sky. He remembered Lut's words: "We never lose touch with those we truly love." Was it true? Oh, he so wanted to believe it. He peered at the two brightest stars, the same ones he'd seen while lost at sea, and closing his eyes, he soon found himself praying and pouring out his soul—to his father, to the gods, to whoever might be listening at this late hour. And then, wonder of wonders, he heard an ethereal voice . . . and lifting his head he saw it: a ghostly image of his father shimmering before him, the familiar red hair and beard fluttering as if blown by an invisible wind. And the spirit of the father spoke to the son.

"Dear boy, what is it you seek?" Voldar asked, his voice echoing as if traveling from a faraway place.

"Father . . . ?" said Dane, transfixed. "Where are you?"

"I'm in Valhalla," Voldar shot back. "Where else would I be?"

"What's it like up there?"

"It's a dream. The weather's pleasant, the food flavorsome and plentiful. There's all the mead you can drink and, well, other amenities I shan't go into now. Did you have a question?"

Dane hesitated, not sure he wanted to hear the answer.

"Father . . . am I fated to be destroyed by Thidrek?"

"Nothing is written until it is done, son. A man can fool his fate."

"That's what Lut told me! So it's true?"

"Yes, it's one of the many truths revealed to me up here. Also, that fruits will keep longer if left to ripen in a cool, dark place. But as to the problem at hand, know this: Your destiny is yours to make. He who fights blindly will be defeated. Be brave, but most of all, be wise. Then you will be worthy of winning back the Shield."

"And if I fail . . . ?"

His father's brow furrowed. "Then you will die a gruesome death, your body hacked to pieces and fed to the dogs, your severed head mounted on a pike for all to see, a rotting, miserable, humiliated failure—"

"O-*kay*, I get it! Thank you, Father."

"Well, you asked. . . ." Voldar's image began to shimmer and fade away. Dane called out to him one last time.

"Father, wait! There's something else!"

"*What*? You want to tell me that you miss me terribly and realize now how wise and loving I was and how much you wish you appreciated me more while I was alive? And that you feel responsible for my death and want to ask my forgiveness and hope there's no hard feelings? And hope we can talk like this again sometime?"

Dane was dumbfounded. "How—how did you know?"

"I know everything, son. And I know that when the time comes, you'll be every bit as brave as I was—maybe even braver. . . ."

Now his father's image faded more and moved farther away. And Dane finally found the courage to tell his father the deepest secret of his heart.

"Father . . . I love you. . . ."

"I love you too . . . ," came the reply, and Dane watched in bittersweet joy as the old man's hair and beard turned into wisps of smoke that dissipated into nothing and his eyes receded into the blackness of the sky, becoming two tiny points of light that merged into stars. . . .

Dane lifted his head with a start and looked around. The pearl-gray light of dawn was peeking through the window. He heard the early birdsong in the trees beyond the castle wall. Had he fallen asleep after all? Had it been real or only a dream? Soon it would be morning, perhaps the morning of the last day he would walk the earth. But strangely, he felt happy, abuzz with vigor and confidence. He drew out the silver Thor's Hammer locket he'd carried for luck, the one intended for Astrid. Even if he had only a few hours to live, there was a chance he'd see Astrid one more time before he died, and this thought further lifted his heart.

At that moment he heard a familiar *crawk!* and was delighted to see an old friend fly down and land on the windowsill.

"Klint! It's you!" The bird's amazing ability to track prey had also allowed him to relocate his long-lost master.

Again the bird squawked, and let drop something from his beak into Dane's palm. Nuts and berries the bird had gathered for his friend. Then Dane saw, out on the window ledge, a pile of berries the bird must've brought while he'd been sleeping.

"Hey, boy," he murmured to the bird. Dane ate one of the berries and set them aside for the others when they awoke. He stroked the bird's glossy feathers. The sight and feel of the bird so close made Dane yearn again for the comforts of home, for the familiar feel of his own straw-soft bed, the taste of his mother's venison stews, and the bright laughter of the village children at play.

The raven cocked his head and looked at Dane, then at the bars. It seemed to Dane that the bird understood his master was in dire straits.

"Good to see you, my friend," Dane said, allowing the bird to perch on his outstretched finger. "But I'm afraid there's nothing you can do. Not unless you've a key to this dungeon. All the same, it's good to be together again."

Behind him, the men began to awaken, and seeing the bird, one by one they came to the window, Drott and Vik and Rik and Fulnir, each reaching through the bars to touch and talk to the raven. They, too, had known the bird since boyhood and looked upon him with the same affection Dane did.

"Eh, Klinty," said Vik, always entertaining thoughts of violence, "why don't you fly down and peck Thidrek's eyes out?"

"And after that," said Rik, not to be outdone, "you can tear his ears off and shove 'em down his throat!"

Klint squawked in reply, as if he understood just what had been said, and the men laughed, cheered by it all. Then Klint flew down into the trees and returned momentarily, his beak full of more berries and nuts, which he deposited on the sill.

"Hey, he's delivering food!" said Drott, eagerly grabbing

and gobbling up a berry. "Klint—gimme a mixed codfish platter and a tankard of your finest ale!" It was silly—like most of the half-formed notions Drott blurted out—but it gave Dane an idea. If the bird could deliver berries, maybe, just maybe . . .

With the others busy divvying up the food morsels, Dane gently took hold of the bird and began to whisper in his ear. He drew something from his tunic and, opening his palm, displayed it to the bird. Klint cocked his head and took interest. Then, taking the item up in his beak, the raven gave a *screek! scrawk!*, hopped off the ledge, and flapped away, swooping out over the courtyard and the castle walls, heading northward, soon disappearing from view over the ramparts. Dane lost sight of him a moment later and turned back to the men, who sat eating the tidbits Klint had brought them. It was a long shot, he knew, but maybe, just maybe the bird could fetch more than nuts and berries.

In her cell in the tower Astrid lay curled in the corner, too tired to weep. Her attempt to kill Thidrek having failed, she, too, had lost hope. She'd fallen asleep and dreamed of her father and mother and a snowball fight she once had as a little girl. Then, from down in the courtyard, she heard the faint squawk of a bird. She could have sworn—quickly she went to her window and looked down. No bird in sight. Strange. For a moment it had sounded like the familiar call of Dane's own Klint, the bird that he'd had since he was a boy. And then she saw workmen with axes and hammers, building a platform. This could mean only one thing. A beheading or a wedding. Or both.

Blackhelmet and Redhelmet stood atop the ramparts, gazing down into the courtyard and out over the castle walls to the valley below, ever watchful for the slightest movement. They held their bows at the ready. They'd been awake all night, doing the usual midnight-to-eight o'clock shift. They were tired and bored and looking for something to occupy their weary minds. Blackhelmet saw it first. A bird, it was, a large black raven, and it swooped down into the courtyard, making a long, looping figure eight. For some reason it seemed like an interloper.

"A silver piece says I hit him," said Blackhelmet to his cohort.

"What? The bird?" said Redhelmet, scoffing. "Five says you don't."

"Make it ten and I'll snag him in one shot."

"You're on."

Blackhelmet drew back his bow, sighting down the arrow at the black bird, following its line of flight as it soared over the wall and out toward the valley. Blackhelmet waited for his moment, then let the arrow fly. *Bzing!* It hit the bird's wing, slicing through its feathers and out the other side. The bird dropped like a stone.

Blackhelmet said nothing. Redhelmet dug in his coin

purse and counted ten pieces of silver into his cohort's hand. He hated to lose, but at least they'd killed something on their watch that night, and he could sign out with a feeling of accomplishment, no matter how small.

24

The Situation Does Not Improve

Thidrek's men had spread the word, and duly terrified of being thought disobedient, all the Norsefolk from the surrounding villages came in droves to witness the event. Shortly after dawn peasants began to appear along the roadsides leading to the castle, children in tow, oxcarts laden with food. By noon the courtyard was jammed to the ramparts with onlookers, anxiously awaiting the festivities.

The day was to start with several beheadings, the royal pronouncement had promised, and then Thidrek's wedding, followed by a grand feast and, if Thidrek's mood permitted, dancing. Some came for the food, some for the pomp and circumstance of a royal betrothal. But mostly, Thidrek believed, it was the executions that really packed them in. "There's something about the spray of blood and the sobbing of women," he'd say, "that grabs 'em like nothing else."

Grelf, being intimately acquainted with the ways of commonfolk, knew only too well the real reason they came. They were scared stiff he'd execute *them* if they didn't show up. But Grelf, who wanted to preserve both his job *and* his life, never burst his master's bubble. He told Thidrek exactly what he wanted to hear and carried out his orders with dashing alacrity.

Except for the order to execute Astrid. Yes, Thidrek had been so angered and humiliated by her betrayal, he'd ordered that she be beheaded and that her head and torso be impaled on a pike and displayed along the battlements with all the others who'd talked back or somehow displeased him. But Grelf had thought this politically unwise, and after some discussion he'd convinced Thidrek to go ahead and marry her anyway. Despite her little assassination attempt.

"But she's a common strumpet!" Thidrek had barked. "A guttersnipe!"

"Exactly," Grelf had purred. "A commoner. And what better way to show the people you are *of* the people and *for* the people than by marrying one of them? Very good for the image, sire. And though this Astrid may be of common blood, she is of *un*common beauty. And that, too, reflects well upon you. It never hurts to woo and win the fairest lady in the land. Shows you're top of the heap. Makes men respect you and womenfolk swoon. Need I say more?" And then to cinch it, he unrolled the poster he'd had painted. It was dominated by the daunting visage of Prince Thidrek, the very picture of imperious power, and above that, painted in large dark letters, the words TEN BEHEADINGS AND A WEDDING.

"Well, sire? What say you? Does it . . . please you?"

Thidrek looked at his image on the poster, then bemusedly at the words above it. He smiled. "'Ten Beheadings and a Wedding.' Not bad, Grelfie, not bad at all."

A few hours later, Thidrek stood in his chamber, admiring his image in the mirror, quite liking the figure he cut in his grand black satin cloak and waxed mustache. Grelf the Gratuitous stood beside him, issuing gushes of praise and approval, making sure that his lordship was feeling as invulnerable as possible.

On a day like this, with so many beheadings on the docket, even a smidge of insecurity could be deadly, and Grelf had to be careful. He'd seen Thidrek at executions before and knew only too well the intoxicating effect they could have on him. He could get so swept up in the excitement, he would order the execution of any old lackey he'd taken a momentary dislike to, just for the sport of it. Grelf was too smart to let that happen to him.

"If I may say, sire, Your Lordship has never looked better. There's not a man in the land more in command of his masculinity than you, sir. You positively reek of class, culture and—if I may say—cunning, sir. A fearless cunning that puts you in a category far above the rest."

"Bootlicker," said Thidrek with a smirk, unable to take his eyes off his image in the mirror. Grelf began backtracking.

"I—I was being totally truthful, sir—" Grelf sputtered. "I meant every word—"

"Well, don't stop then! Get toadying with all due dispatch! Fawning sycophancy is what I live for, Grelf. You of all people should know that by now. I positively thrive on it. It's the air I breathe, the water I drink, the chariot I ride. And you're Grelf the Gratuitous! The best bootlicker in the land! So c'mon!"

"Yes, yes, of course, sir. You—you radiate a kind of animal magnetism, an attraction like no other. Indeed, you give off an—an aura of perfection that is almost godlike." He caught himself. "Did I say 'almost'? It *is* godlike, it absolutely is. Your aura. You, sir, are a paragon of perfection unparalleled on this plane of existence." Grelf stopped to take a breath, hoping he hadn't overplayed his hand.

Thidrek turned to face Grelf, eyed him for a moment, then gave him an affectionate pat on the cheek. "Oh, Grelfie, what would I do without you?" Thidrek swept out of the room, Grelf feeling that, for now, he still had job security.

⚡

The boy carried the basket down the winding stairs, watching the rats scurry off into the darkness. The deeper he went, the colder the air grew, and a dank odor penetrated his nose. He noticed dark stains from the moisture that seeped through the ancient stone walls, as if the stones themselves were weeping. He, on the other hand, had nothing to be sad about, if he actually ever stopped to think long enough to be sad. He had long ago stopped reflecting on much of anything, for reflection gave way to troubled dreams.

When the boy reached the dungeon, the guard stepped aside, letting him walk right up to the bars and look in. The men inside, the ones he knew would that day die, were oddly cheerful for those so soon to meet their doom.

A sturdy young man came to the bars, anxious to talk. He had red hair and a broad smile. Recognizing him as the one he had shot with his arrow just days before, the boy busied himself with opening the basket and said nothing, having learned from Thidrek that it was best a boy speak only when commanded to by his lord and master. He reached into the basket and began throwing the tunics in through the bars.

"What's this?" the young redhead said. "We gotta wear uniforms?"

"Lord Thidrek likes victims to wear clean shirts. Blood spatter looks better on white." He began passing them inside, while the young man continued to stare.

"Well, 'tis a good day to die," said the redhead.

"You should be dead already," said the boy, with an edge of irritation.

"Oh, yeah," said the red-haired one after eyeing him more closely. "You're the one who shot the arrow, eh?

Glad your aim wasn't true."

And now, with his marksmanship impugned, the boy was compelled to speak. "If I'd wanted you dead, you wouldn't be here."

Dane had an impulse to chastise the boy for being a braggart, but realized that, perhaps, the boy had deliberately wounded him, had let him live, and so must be somewhat sympathetic to his plight.

Dane smiled, studying the boy's features. The freckles. The soft sandy hair. What was he? Nine, ten years of age at most? What was *he* doing with trash like Thidrek? Had he no family? In a flash Dane saw it on the boy's face, the conflicted expression in the eyes, the mouth that needed to speak. Dane took a chance.

"Lost your parents, huh? Must be hard." The look on the boy's face when he met Dane's eyes told him all that he needed to know, and Dane continued as if his life depended on it—because it did.

"I lost my father, too," Dane said. "Thidrek, the dastard, did the deed himself. Got him in the back, he did, coward that he is. And every night I dream of revenge. To end his life with my own hand. The only way I'll be at peace. But I can't kill him if he kills me first. And killing him wouldn't just bring *me* peace—it'd free all the other people he's enslaved. Even you, boy. Even you." Dane paused. The boy's eyes were fastened on his.

"But Thidrek has given me a home," he said, his jaw

trembling. "He has fed me. Clothed me. He has promised that one day I shall ride beside him in battle!"

"Is that what you wish?" Dane asked "To serve a tyrant who rules through fear and cruelty? You could have killed me, but you didn't. And that tells me there's good in your soul yet, that you'd rather fight evil than ride with it." The boy was silent, thinking about Dane's words. He turned to go, then looked back.

"Them dreams you talk of? I have 'em too."

"My name's Dane. Dane the Defiant."

The boy looked at him a moment, making a decision. "Mine's William," he said.

"No nickname?"

The boy shook his head.

"How does William the Brave sound?" Dane asked.

The boy seemed about to smile but abruptly turned and strode away. Dane listened to the boy's footsteps on the stone stairs, knowing now that he'd been right about the boy, that the boy hated Thidrek as much as he did for just the reason he'd surmised. But would the boy actually *do* anything about it?

Dane then heard a murmur of voices and turned to see Ulf the Whale and Fulnir helping Lut the Bent get to his feet. Though pale and weak and barely able to stand, Lut seemed determined to make a speech to the men, and they respectfully gathered round the old one, waiting for him to speak.

Lut cleared his throat and, in a cracked whisper of a voice, said, "On this, likely our last day alive, I am glad hearted . . . for I feel privileged to have known you men . . . and knowing you as I do, I have come to regard you all as sons of Thor. . . . Though not godly in flesh, in your hearts you have lived fully and bravely. You have loved well and fought for the love of your kinsmen . . . and in my eyes, that makes you as fine and good as the gods above. Yes, you are all sons of Thor, and my heart swells with pride to have seen the starlight in your eyes and to have walked among you, lo these many winters. . . ."

After a long and powerful silence, a hand was raised. It was Drott's, once wise and now dim again.

"Uh, Lut, quick question. Did you mean everyone?" Drott asked. "I mean . . . am *I* one too?"

"Yes, my son . . ." came the old one's reply, "even you."

And Drott's smile beamed the brightest of all.

25

Thidrek Rules!

It was nearing noon. The courtyard was jammed. Upward of a thousand villagers were on hand, the ticket takers said, with hawkers walking through the crowd, selling all sorts of items bearing Thidrek's likeness—tunics, pennants, even undergarments. One food vendor was handing out "official Prince Thidrek figurines" with each meal, carved wooden dolls made to look like Thidrek with a *T* painted on the back of a long black cloak.

The selling of what was termed "merchandise" at public events was a new phenomenon in these parts, something Grelf had dreamed up to help smooth his lordship's transition to the throne. Just one of the many new ways a despotic ruler could boost his popularity *and* create a revenue stream he could profit from personally. Creating a cult of personality was hard work, Grelf knew, and you had to work every angle. To that end, he'd plastered Thidrek's image everywhere, and for maximum effect, he'd ordered local artisans to create a huge banner forty feet wide bearing Thidrek's likeness and the words THIDREK RULES! and had it hung across the upper balcony seating. Although most of the villagers on hand that day couldn't read, the basic idea came through with dazzling clarity.

The place was abuzz with activity. Against one wall of the courtyard stood a giant platform, a kind of stage upon which all the main events would be presented. It was gaily decorated with long twirling strands of flowers and ribbons, the pink and yellow blooms of the flowers contrasting nicely with the black-and-bloodred-colored uniforms of Thidrek's guardsmen who patrolled the walkways above, armed and ready to kill anyone who might do anything to disturb the day's festivities.

A band of musicians stood in a roped-off area beside the stage, surrounded by the sea of commonfolk, who were now growing restless with anticipation, having waited all morning for the show to begin. So when Grelf appeared onstage and the music stopped, a cheer went up from the crowd. Grelf waited for them to fall still, and soon the only sound was that of his voice addressing the assemblage.

"Ladies and gentlemen!" Grelf shouted. "Boys and girls! How good of you to gather on this fine day! Welcome to Ten Beheadings and a Wedding!" Another huzzah and the waving of pennants. "A day that promises to bring the color and pageantry of many fine executions! Brought to you in part by Prince Thidrek"—so cued, the crowd cheered again—"and many fine local tradesmen who've so generously agreed to endorse the proceedings!" Ever the innovator, Grelf had also convinced some of the local innkeepers, cobblers, and tinsmiths to sponsor parts of the event, allowing them to hang what were called "advertisements" around the inside of the castle courtyard in exchange for certain cash gifts that he and Thidrek had then redirected into their own purses, all done for the good of the people, of course. "And we hope you show your support by frequenting their establishments after the show!"

Grelf paused and threw a look to the musicians. They struck up an introductory fanfare and then, on his signal, abruptly went silent again. "And now, it is my great honor and privilege to present—your lord and leader! That god among men! The potentate whose personage graces the earth each day he walks upon it! No longer a mere prince—behold your new ruler! The one! The only! *King* Thidrek the Terrifying!"

Thidrek took the stage to rather underwhelming applause. A few pennants waved. A smattering of people chanted his name. One could see that Thidrek was dismayed at this less-than-roof-raising reception, though he tried not to show it. Grelf sensed disaster and snapped into action. Behind Thidrek's back, he gestured to the crowd, trying to boost their reaction. Some louder cheers were heard. And then, grabbing a nearby basket of Thidrek merchandise, Grelf began throwing the dolls into the crowd, causing something of a frenzy, since people always want to get something for nothing, even if it is just a worthless figurine of a ruthless and despicable ruler.

The hubbub seemed to please Thidrek, and he gave a great gallant bow to the crowd. They fell silent. Thidrek spoke.

"My friends! You honor me with your presence. As promised, we have a big day planned. A celebration of love and death, not necessarily in that order. But first, a few pronouncements . . ." He drew out a small vellum scroll. "Will the man with the green wagon please move it—it's blocking the entrance . . . and some of the Thidrek-themed merchandise may not be suitable for young children—they have small parts that could be swallowed—so I caution any parents out there to be advised. . . ."

A few babies began to wail as parents took away their toys.

"So! Let's get this party started!" shouted Thidrek. "First, let's put your hands together and welcome the men whose lives we'll be taking today!" He gestured grandly as out of a nearby doorway Dane and the others were led in, guarded by four particularly nasty-looking Berserkers. This drew the requisite applause level that Thidrek was seeking, and a sickening look of pleasure appeared on his face. "Yes, let's really hear it! These men are making the ultimate sacrifice—for you! C'mon, let's give it up now!" Thus prompted, the people responded with great waves of applause. Thidrek seemed to feel that this ovation was an outpouring of the people's appreciation for the entertainment value he, their beloved leader, was so generously providing. But in truth, their wild applause was but an expression of the terror in their hearts, the fear that someday it might be them up there about to lose a key appendage.

Dane, too, felt terror, but endeavored to keep it in check for the good of his men. He glanced at Drott, Fulnir, Jarl, and the others, all of them looking strong and resolute, like the sons of Thor they were—all except Lut, whose palsied hand wouldn't stop shaking until Orm reached out and took the hand in his.

"We'll get to them in a minute," Dane heard Thidrek shout. "But first, a little surprise . . ." The crowd quieted in expectation. "Well, it's not really little at all. In fact, it's huge. And the fact that *I* possess it promises peace in our land for generations to come!"

And with a sweeping gesture, Thidrek beckoned to the THIDREK RULES! banner that bore his visage. The banner was flung aside to reveal an awesome sight: There on the upper ramparts, set upon a giant wooden catapult, was Thor's Hammer. Fifty feet long from the end of its roughhewn wooden handle to the tip of its massive iron head. And most breathtaking of all, it glowed with an unearthly light. A thousand rays of multicolored light burst forth from the Hammer, a luminous aura crackling and sparking up into the sky like miniature bolts of lightning.

So it was true! Dane could scarcely believe his eyes. Thor's Hammer was real! It *did* exist, just as his father and the elders had always said. A hush fell over the crowd as the peasantfolk kissed the charms they wore round their necks, touching them to their foreheads in awe. For the longest moment one could only hear the buzz and sizzle of the otherworldly sparks the Hammer gave off, all eyes glued to its radiant glow. Dane gazed upon it, marveling at its magnificence. The frost giant was a wonder, but this literally took his breath away. Then his awe gave way to an awful dread as he remembered the man who possessed it.

Thidrek stood on the stage like a pleased parent, beaming with pride.

"Kind of puts things in perspective, doesn't it?" Thidrek crowed, his eyes agleam. "It's what we royal rulers call 'a weapon of . . . of' . . . oh, what's that phrase, Grelf?"

Grelf quickly whispered in his ear and Thidrek nodded in recognition.

"Ah, yes, 'a weapon of mass destruction'! That's it. And as you can see, using the latest in catapult craftsmanship, we do, in fact, have the capability to launch it rather effectively, at whichever village might be so pigheaded as to disobey, disrespect, or displease me in any way. And seeing as how it's a weapon of mindboggling destructive power, well, I'd rather not ever have to use it."

The crowd gave a gasp. Thidrek saw the looks of fear on their faces.

"You're frightened? Of course you are! Who wouldn't be? But that's the beauty of it, you see? *Because* it's so stupendously terrifying, the man who possesses it need never use it. It acts as—"

He stopped, and Grelf again whispered in his ear.

"It acts as a 'deterrent,' almost ensuring that it will never be used. Which is just a fancy way of saying that you are safer now than you ever were before!"

A deadly pall fell over the people, a terrible dread having silenced them. But Thidrek seemed happier than ever before now that he'd indeed become Thidrek the Terrifying.

At that moment, high in his mountaintop cave, Thrym sat alone, thinking of Astrid. He cradled the ice carving of the winged horse that Astrid had left for him. It comforted him to hold and touch the delicate ice creature, because he knew she'd made it for him and him only. And that she'd made it out of love. For only love could create something this beautiful.

He heard a sound. *Crawk!* He looked up to see a large black bird had found his way into the cave. A raven. Yes, it was Klint himself, the very bird seen plummeting into the trees earlier. Although the guard who shot him had been sure the bird was dead, in fact he'd only been hit in the wing, losing a feather or two, and, after regaining his wits a short time later, he'd flown off again toward his intended destination, for such was the fortitude of Dane's fine feathered friend.

Flapping his wings, the bird hopped up on the tabletop, cocked his head, and stared up at Thrym, squawking as if trying to tell him something. *Screek!* Thrym marveled at the creature. His beak looked so sharp, his feathers so black and shiny. He'd never seen a bird so beautiful. He didn't know what the creature was trying to tell him, but all the squawking made him think the bird was lost and trying to find his way out of the cave.

He was reaching for the bird to take him outside when he caught sight of something else. A tiny trinket lay at the bird's feet. The frost giant leaned down for a closer look. It was a locket of silver and turquoise in the shape of Thor's Hammer. As he picked it up, the locket fell open. And inside, Thrym was struck to find the one face he'd thought he'd never see again. The tiny etched portrait of Astrid.

26

Dane the Defiant Lives up to His Name

Standing in a small portico just offstage, peeking through curtains that separated her from the crowd, Astrid could see the horrified looks on the faces in the courtyard.

"Who's ready for romance?" she heard Grelf crow. "I know *I* am!" She felt a cold emptiness rising inside her as handmaidens began tossing flowers into the crowd, and Grelf, gesturing, cued the musicians. Now Astrid heard music, a sweet sprightly melody that further sickened her. Then all at once the curtains drew aside and Thidrek had her by the hand and was drawing her out onto the open stage. And now, with all eyes upon her and her snow-white dress, teal taffeta headdress, and elbow-length white velvet gloves, she was further shocked to hear the people actually cheering her!

"Isn't she magnificent?" she heard Thidrek cry. "Behold

your queen!" The cheers grew louder now, the people chanting her name and waving the little Astrid figurines that had also been for sale. Hrolf, the royal clothier, beamed too as she passed him onstage, his mates in the crowd cheering, appreciating fine design when they saw it.

She wanted to stop the music and scream out that it was all a charade. That she detested Thidrek and would rather die than marry him. But she knew it was for naught. Grelf had made a private visit to her chamber that morning and made it clear that either she submit to marriage to Thidrek, or Dane, her father, and everyone else would be hideously tortured before being put to death. But if she smiled to the crowd and pretended to be a willing bride, then the executions would be quick and painless—or relatively so, given Thidrek's penchant for theatricality.

Now, as Thidrek paraded her by the hand before his cheering subjects, showing her off as if she were but another trophy for his wall, her flesh crawled at his cold, reptilian touch, and she tried her best to smile and appear every bit the shining picture of poise she knew the people needed. After the awful business of the Hammer, they desperately craved a diversion, a story of love, a lie, an illusion—anything to quell their terror. And so she beamed a smile and waved to the crowd and patted Thidrek's arm, a tiny reassuring voice deep inside her saying that at least Dane would die having seen her looking more beautiful than she ever had before.

Dane watched in agony. There stood his beloved Astrid in all her wedding finery, looking more radiantly lovely than he ever could have imagined. He ached to hold her, to tell her all the secrets of his heart, but—how was it possible? She was soon to wed Thidrek. It was all too monstrous. At that moment Astrid passed by him, and his eyes met hers, and the pained look he saw there was too much to bear. And before he even knew what he was doing, Dane stumbled forward and shouted out the single word that overwhelmed his heart.

"*No!*"

The music stopped. Thidrek dropped Astrid's hand and turned to face Dane. All eyes in the castle courtyard fell on Dane now as they waited for Thidrek's reaction.

"No?" said Thidrek, chuckling in amusement. "No *what*, pray tell?"

"No, you can't have her—she's *mine*!"

"Dear me!" Thidrek said, turning to the crowd, putting his palms to his cheeks in mock shock. "I almost forgot to introduce him. M'lords and ladies, the man responsible for Thor's Hammer falling into my possession. He as good as handed it to me himself! None other than Dane the Defiant!"

Dane began to speak again but was hit from behind by a guardsman. He fell forward, feeling a sharp stab of pain as his jaw hit the stage floor. Sprawled there, he spied a familiar face in the crowd. The boy with the basket, William the Brave! The boy stood beside the platform, eyes glued to Dane. And in a span of time too brief to measure, something passed between them—a look, a decision.

"Tell you what I'll do," Thidrek continued. "Just to show I'm not the coldhearted guy everyone thinks I am. I'll make you a deal. My regular executioner is out sick today. I'm promoting you to first assistant executioner. You kill whoever I say and I'll let *you* marry the girl. How's that?" For a brief moment it actually sounded good to Dane. Well, the part about him getting Astrid did, at least.

"How 'bout I kill *you*?" Dane suggested, delighting the crowd.

Thidrek just issued a poisonous smile and, to Dane's horror, pointed to Blek the Boatman, Astrid's father. "*Him*, for instance. Cut off *his* head and you're home free. Take the girl and all your friends and live happily ever after. On my honor. How's that for mercy, huh? Here"—Thidrek threw an executioner's axe to Dane—"show us your stuff."

A guardsman pushed Blek's head down onto the chopping block. Dane looked at Astrid, then down at Blek. Kill the father of the woman he loved? How could he?

"Oh, come, come," Thidrek clucked. "You call yourself a man? A *Viking*? One teensy little swipe of the axe and it's done. And you can't do it?" He turned to the crowd. "Well, I guess he doesn't love her after all." The crowd let out a deflated sigh; if there had to be killing, at least it should be for love.

"I suppose we'll have to call him Dane the Indecisive," said Thidrek, drawing more sniggers from his men, "or Dane the Incredibly Doubtful," drawing more laughter still.

Dane was in torment. He looked down at Blek, surprised to hear him say, "Go on, son. Do it. I've lived a good life. It's the only way I have to save my daughter. Just make it quick." But *would* it save Astrid's life? That was the question. What assurance did he have that Thidrek would keep his word?

Dane stood hefting the executioner's axe in his hands, feeling the weight of it, its long spruce handle worn smooth by countless beheadings, its blade honed to a gleaming edge. Time seemed to stand still. A kaleidoscopic swirl of images ran through his head, memories of all he and his friends had been through in tracking Astrid. The storm on the ship, the finding of wisdom, the escape from the doomfish, freeing Astrid from the frost giant, only to be captured again by Thidrek.

And now this—an impossible impasse.

All he need do was kill one person to have his heart's desire. Only trouble was, it wasn't the right person. And as the moment seemed to stretch into minutes, he caught the eyes of the boy with the basket, of Astrid, of his friends Jarl and Drott and Fulnir and the others, and it seemed his hands knew what they were doing before his mind had realized he'd made his decision.

"Forgive me, brother Blek!"

Dane raised the axe up to chop off the man's head. In one terror-stricken moment, Blek's eyes shut. Thidrek felt the satisfaction rising in his throat. And what happened next happened in the blink of an eye. Dane swiftly brought down the axe, deliberately *missing* Blek completely, and threw it behind him—to Astrid! Being the Mistress of the Blade, she handily caught it and—catching all by surprise—she slashed and flashed it, dispatching three guards, their long spears falling to Vik and Rik the Vicious Brothers, who swiftly began their own campaign of destruction.

At this same moment William threw the basket up onstage. Dane grabbed it, pulling out the many weapons that he'd known from the boy's look would be inside. Daggers, knives, cleavers, clubs—Dane threw one of each to Jarl, Drott, Fulnir, Orm, and Blek, and in a wink the stage was mayhem. With arrows from above whizzing by their heads, Dane and his kinsmen hacked away at the guards, pushing them off the platform and into the crowd. Thidrek disappeared in the ensuing chaos. Then, following Dane's lead, the men rushed through the archway into the castle proper, thereby taking themselves out of range of the bowmen on the parapets.

Barring the door behind them, Dane barked orders as they dashed down the stairs, saying that he'd stay behind, giving Jarl and the others time to spirit Astrid safely away. And as they got to a fork in the hallway, he couldn't understand why Astrid was still standing with him and not going with Jarl and the others. "Astrid? Go!"

"We fight together or not at all," she said in irritation, pulling off her veil and gloves.

"But—"

"But what? Just because I'm a girl you're supposed to die trying to protect me? Hog pizzle! I say we die trying to protect each other!" They could hear the chaos of screams outside—the sound of the people in revolt—and the pounding of Thidrek's men against the door, its creaking hinges about to give way.

"And no matter what happens," said Jarl, "we can't let Thidrek launch that Hammer!"

"Right," said Astrid, hefting her executioner's axe. "Now let our blades taste blood!"

Moments later, the door was broken open, and down the steps ran four of Thidrek's guardsmen, spears and swords in hand. But Astrid stood firm with Jarl, Dane, and the others. Orm fired two arrows, one right after the other, quickly felling two of the guardsman, as Dane and Astrid worked their spears and swords to kill a third.

When the last remaining guardsman raised his hand to throw a knife at Blek, who'd fallen and lay defenseless in the open with no cover, Astrid let fly a hatchet—*whoosha! whoosha!*—and it sliced the man's arm clean off. And with these four dispatched, Astrid, Dane, Drott, Blek, and Orm took the men's weapons and ran off down the corridor toward the southern ramparts, Jarl and his men having already run to the stairway leading to the north wall and the Hammer.

27

Courage, Blood, and Cabbages

Dane and Astrid, fighting shoulder to shoulder with Blek, Orm, and Drott, found resistance as they hacked their way toward the winding staircase that led to the southern rampart wall. Thidrek's guardsmen fought hard and well. But Astrid's axes and Dane's slashing sword overpowered the first line of defense, and soon Dane and company were moving up the stairs.

Halfway up, however, they encountered more of the enemy and had to fall back. Splitting apart a tabletop and fashioning shields from the broken slabs of cedarwood and bits of rope, they mounted another attack, slowly advancing higher and higher up the stairs. After some hard fighting they finally reached the upper ramparts and could look down into the open air of the compound.

Crouched behind the stone wall, Dane could see, all the way across the courtyard, more of Thidrek's men and the

Hammer atop the north rampart, its power jolts sparking. But where was Thidrek? And what had become of Jarl, Fulnir, and the Vicious Brothers? He worried an ill fate had befallen them. He was about to call a command to his crew to retreat down the stairs and make their way to the north wall—sensing he'd find Thidrek there, near his precious Hammer—but then he heard footsteps on the stairs behind him. More guardsmen appeared. Then faces appeared in the windows of the castle tower, two stories above them, and bowmen began firing arrows down upon them.

Taking cover behind the low wall, they were trapped there, pinned down by arrows raining from above and the guardsmen on the stairs. For now, they could neither advance nor retreat. Though in desperate straits, Dane was comforted to see that all those with him—Astrid, Blek, Drott, Orm, and Lut—were, as yet, safe and unharmed. Thoughts of Jarl and the others flashed through his mind, and he hoped for their sakes that his friends were fighting well that day.

Meanwhile, beneath the tapestries in the great north hall, Jarl fought like a demon, taking on two, even three men at a time. With Fulnir's help, and the aid of Vik and Rik, Jarl broke through Thidrek's first-floor defenses and ran up the stairs to where the Hammer's launch catapult was stationed. He had a hunch Thidrek would hasten to the source of his power, and he was right. Rounding the top of the stairway, he spied Thidrek out on the ramparts, gesticulating and shouting to his men, who were straining to prepare the Hammer for launch.

The Hammer itself was majestic, and the sight of it momentarily held Jarl rapt, its radiating glow a wonder to see. To be so near to something the gods had touched, something of such awesome, otherworldly power, was nearly overwhelming. Mesmerized, Jarl was unable to take his eyes away from it. But then he heard a scream, and behind him on the steps he saw Rik fall, the sight of this sending him into a fury. With a bloodcurdling war cry, Jarl ran out onto the ramparts, heading straight for Thidrek.

No one fought with more ferocity than Jarl the Fair that fateful day. Stories of his singlehanded attack on Thidrek and the five guardsmen who rushed to protect their lord and master became legend in the years to follow. Little children were to hear endless stories of the courage Jarl showed in fighting off five heavily armed men. How with his Demon Claw dagger in one hand and a newfound broadsword in the other, using all his considerable strength and agility, one by one he ended each man's life. And then turned at last on Thidrek.

And Jarl, they say, would have easily taken Thidrek apart had Thidrek not had the one thing Jarl could not defeat: the Shield of Odin. For as Jarl made his final attack on Thidrek, Thidrek brought forth the Shield, and as the stories go, no matter where Jarl's sword struck, the Shield, by some unseen force, was there to shield its owner. And soon, fatigued by the fearsome battle, gasping for breath, Jarl fell to the stone floor, where Thidrek easily kicked away his weapons, spiked him in the face with a boot, then knocked the poor boy over the battlements.

Thidrek watched Jarl's body plummet from the high battlements and splash into the murky waters of the moat. He then ordered Redhelmet and Blackhelmet to fish out the body and cut off its head so that it could be stuck on a pike and placed atop the castle wall, the displaying of his enemies' decapitated heads being one of Thidrek's most favored pastimes.

Dane heard Jarl's war cry, and spurred by the sight of his friend fighting alone, leaped into action. Braving the barrage of arrow fire, Dane vaulted the ramparts, and spying a cabbage cart in the courtyard directly below, he gave an angry cry as he jumped, landing safe amid the green heads of cabbages. He grabbed a bow and a quiver of arrows off a dead guardsman, calmly took aim, and knocked out the two enemy bowmen in the tower. Then he threw a rope up and over the south rampart wall, helping Astrid, Orm, Blek, Lut, and Drott to rappel down into the courtyard to safety.

Slowed by an onslaught of more arrows, they took cover behind the cabbage cart. Trapped, with nowhere to go and no way to help, all Dane and the others could do was watch in agony as Jarl tried in vain to defeat Thidrek. They bore witness to Jarl's final moments of heroism. And when the awful end finally came, and his body went toppling over the battlements, disappearing from view, Dane felt a sudden pain in his chest, as if an enemy arrow had just pierced his heart.

Moments later, Dane was shaken to his senses as Orm pulled him up onto the cabbage cart. His head clearing, Dane saw that Drott had secured a team of horses to the cart and that Astrid and the others were already aboard.

"Ho!" Drott bellowed to the horses. He snapped the reins and the cart took off, clattering across the courtyard. Still dangerously outnumbered, with arrow fire raining down upon them, they raced past rubble and throngs of villagers streaming out the castle gates. Two Berserkers ran up raising broadswords, but Astrid flung her last axe to finish one off and Dane speared the other. Orm hurled a barrage of cabbages, knocking several more in the head, and soon they were through the castle gate and on their way to freedom.

28

Thidrek's Thrill for the Kill

Once past the rabble streaming from the castle, they sped up. Drott drove the horses hard down the rutted dirt road, winding round the base of the mountain toward their village, where Dane's people were in hiding.

Dane's mother and the other families were in mortal danger and had to be warned. For now, like a nest of vipers disturbed, Thidrek's death squads would be sent in all directions, wreaking vengeance on those villages that had shown the poorest attendance at the day's festivities. And since Dane and his folk had caused the uprising and escaped, it would no doubt be Dane's village that would first feel the brunt of Thidrek's wrath.

No one in the cabbage cart spoke, still grieving over Jarl's demise.

Dane, lost in worry, felt Astrid take his hand. Their eyes met.

"It's not over, is it?" she asked, already knowing the answer.

Dane shook his head no but mustered a brave smile. He pulled her close and kissed her forehead. The soft wisps of her hair brushed his lips, giving him momentary comfort.

"Will he send men?" she asked.

Dane grimly nodded, throwing a look back at the castle, fearing Thidrek would send more than just men.

Back on the battlements, Thidrek was in an exhilarated rage. He'd just killed Jarl, the kid with the great hair, and watched his limp body fall into the waters of the moat. Oh, the joy of killing! With the Shield he'd felt invincible! But the girl? Where had she gone? How could she have slipped from his grasp? She was the prize he yearned to possess!

He scanned the horizon, desperately scouring the countryside for a glimpse. And there, on the road northward, he spied Dane and Astrid escaping in a wagon with the other renegades.

"There she is, Grelf!" he cried. "With the defiant one and his friends, in the cabbage cart!" Thidrek's eyes were ablaze with vengeance as Grelf came rushing up, anxious to report.

"Sire, I'm afraid the people are rioting," said Grelf, breathless. "We've lost three quarters of our men, the Berserkers have deserted us, and our manpower is running dangerously low. And the shopkeepers—well, the sell-through on the merchandise wasn't great and they all want their money back. I say we cut our losses and retreat, sir, before they overrun us and we wind up in the dungeon ourselves!"

"Retreat? *Retreat?*" Thidrek's eyes burned in their sockets, his cheeks aflame with fury. He took Grelf by the throat, choking him. "I am Thidrek the *Terrifying*! I don't retreat, I *attack*!" Thidrek then shoved Grelf aside and turned to Redhelmet and Blackhelmet, who'd just appeared on the battlement.

"Proceed with countdown. We launch in thirty seconds!"

"But sire—" said Grelf, as the awful truth sank in. "The Hammer! You're not actually thinking of *using* it, sir! It's strictly a deterrent!"

"Yes! I'm using it to *deter* those bloody bastards from escaping! And that girl—no one runs out on me, understand? My kingdom could *use* a little fireworks!" Thidrek's eyes then went to the Hammer. "And so could I!" Mesmerized by its magical halo of light, drawn to its supernatural power, he moved, unafraid, directly into its shower of sparks, bathing in the glowing energy field, as if wishing to become one with the Hammer itself. He reached out to touch the Hammer, and his body arched backward and shook, as if seized and shaken by the gods themselves, sparks dancing across his body. Grelf heard a mad cackle issue forth from his master's lips and then watched as Thidrek stumbled, released from the

Hammer's otherworldly grip.

And when Thidrek turned again to face them, Grelf and his men recoiled in shock. Thidrek's face was now the mask of a fiend, a man possessed. As if all the perverse and deviant desires inside him, all his hatred, all his destructive impulses, had been made manifest at last and could be seen upon his face, his true nature revealed. His eyes burned madly as he continued the countdown, intoxicated by the power he soon would unleash.

"Fifteen! . . . Fourteen! . . . Thirteen! . . ." he shrieked, eyeing his target, doing last-second calculations as to distance and trajectory, and shouting instructions to his guardsmen as they moved the catapult into position.

Grelf stood back in horror, now realizing where Thidrek was aiming the weapon and what he intended to do. The wagon was speeding down a road that led to a small valley of tiny villages scattered along the base of the snow-covered mountain. If the Hammer were to hit high on the mountaintop, near the outcropping of granite peaks, the resulting avalanche, comprised of both glacier ice and huge boulders, might be of such monumental proportions as to—well, it could be catastrophic. Grelf gulped. The death toll would be . . . in the thousands. Mass destruction, indeed. Oh, my, he thought, am I to be a party to such wholesale devastation? "Five! . . . Four! . . . Three! . . ." But then he thought of the unique opportunity to be had in plummeting land values, which would allow certain savvy speculators, like himself, to snap up most of the valley at bargain prices, thereby giving him the comfy retirement property he had for so long coveted.

So he just stood and watched as Thidrek screamed, "Two! . . . One! . . . Fire!" and Redhelmet threw the launch lever and the catapult sprang loose, unleashing the unknown upon the world. . . .

The flight of Thor's Hammer was like nothing Grelf had ever seen. End over end it spun, soaring through the sky, arcing ever upward on its trajectory, spinning faster and faster, blue sparks radiating off it like miniature bolts of lightning. As it reached its apex, the Hammer itself began to glow redhot from within, as if some inner force at its core had been triggered. And then an even more amazing thing happened. From directly above it, bolts of lightning shot down from the clouds and zapped the Hammer, instantly turning it whitehot and sending out a silver-and-blue light show of sparks, connecting and commingling with more jagged bolts from above, as if the Hammer were getting recharged by the gods—its source of power.

And then far, far in the distance, at the very peak of the mountain where snow met rock, the Hammer struck, exploding, sending an apocalyptic cloud of fiery smoke and debris into the sky. Even miles away, the concussive sound it made was thunderous. Grelf heard a yelp of pleasure from Thidrek. And then, getting a sick feeling in the pit of his belly, Grelf saw that his worst fear was coming true. The explosive power unleashed in the Hammer had been of such an earth-shattering magnitude, half the mountainside had been blown away and was now slowly, inevitably rolling down, a gigantic wall of rock and ice that looked like it would not only swamp the wagon with Dane and Astrid, but easily engulf all the villages of the valley as well.

29

A Gigantic Turn of Events

Astrid's hand found Dane's and held fast. The horses pulling the cabbage cart stopped and they, too, looked up to see what had caused the thunderous noise. Was it a volcanic eruption this far north?

"The Hammer . . . ," said Dane, realizing what had happened.

And then they saw what was coming. Though the avalanche was still high above them on the steeply sloping mountainside, Dane quickly calculated that there was nothing they could do. The avalanche was too high and too wide and coming too fast for them to get out of the way, even on horseback. He grabbed the reins of the horses and urged them on, faster and faster. But in his heart he knew he was finished.

Then the wagon wheel hit a rock and broke, and the cart

itself fell apart, and Astrid, Drott, Fulnir, Blek, and Dane went tumbling to the ground, as the horses ran on with the remains of the cart dragging behind them. Instinctively taking Astrid by the hand, Dane stood there and looked up, unable to take his eyes off the descending wall of ice and rock. The sound of it was now deafening.

No one spoke. With the certain knowledge that these were the last precious moments of his life, Dane turned for what he believed to be his final act: kissing the woman he loved. But he was surprised to see Astrid turn away and point up the slope. What now?

Then Dane saw it too. Something moving down the mountain. It wasn't the avalanche. It was Thrym the frost giant! Dane's heart lifted at the sight. Obviously, he'd gotten the message and traveled south along the snowcapped range of mountains that connected his Mount Neverest to their much smaller peak, traversing in mere hours what men would take days or even weeks to travel. And now, carrying what looked to be an armload of fir trees, Thrym was bounding down the mountainside, crossing far too low below the snowline for his own safety.

He stopped at a ridgeline at a dangerously low elevation, putting himself right in the path of the avalanche, above the spot where Dane and his friends stood. And then, *Plop! Plop! Plop!* The giant jammed the trees upright into the snow, one right next to the other, quickly forming a rather crude but serviceable wall, a barrier with which to brake the onrushing calamity.

Would it work? They held their breath.

The thundering mass of snow and rock hit the wall of trees with a deafening crash and, to Dane's utter amazement, it held. Dane, Astrid, and the others cheered as they saw the avalanche churn to a grinding halt, the rock and ice boulders piling up behind the tree wall. *Hurray!* Thrym's plan had worked! But no!

The huge avalanche piled up and up and *spilled over* the tree wall. And now, like water through a spout, a mass of countless ice boulders, many more than ten feet tall, came rolling and tumbling straight for Dane and his friends, and straight for the village behind them—Dane's village.

All at once Thrym bounded forth—*Boom! Boom! Boom*!—and in one heroic leap he flung himself in front of the advancing avalanche, using his own body as a shield to block its flow. And this *did* work, though sadly, all too well. Hitting his body, the avalanche lost its momentum, and the onrushing rubble of rock and snow came to a rumbling stop. The giant's entire body disappeared under a great mound of ice and trees and other fallen debris. The village was saved, but the giant had been buried alive. The last Dane had seen of Thrym, before he disappeared under the heap of ice and earthen rubble, had been the giant's left hand, balled into a fist, bashing in vain at a boulder that had fallen on top of him, and soon that boulder too had been covered, and Thrym was gone.

They waited, hoping for some sign of life or movement, but nothing stirred.

Finally, Thor's Hammer itself came tumbling end over end down the slope and landed with a thud on the pile of rubble. The long handle was dented in one or two places and the iron of the hammerhead scuffed a bit, but otherwise it was none the worse for wear, a few sparks still buzzing off it.

The whole of the sky now eerily darkened with storm clouds. Rain began to fall, a light pitter-patter at first, spattering Dane and Astrid and the others as they ran to the mound of rubble and began to dig furiously, trying to get to the frost giant in time. Dane did not know if the wet spots on Astrid's face were from the pelting rain or from the love she felt for the giant, and he did not ask.

For several minutes they worked side by side in silence, digging furiously, lifting off the chunks of glacier ice and granite rock, the rain sheeting down now as the sky opened up and shed its own tears for the fallen giant. Soon they found him, lying motionless beneath the rubble, his deep-freeze sheen beginning to melt in places from having come down too far into warmer climes.

Astrid touched his face, and a piece of his beard broke off in her hand. His features began to dissolve into watery slush. The pelting raindrops only worsened it, drenching them all and washing away the tears of those who were crying, which was pretty much everyone.

Thidrek sat atop his horse at the rise in the road, watching this pathetic display of sentiment. *Pig slop*, he thought.

Putting yourself out to save anyone but yourself? What a pointless waste of time and effort. This was weakness of the worst order. Feebleminded frailty. Something his father most certainly would have approved of—and at the thought of this, Thidrek spat in anger.

Thidrek dismounted. He stood in the rain, waiting for Dane and the others to finish, a bitterness rising in the back of his throat. The boy known as Dane was to die: that was all he knew. All he craved. Drawing his sword from his scarred leather scabbard, Thidrek strode down the muddy trail toward the shambles of huts they called a village. Amid the hard rain, all Thidrek felt was the cold hatred rising inside him and the anticipation of blood about to flow.

"You dare defy ME?"

Dane's whole body went rigid, the voice sending a jolt up his spine. He turned to face the one man he hated with all his heart, the man who had killed his father.

Prince Thidrek stood in the sheeting rain, holding the Shield of Odin in his left hand, a broadsword in his right. His usual smug smirk now gone, Thidrek's face, Dane saw, resembled a death's head, with a cruel grin and eyes incandescent with rage.

"Thidrek, you're not looking too well."

"Well enough to kill you, boy," Thidrek muttered, stepping toward him with purposeful strides. "It'll be an unspeakable pleasure to rid this earth of you once and for all."

"Funny," Dane said, "I was thinking the same thing about you."

The fight then began, and a great one it was. A furious clatter of sword against shield, of steel against steel, of man against monster—at least that's how the storytellers were later to tell of it. An epic battle between right and wrong, between him who saw love as the source of human strength and him who saw it as the source of human weakness. Armed with only a broadsword, and a dented one at that, Dane delivered his own share of terrible blows. But the Shield of Odin that Thidrek had firmly in his grasp turned away each thrust, blocking every move Dane made, no matter how much strength or speed the young man could muster.

And as the fight grew fiercer, so did the storm, the sky turning so black with roiling thunderclouds, it blocked the sun. A great gale began to blow, taking the roofs off huts in the village, bending back trees, and blowing down fences. Soon the ground had grown so soupy with mud, the two men kept slipping and falling in it as they fought, so begrimed and bespattered with mud and slush, Dane's friends could barely tell them apart. Those watching from the village would later say that, in the end, all they could see were the silhouettes of two mud-darkened figures, one standing with a shield, the other on his knees, as they were illuminated in the flashes of lightning that came more and more frequently.

Scarlet slashes of blood ran from Dane's wounds as the

gleaming purple light of the Eye of Odin stared out at him, all-seeing, all-knowing. His clothes hung in tatters from his rain-slicked body, as with his last bit of strength Dane brought his broadsword crashing into the Shield, breaking the sword in two.

Thidrek gave a grunt of pleasure. Dane, now without any weapon or strength to continue, fell back and lay in the mud, his spirit broken. Looking up into the heavens above them, he could see that a cyclone-like funnel had descended from the lead-gray sky. He and Thidrek were standing in the very eye of the storm, the winds whipping round them with such force, they created a deafening roar.

Then Dane saw Astrid. She'd run out to him from the safety of one of the huts she'd been watching from. Another figure—Fulnir, it was—ran behind and grabbed her, trying to pull her back to safety, but she wouldn't budge. She stood there, fighting the winds, shouting something to Dane. But no words reached his ears, for he could hear nothing save the howling wind. Objects were being sucked up into the funnel now—leaves, twigs, chunks of ice. Then Dane saw what she was trying to do. She'd taken a knife from her boot and was reaching out with it, trying to give it to Dane. Once she saw that *he* saw it, she threw it; but the knife itself was so light, it was sucked straight upward into the tornado. And she was pulled back to the huts by Fulnir and out of harm's way.

Thidrek stepped toward Dane, raising his sword. The

closer he came, the closer came the Eye of Odin, its bejeweled centerpiece agleam, Dane's gaze fixing upon it; it seemed to be calling out to him. All the world dropped away then, and all he could hear was the shrill and wailing cry of the wind; all he could see was the glittering bits of starlight in the Eye. Then it seemed that his mind had entered the Eye itself, had *become* the Eye, in fact; for now, from a completely different vantage point, he could see himself lying there in the mud, the wind whipping his hair and his tattered tunic. And then even the wind seemed to fall away, and the only sound that came to him was the voice of his father intoning the words, "He who fights blindly will be defeated."

In a flash of pure white light Dane saw what he must do.

He tore from his body his mud-spattered tunic and, in one swift movement, flung it deftly over the Shield, covering up the Eye. Now covered, it could no longer see! Thidrek tried to shake the Shield to remove the rain-soaked tunic. But it stuck there, as if glued, the mud adhering it to the Shield. In a flash Dane was up and fighting again, surprising Thidrek with his speed, and before Thidrek could react, Dane had kicked the Shield of Odin from Thidrek's grasp and grabbed it up in his own left hand.

Now the tables were turned. Thidrek slashed away with his sword, but wherever the sword went, Dane's unveiled Shield was instantly there, blocking the blow. And finally, when Thidrek raised his sword to strike, the very sword itself was swept out of Thidrek's hand by the force of the cyclone and sucked up into the black hole above them.

Thidrek panicked, defenseless now, and looked around for something to use as a weapon. His eyes fell upon the Hammer. He ran to it. In a desperate frenzy, he climbed up on it and clung to it, pleading with the gods to please unleash its powers again to defeat his foe.

And then, as if in answer to Thidrek's plea, Thor's Hammer began to teeter upward, the handle end beginning to rise up into the sky. Seconds later, the force of the gale was so great that the entire Hammer, with Thidrek still astride it, lifted off the ground and was sucked up into the vortex, whipping in circles, tighter and tighter, and soon disappeared completely into the maelstrom as if gulped into the maw of a giant beast made of wind. And both Thidrek and the Hammer were gone. . . .

30

Many Happy Returns

Dane lay there on the ground, slowly regaining his breath, feeling washed clean by the rains. Slowly the winds subsided, the rain abated, and the blackish clouds blew away, the dark and angry skies turning bright with golden light.

"I guess Thor wanted his Hammer back," said a voice. It was Fulnir, looking down at Dane and helping his friend to his feet. Then from the heavens they heard resounding claps of thunder. The booming rumbles were a welcome sound to their ears, for they meant that the Hammer was indeed back in Thor's mighty hands and all was right with the world. All Dane could do was smile a big stupid grin as everyone came out from the rubble and gathered round him, hugging and kissing him—well, the women, at least—and his whole body, he realized, felt warm and good all over.

His mother enfolded him in her arms and whispered loving words in his ear. "So good to have you home, Son. You've made us proud."

Dane and the villagers felt even happier when they spied Vik and Blek and Ulf the Whale, who'd stayed behind to fight Thidrek and his men, as they appeared, holding knives on Grelf and the last few guardsmen who'd surrendered. The ragged-looking Grelf wore a particularly sour look on his face, though it was hard to tell if this was due to the beating he'd received or the disappointment he felt over losing his potential real estate empire.

Then Dane saw Orm the Hairy One and Rik the Vicious straggle up behind the others, Rik limping on the bandaged leg he'd injured. Happy to be reunited, Vik the Vicious and Rik the Vicious bumped chests and embraced, then broke out a cask of mead and began serving drinks to everyone. Fulnir and Ulf the Whale broke out their wood pipes and there was music. Drott the Dim issued a belch and there was laughter. And one by one, with an outpouring of affection, the villagers welcomed Astrid home.

Even William the Brave, the boy who'd thrown the men the weapons, showed himself amid the merriment, asking for mead and grinning in amusement at Dane, who was performing a mime of Thidrek to the delight of the gathering. When the boy's eyes met Dane's, the warmth of the boy's smile told Dane that William had found a new home in the village.

Then from out of the crowd, a weary-looking Lut the Bent shuffled up to Dane. The expression in the ancient man's eyes was grave as he gave Dane a long stare, as if he were about to share some long-held secret. Dane waited for him to speak. Finally, Lut crinkled his lips into a smile. "Well done, son," he said. "I wouldn't be surprised if they called you Rune Warrior someday." Then, mumbling that the voyage had been far too arduous for a man of his advanced years, Lut the Bent excused himself and went off for a long-overdue nap.

And before he had time to reflect on what Lut had said, Dane heard a voice he'd thought he'd never hear again.

"Mate," it said, and a firm hand found his shoulder. Dane turned to see Jarl there, his hair long and glossy and his grin as toothy as ever. The two men knocked fists, both feeling it was good to be home.

New tears of joy were shed as the villagers gathered round Jarl the Fair, touching his hair and cheeks and welcoming him home. The men who'd seen him fall were especially moved to find him alive as ever. For, as Jarl soon explained to his awed friends and family, he hadn't died at all. Yes, after losing his footing while fighting Thidrek, he'd fallen from the battlements. But as fate would have it, he'd splashed into the marshy waters of the moat below and a thicket of reeds had cushioned his fall. He'd come to, dazed. Without a weapon and knowing that Blackhelmet and Redhelmet would soon be fighting over who'd get to chop his head off, he'd quickly swum away to the other side of the castle and hidden amid the high grasses there, awaiting his fate. But he'd never been found. He'd heard the terrible explosion of the Hammer, the rumble of the avalanche, then all had grown quiet. And after a time he'd ventured forth, found a horse by the side of the road, and ridden home.

Later that afternoon, everyone gathered in the home of Dane and his mother. It was there, in a solemn voice, that Dane the Defiant, son of Voldar the Vile, grandson of Vlar the Courageous, addressed his fellow villagers.

"The gods have looked upon us with favor and given us victory . . . and our own dear Astrid," he said. His eyes met Astrid's, and she returned his look of love. Then, holding up the Shield of Odin for all to see, he said, "And I return to all of you the sacred Shield of Odin, the protector of our people." Reaching up, he hung the Shield on the wall above the fire, and all stood in reverent silence for a moment.

Jarl then stepped forth. He clasped Dane's shoulder and said the words they all were thinking: "You're our protector now."

And at that moment an odd thing happened.

It began snowing. Great big fluffy flakes floated down, and everyone went outside to romp and play in the last snowfall of spring. Dane heard the *scrawk!* of a bird. Sure enough, it was Klint, his raven, circling the sky high overhead.

"Well, I'll be dipped in weasel spit," said Dane, his heart lifting at this sight. The bird swooped down and landed on Dane's arm, squawking a greeting. Dane said hello to his friend and held out his palm, and the bird dropped something into it: the Thor's Hammer locket. And now both the bird and the locket were safely home once again.

CHAPTER LAST

Happily Almost Ever After

The moon shone clear and bright that night and laid a blanket of silver across the newfallen snow. Dane and Astrid walked hand in hand through the woods, not needing to speak; they were together again, and the mere sound of each other's breathing was enough to make them happy.

Reaching the rim of the forest, they stopped and looked out over the frozen lake.

After a moment, Dane drew something from his pocket and, pulling up Astrid's hand, placed it in her palm. She looked down and saw it was the silver Thor's Hammer locket he'd tried to give her not so many nights ago. At last he was to place it where it belonged: round the throat of his intended.

He gazed down at her, so full of love, and when he heard her say the words, "I accept," he could have sworn he saw the faces of his children in her eyes. He drew it up and clasped it round her neck. And then he kissed her . . . and she kissed him back.

And as they walked back through the woods, Dane began to set forth what he called the "rules of their relationship," telling her that wearing his locket meant she was his and his only and that she could not be seen walking alone with any other boy. Astrid said that was fine with her. "That means no boating or horseback riding with anyone else, either," he continued. "And at festivals you won't sit or dance with anyone but me." Astrid stiffened and stopped walking, not liking the sound of this. But Dane, too busy to notice, walked on, saying, "And if I want time alone or want to go out hunting or fishing with my friends, you'll not complain and—"

—*Whomp!* The axe she threw whizzed by his ear and embedded with a *whack* in the trunk of the tree right behind him. Dane's eyes went to the axe and then back to Astrid. "On second thought," he said, "who needs rules?"

And then they heard a commotion, a clamor of voices coming from the village, and Drott the Dim came stumbling up to them, all in a tizzy, barely making sense, he was so excited.

"You're never going to believe it, c'mon, you've got to see—it's the snow, the cold weather, it's—well, c'mon!" And off they ran through the woods.

He was sitting up and talking to the children when she and Dane came round the corner and saw him. It was Thrym the frost giant, alive and doing just fine. The snow that had fallen that night and the sudden freezing temperatures had refrozen his thawing limbs and brought him back to life. When he'd awakened and poked his head out of the rubble, the villagers reported, the first thing he'd said was "Astrid."

She came to him and touched his cheek. It made him smile to see her, and she smiled at him and told him how happy she was to see him again. She thanked him for what he'd done for them, for saving their lives, and he seemed to blush a darker shade of icy blue.

Astrid introduced Thrym to all the other villagers, making a special point of introducing him to Lut, to her father, and of course to Dane.

Dane apologized for stealing his porridge bowl, and the giant said it was all right, he'd already carved another. Thrym said he was sorry for having frozen Astrid to the floor, and she said she knew he hadn't meant to harm her. Soon it was time for him to go. He had to return to the mountaintop or else he might melt for good. He said good-bye to everyone, and then Astrid walked off a little ways with him, wanting to be alone for a moment with the frost giant when she said her farewell.

She patted him on the arm and kissed him on the cheek.

"You'll always be in my heart, Thrym," she said.

"And you mine," he replied.

And with that the frost giant turned and, stepping over the big pile of rubble, made his way back up the mountain, while Dane, Astrid, and the others silently watched him go. Just as the giant was disappearing from view, Klint the raven, circling high overhead, squawked a goodbye. Thrym turned and waved, and the villagers all waved back, their hearts too heavy to speak. Then the giant gave another wave to his messenger friend, turned, and soon was gone from sight. The raven flew down to where Dane stood arm in arm with Astrid and landed on Dane's shoulder. Dane lifted his mead cup and let the raven dip his beak, and refreshed, the bird flew back to his nest atop the thatch roof of Dane's family hut.

And soon the crowd of people broke up, all returned to their homes for the night: Drott the Dim and Fulnir the Stinking and Orm the Hairy One and Vik and Rik and Lut and Jarl the Fair and Ulf the Whale and all the others, back to the warm and welcoming arms of their families. Dane opened the door of his home to let his mother in, as well as William the Brave, whom Dane had taken in as family. Then Dane walked Astrid, too, across the threshold, and there before the hearth fire, they came together for another kiss, each safe at last in the arms of the other.

And so it was that a boy became a man, found love, and brought peace again to his people. As prophesied, he'd found wind, wisdom, and the thunder in his heart, and now life could go pretty much back to normal for this little village by the sea. The men hunted and fished, braving the dangers of sea and forest, and the women gave birth to children and did all the really hard and important work.

And what of Thidrek's fate? No one really knows. Some believe that, after being sucked up into the center of the cyclone, his body was no doubt torn to itty-bitty bits and the pieces scattered to the four corners of the world. Others say he was sucked straight up into the heavens and into the hands of Thor himself. And if so, what do you suppose Thor *did* to him? The answer, perhaps, is best left to the imagination, but whatever his fate, you can be sure it wasn't pleasant.

As for Blackhelmet and Redhelmet, an odd fate befell them. After Thidrek had released the Hammer and hurried off to have it out with Dane, his castle fell into chaos. The commoners rioted, setting the place on fire, torching the tapestries and timbers, cheering as the giant poster of Thidrek's face took flame, looting and pillaging and tearing the place apart. Blackhelmet and Redhelmet, the only two guardsmen not killed or scared off by rioters, made it to Thidrek's upper rooms, intending to make off with their master's hoard of silver. But the Berserkers, who had been the first to desert, had already broken into Thidrek's cash vault and carted off his entire cache of coins and art objects. People had stripped the rooms bare of most everything else, even the bedclothes and Thidrek's knitting needles. Blackhelmet and Redhelmet went from room to room in mounting frustration, tearing through closets, rifling drawers, pulling up floorboards in a vain search for something, anything, of value, but to no avail. And then under the bed they found a wineskin, still heavy with liquid, and, knowing Thidrek's tastes, they both assumed it was filled with fine wine. Unbeknownst to either, this was the very same wineskin Astrid had tried to poison Thidrek with, the one with the idiot water inside it. And so, being thirsty and desperate for booty of any kind, the two guardsmen fought over who would get to drink from it. Blackhelmet pulled it free and managed several long swallows before Redhelmet wrenched it away and guzzled down the rest. And though no one was there to see the initial effects the idiot water had upon them, it is said that they lived the rest of their lives in a comical state of abject imbecility, aimlessly wandering about, slack-jawed and drooling, suddenly laughing for no apparent reason, mumbling half words and bits of songs they'd learned as children, making no sense whatsoever.

The Berserkers, duly impressed by Dane's defeat of Thidrek and by his forgiveness, swore allegiance to the new village chieftain and promised to live in peace and harmony and not steal too many of the village goats. And although they were to keep this blood oath for many years, on nights when children awoke and were frightened by the eerie howl of wolves nearby in the forest, parents told them these weren't wolves at all, just the wailing cries of bloodthirsty spirits who'd been cast out of the bodies of the

Berserker warriors by Dane's magic and now roamed the forest looking for someone to eat. Dane thought it strange that parents told their children these kinds of bedtime stories, and he vowed if he were ever a father never to tell scary tales after dinnertime.

And speaking of nightmares, Lut the Bent never did tell Dane of the dream he had had so long ago, deciding there was no point to it, the young man having more than proven that it was possible to change your fate if you believed in yourself and got a few lucky breaks. Fulnir switched to a vegetables-only diet, as the smartened-up Drott had advised, and, lo and behold, it quelled his intestinal disquietude for a whole week. And whenever Jarl the Fair talked of his fight with Thidrek on the ramparts, which was as often as anyone would listen, he so embellished and embroidered the facts that in only a matter of days it became known as the *Folkesagn av Jarl Fager og Fryktløs og Kjekk*, or the "Legend of Jarl the Fair and Fearless and Handsome."

And Drott? Well, every once in a while, when the moon was full, he'd get a flash of the old wisdom and he'd amaze and astound the villagers with new insights about the world, like how to get bloodstains out of animal hides and how long after eating you should wait before taking a swim. But then, just as quickly, these flashes of knowledge would vanish and he'd go back to belching and laughing and drinking ale with his friends, the same old lovable dunce he had always been.

And thus we leave these sons of Thor, each having gained the strength and courage to face death and the wisdom to greet each new day as if it were to be his last. Finally reunited with family and friends, they settled down, expecting to enjoy the long period of peace and prosperity the prophecy had promised would be theirs.

But, unfortunately, that's not what happened.

One night just a few weeks later, Dane the Defiant awoke, his sleep disturbed by a dream of his own, a terrible dream that left him too troubled to sleep. He lay for a time in his bed-straw, listening to the night sounds and wondering what to do. At last he rose and put on his coat, intending to take a walk in the woods as his father often had, knowing the fresh air would help to clear his mind. But soon his footsteps took him past the hut of Lut the Bent, and there he stopped, somehow unsurprised to find Lut awake too.

Invited in, Dane sat on the dirt floor and took the mead horn Lut offered him. The hut smelled of rosemary from the tallow candles Lut had lit. Dane began to tell the old one of his dream, Lut listening intently, the candlelight reflected in his eyes. And when Dane halted at the most disturbing part of it, not sure how to continue, he was startled to hear Lut finish the dream for him, as the old one described every detail, as if he had had the very same dream himself. Which, as Dane soon realized, he had.

"What does it mean?" Dane asked.

Lut held his searching look for a moment, then tossed a

small sealskin sack into Dane's lap. "You tell me," said Lut.

Dane loosened the leather drawstring from the top of the sack, and out fell a new set of runes, each one smooth and shiny and made of whalebone. Having lost the old set in the storm while aboard the ship, Lut explained, he had just finished carving these that very afternoon. Dane said he knew that to cast the runes was the only way to read the true meaning of his dream and, thus, the future as writ by the fates. But why should *he* have this honor? Wasn't that Lut's job? It didn't feel right.

Lut said that now it was his turn to take on this new responsibility. By his actions, he had earned the villagers' trust, and as their chieftain it was his honor and duty to perform this task. Still, Dane hesitated.

"Knowledge is scary, son," said Lut. "But it's the burden we carry for our people." Dane nodded. He *was* frightened, but knew what he must do. Kneeling, he closed his eyes and drew a breath to clear his mind, as he had seen Lut do so many times. And then, in one purposeful motion, he tossed the runes in the air. They landed on the earthen floor. He felt a tingle on the hairs of his neck. Afraid of what he might see, he opened his eyes and stared down at the runes gleaming in the candlelight. Carefully, one by one, he read them, and as he did so he felt a chill crawl up his spine and into his belly. There they were. The very things in his dream mirrored there in the runes themselves. His worst fears confirmed. His dream would indeed come true, and soon. A heinous fight for survival that might prove even more harrowing than the last. A wave of fatigue overtook him. His eyes met Lut's.

"Boys play," the old one said, "but men must worry."

Leaving the hut moments later, Dane looked into the night sky and saw the misted-over moon. It was round and pink and looked mysteriously like the bloodshot Eye of Odin himself. Though Dane knew a new darkness was coming, the what, when, and where of it were things only Odin himself could see. It wasn't fair. Why were men kept blind to the very things they most needed to see? As he walked through the quiet village toward home, feeling weighted by the heavy cloak of new responsibilities, there was yet a lightness to his step, for he realized that now he truly walked in the footsteps of his father.

Acknowledgments

With deep gratitude, the authors would like to acknowledge the many friends and colleagues—and actual Norsefolk—who helped make this book possible. First, kudos are showered upon the fabulously talented team of Laura Geringer, Lindsey Alexander, Jill Santopolo, and Carla Weise (*aka* Laura the Seer of the Tale, Lindsey the Slayer of Sloppy Syntax, Jill the Incredibly Patient, and Carla the Artful), whose creative efforts and devotion to detail can only be described as "strangely inhuman." Many thanks, as well, to *uber*-agent Jodi Reamer, for the great judgment she showed in agreeing to represent us, for her wise counsel, and for her insistence on always picking up the check at Katz's. A tip o' the war helmet to our Norwegian friends Veslemoey and Harald Zwart for their tireless help in answering questions about all things Old Norse (and the

Fårikål). Furthermore, Jim would like to thank his dear friends Jamie, Chris, and Tom for their treasured friendship and support, and his mother, Thelma, for having been there with books from the beginning. He also throws a hug and a kiss to his wife, Allison, and son, Jake, who, for years, have shown great patience and fortitude in sharing his home with so many Vikings.

SHIELD OF ODIN

A Conversation with the Authors

Viking Fun Facts Quiz

A Poem by Ragnar the Ripper

A Sneak Peek at *Runewarriors: Sword of Doom*

A Conversation with Jim Jennewein and Tom Parker

It's hard enough for one author to write a novel, but *RuneWarriors: Shield of Odin* has two authors.

TOM: One of us has to make the coffee while the other types.

Is this collaboration a difficult process, or did it come naturally?

TOM: On the first draft of the book, I write the consonants and he writes the vowels. On the second draft we switch.

JIM: We have been working Hollywood screenwriters—and writing partners—for nearly twenty years. Together, we've written scripts for all the major studios and have several movies to our credit.

TOM: Such as *The Flintstones, Ri¢hie Ri¢h,* and *Getting Even with Dad*.

JIM: And although the mediums are as different as night and day, oddly, our process for writing novels is the same as writing movies. Basically, once we develop the story idea, one of us sits and writes up a synopsis—anywhere from two to twenty pages long. We go back and forth, tweaking the synopsis, breaking it down into scenes, fine-tuning it all. Then we begin the actual writing, taking alternating chapters.

TOM: Once we're done, we each might rewrite certain parts of what the other guy wrote and send them back, and we go like that all through the first draft. Once that's completed, we start again at the beginning and repeat the process all over again, refining language, adding comedy, clarifying character and theme as we go. We don't always agree at first on how certain scenes should be written or what characters should say. But disagreement leads to discussion; it forces us to better articulate and communicate our ideas.

JIM: And if talking doesn't work, there's always another option: water balloons at twenty paces.

Are any of the characters in *RuneWarriors: Shield of Odin* based on anyone you know personally? Are these the types of characters you were drawn to when you were growing up?

JIM: Every story we write is informed, in some way, by the lives we have led, the people we have known. But we wouldn't say that characters such as Drott the Dim or Fulnir the Stinking are literally based on actual people. They are people who spring from our imaginations, uniquely crafted to entertain and to enliven the story as much as possible.

TOM: When growing up, we read everything we could get our hands on. Especially the adventure stories of Jack London, Sir Arthur Conan Doyle, Mark Twain, and Robert Louis Stevenson. Plus sci-fi writers like Ray Bradbury and Jules Verne.

JIM: Dickens and Vonnegut, too.

TOM: So we looked up to our own fictional heroes—and the writers who created them—as much as young readers do today.

JIM: In real life, interesting characters are everywhere; all you have to do is pay attention. The most important thing when creating characters is to make them identifiable in some way. You have to believe the people are real; you have to understand what it is they want or need or are obsessed by in order to care whether they succeed.

TOM: Villains are a whole different story. You don't have to like them *per se*, but you should understand what it is they want and why. Or at least be fascinated by them.

Well, what made you want to write about Vikings?

TOM: We like adventure.

JIM: And violence.

TOM: And violent adventure.

JIM: The two do seem to go hand in hand, and nobody was better at bloodletting than the Vikings.

TOM: We also fell in love with Norse mythology. The gods, the monsters, the trolls, the frost giants, the Valkyries—it felt like a fresh new world to have fun with and build a series around.

JIM: Yes, Greek and Roman mythology have been taught in school for years, and kids have learned about it from books, movies, video games, what have you. But we feel the tales found in Norse mythology are totally fresh and just as enriching, and *RuneWarriors: Shield of Odin* will give teachers a way to let kids discover that.

TOM: Teachers, I think, will find a lot of interesting themes to discuss in this book. The hero's journey to manhood, his struggle to accept the responsibilities of adulthood.

JIM: And the farting scene.

TOM: If you can't have a scene featuring "personal breezes," what's the use in writing a book anyway?

The Vikings in your book are very funny, yet they remain quite believable. How do you use humor to further the plot and show the Vikings' depth of character?

TOM: Iconic heroes must be humanized in some way—made flesh and blood. And one of the best ways to humanize a character is through humor. If our protagonist can make funny observations or can laugh at himself, it not only makes him more likable, it makes him more unpredictable. Because the essence of humor is unpredictability.

JIM: Right. If you already know the punch line, you're not going to laugh.

TOM: Comedy can also come from a character who has no sense of humor. For instance, if the big, bad, self-important villain strides in and everyone sees he has toilet paper stuck to his shoe, he's comically brought down a notch and made more real to the reader.

JIM: But we don't use this gag; in the Viking Age toilet paper hadn't been invented yet.

You both have been writing movies for several years. How does writing a book differ from writing a screenplay?

JIM: Movies, by their very nature, have to move. Characters have to do things—take action—in order for the audience to understand and care about what's going on. So, generally speaking, movies are less about the internal lives of characters and more about the external kinds of problems they get into. Novels can and should take you into the minds of the characters and allow you to share in their deepest thoughts and feelings. There's an intimacy and a kind of absorption in character that a movie usually cannot deliver. Ultimately, nothing beats the satisfaction of writing books. Because it's just the author's words going right into the reader's brain; it's a direct connection. There is only one interpreter of the work—you, the reader. You get to escape to this other world the writer has created for you, building your own mental pictures of all that unfolds. It's a special kind of magic that happens when you read a book—a special kind of power that both the reader and the writer tap into—and we're happy to be a part of it.

TOM: Yes, the human imagination is the ultimate special effect.

Viking Fun Facts

Test your Norse knowledge with this true-or-false quiz. (Then check your answers at the end.)

1. Vikings were dirty brutes who never bathed.
   True_____ False_______

2. Many of the names of our days of the week come from the Vikings.
   True_____ False_______

3. Vikings discovered America.
   True_____ False_______

4. Vikings could not read or write.
   True_____ False_______

5. In Viking culture, it was considered wrong to own slaves.
   True_____ False_______

6. Vikings invented the honeymoon.
   True_____ False_______

7. A Viking woman was free to marry whomever she wished.
   True_____ False_______

8. Vikings were dour, serious dudes with little sense of humor.
   True_____ False______

9. A dog was once a Viking king.
   True_____ False_______

10. The Vikings used urine to keep fires going.
    True_____ False_______

11. Vikings were the first guys to "go berserk."
    True_____ False_______

12. Our word "cholesterol" comes from the Viking word "kohlastroll" which meant "trolls for breakfast."
    True_____ False_______

ANSWERS TO THE QUIZ

1. FALSE. Vikings were surprisingly *clean.* They bathed frequently—Saturday was known as Washing Day—and often taught those they conquered the benefits of good hygiene. They also used something called "ear spoons" to clean the wax from their ears.

2. TRUE. Many of our modern-day names for the days of the week are of Viking origin. Tuesday: "Tyr's day," Tyr being the Norse god of heroic glory. Wednesday: "Wodin's Day," an Anglicized spelling of "Odin's day." Thursday: named for Thor, the Norse god of thunder. Friday: "Freyja's day," Freyja being the goddess of love, beauty, and fertility.

3. TRUE. Almost 500 years before Columbus sailed, Norse explorer and outlaw Leif Erickson discovered the North American continent. He landed on the northernmost tip of the island known today as Newfoundland, Canada. Archaeological evidence recently uncovered suggests that Erickson and his men may have sailed as far south as Boston Harbor.

4. FALSE. The early Vikings had a rich language all their own using letters called runes. Using this alphabet (shown on the next page), also called Futhark, the Vikings carved stories of their heroic tales on giant slabs of stones they called runestones. Hundreds of runestones still exist today.

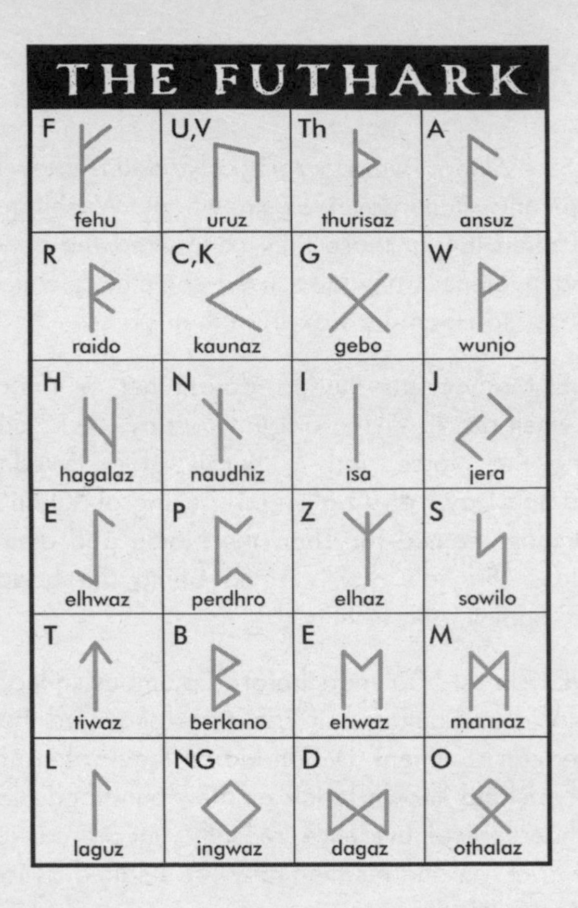

5. FALSE. Like most societies of the era, the Vikings did own slaves, called "thralls" (the origin of our word "enthrall"). Used as laborers, thralls were kept as livestock and their masters had absolute power over their life and death. Worse, thralls were never offered a good dental plan.

6. TRUE. The traditional drink at a Viking wedding was the "bridal ale," which was ale flavored with honey. To ensure happiness and fertility, the married couple

would share this concoction for the entire month following the wedding, through all four phases of the moon. Thus it became known as the "honey-moon" period.

7. FALSE. Women in Viking society usually married whom their parents told them to. Her father would negotiate her "bride price," the amount her prospective husband would have to pay. If her father was deceased, the job would fall to her older brothers, which sometimes led to trouble because the brothers would reject suitors so as to keep their sister working on the family farm. In this case, the law stated that the woman could marry the third suitor her brothers rejected. Once wed, however, Viking women could freely divorce and even own property. Wow, what a life, huh?

8. FALSE. Vikings loved to laugh and excelled at telling humorous stories. Their sagas are filled with amusements of all kinds. Adept at the use of language, they were also skilled in the art of the insult, producing such zingers as "You have the breath of a goat's backside!" and "May your sister's head grow horns and her feet hooves."

9. TRUE. According to one tale, the Swedes installed a little dog—a terrier named Rekkae—as king of the Danes. They forced the Danish to swear fealty to their new canine king, giving it the best food and drink. After this dog-king died, the conquering Swedes crowned a new pooch as king, a poodle named King Snio, who was eventually eaten alive by lice.

10. TRUE. Vikings harvested a substance known today as touchwood fungus. This fungus was beaten into a flat, feltlike

material that was charred by fire and then boiled in urine. Urine contains sodium nitrite, a chemical that slows the burning process. When urine was infused into the touchwood, it allowed it to slowly smolder but not burn, so fire could easily be transported during a journey.

11. TRUE. Berserkers were Norse warriors who fought with uncontrollable rage. Some believe the word stems from the Old Norse "bare-sark," which meant "bare of shirt" and referred to the berserkers' fearless habit of going into battle without armor. Others believe that the word "berserkir" referred to those who wore the skins of bears or wolves when making war so as to strike fear into those they attacked. Still other evidence suggests that many of the era believed Berserkers to be shapeshifters who could actually turn into bears and wolves. Whatever the origin of the word, the modern translation is still the same: Berserkers kicked butt.

12. FALSE. Although hundreds of our most common English-language words had their origins in the Viking tongues of Old Norse, Danish, or Swedish, cholesterol is not one of them. Here are a few that are: anger, awkward, bark, crawl, crazy, dirt, egg, gawk, geyser, glitter, guest, gust, haggle, hurry, ill, knife, law, leg, loan, loose, muck, mug, odd, ransack, reindeer, root, Russia, saga, scab, scare, scold, scrape, scythe, sister, skeet, ski, skill, skull, sky, sleuth, smile, stagger, thrive, thrust, troll, ugly, wand, whirl, window, wrong.

A Poem by Ragnar the Ripper

A poem inspired by the exploits of Dane the Defiant in book one (penned by Ragnar the Ripper—a character you'll meet in Book Two)

Son looked not to elder
'Ere his wounded father fell.
And in his heart e'erafter
A bitter guilt did dwell.
Breathing in his father's dust
Son swore he would behead
The one who struck his father dead;
For glory's sake, he must.
He journeyed forth, still mere pup
Vowing not to rest a wink
Till with his enemy's skull as cup
His warm blood he did drink.

To view author videos and other fun extras, visit the RuneWarriors website: www.runewarriors.net.

EXTRAS

A Sneak Peek at the Next Thrilling Book, *RuneWarriors: Sword of Doom*

The village has been attacked . . . and Dane has been summoned to the palace of King Eldred!

Later that night Dane sought out Lut the Bent and found the old one in his hut, recovering from his bout with the invaders. They sat by a smoky fire, sipping barley ale, Lut applying a yarrow-root paste to the scrapes on his arm as Dane relayed news of the white-cloaked one and his father's war chest.

"I knew of this chest," Lut said, "but nothing of its contents. Your father rarely spoke of it to me, nor to anyone else, I gather." The old one's eyes grew misty. "It was as if his war chest held something he no longer wanted to possess or be reminded of. A part of his past—a piece of himself—that he wanted to keep locked and hidden away, perhaps as much for his own good as anyone else's." Lut gave Dane a penetrating look. "I believe your father would never have opened that chest again," he said with emphasis, "and perhaps neither should you."

"Not *open* it?" said Dane in surprise. "But if there's treasure inside—"

"Some secrets are best left unknown, son." Dane wanted to speak, but the fire in Lut's stare silenced him. "That which happened in your father's past, before you were born—how much do you know of it?"

Dane shrugged. "I know that in his youth he followed the sword path. He was a brave warrior who served with distinction and honor, but he spoke little of it to me."

"True, your father sent many to their deaths."

Dane took this in and then said, "I must have asked him a hundred times to tell me of his glories and victories. But he would only laugh and change the subject. It hurt me, like he didn't believe I had the stuff to fully understand what he had done. Or do it myself."

"Perhaps he was protecting you," said Lut, "from something he knew might only cause pain. Fathers are funny that way, only wanting the best for their sons." This last was said with a playful smile. His mother, Dane knew, had respected her husband's wishes to let the past be and had rarely spoken of it, at least in Dane's presence. But oh, how Dane had yearned to know all he could about the man he revered. And why not? Wasn't it natural for a son to learn all he could about his father? To hear of his grandest exploits and, yes, even his lowest failings? To examine every broad stripe and torn thread from the tapestry of his life? How else would he ever come to know the one who had fathered him—or come to know himself, for that matter? And with his father dead, that chance was gone forever. But now the chest gave him a final opportunity to peer into his father's mysterious past.

"I *must* know what's in the chest," said Dane. "Perhaps we should consult the runes."

"I already have."

"You *have*? But how'd you know—"

"—that you'd come pestering me with questions? When *don't* you?"

Dane smiled. It was true. Hardly a day went by that he didn't ask Lut's advice on any number of subjects, from girls to cures for scalp itch. Despite being decades older than most elders, and having a long white beard and more wrinkles than a bucket of prunes, Lut possessed the light heart and playful nature of a much younger man.

"So," said Dane, staring at Lut in the firelight, "*was* there a message in the runes?"

Lut stifled a yawn, then nodded soberly. "They said, 'The secret of the chest will change your life.'"

Dane took a long moment to consider this; then he spoke.

"So it means I might find treasure, or . . ."

"Or something," Lut said with finality, "you'll wish you'd never laid eyes on at all."